Scorched Eggs

·LAURA CHILDS·

Scorched

Eggs

BERKLEY PRIME CRIME, NEW YORK

THE BERKLEY PUBLISHING GROUP
Published by the Penguin Group
Penguin Group (USA) LLC
375 Hudson Street, New York, New York 10014

USA • Canada • UK • Ireland • Australia • New Zealand • India • South Africa • China

penguin.com

A Penguin Random House Company

This book is an original publication of The Berkley Publishing Group.

Berkley Prime Crime Books are published by The Berkley Publishing Group.
BERKLEY® PRIME CRIME and the PRIME CRIME logo are trademarks of
Penguin Group (USA) LLC.

Childs, Laura.
Scorched eggs / Laura Childs.—First edition.
pages ; cm.—(A Cackleberry Club mystery ; 6) ISBN 978-0-425-25559-9
(hardcover) 1. Women detectives—Fiction. 2. Arson—Fiction.
3. Murder—Investigation—Fiction. I. Title.
PS3603.H56S365 2014
813'.6—dc23
2014031991

FIRST EDITION: December 2014

PRINTED IN THE UNITED STATES OF AMERICA

10 9 8 7 6 5 4 3 2 1

Cover illustration by David Leonard.
Cover design by Sarah Oberrender.
Interior text design by Kristin del Rosario.

This book is for all my terrific teachers at JHS. Especially the ones who taught social studies (sorry I voted for Nixon), chemistry (apologies for that lab explosion), higher algebra (my favorite pi is still apple), English (Steinbeck, yes; Beowulf, no), speech (I still use your tricks!), and typing (a skill I use almost every single day).
Thank you very much.

Acknowledgments

A major thank-you to Sam, Tom, Amanda, Bob, Jennie, Troy, Dan, and all the designers, illustrators, writers, publicists, and sales folk at The Berkley Publishing Group. You are all such a wonderful team. Thank you also to all the booksellers, reviewers, librarians, and bloggers. And special thanks to all my readers and Facebook friends who are so very kind, supportive, and appreciative. I truly love writing for you!

Scorched Eggs

CHAPTER 1

SUZANNE didn't know how she felt about Blond Bombshell No. 4 as a hair color, but she was about to find out. Especially since she was sprawled in a red plastic chair roughly the size of a Tilt-a-Whirl car, bravely enduring her "beauty experience" at Root 66, downtown Kindred's premier hair salon. Silver foils that looked like baked-potato wrappers were crimped in her hair, while a sparkly pink '50s-era bubble-top hair dryer hovered above her head, blasting a constant stream of hot air.

Yup, the foils were bad enough, but the droning dryer made Suzanne feel as if her head were being sucked into a jet engine.

Jiggling her foot, tapping her fingers, Suzanne knew she should try to regard this as "me time" as so many women's magazines advocated.

But, all cards on the table, Suzanne felt restless and a little guilty about ducking out of the Cackleberry Club, the cozy little café she ran with her two partners, Toni and Petra.

She'd dashed away this Friday afternoon claiming a dire personal emergency. And when you were a silvered blonde who was a tad over forty, the emergence of dark, scuzzy roots all over your head definitely qualified as an emergency.

But now, after all the rigmarole of mixing and tinting and crimping and blow-drying, Suzanne just dreamt of sweet escape.

She glanced around at the five other women, customers in the salon, who seemed perfectly content to sit and be beautified. But scrunched here, paging through an old copy of *Star Whacker* magazine and reading about the questionable exploits of Justin and Miley, didn't seem like the most productive way to spend an afternoon.

"How you doin', gorgeous?" cooed Brett. He bent down and flashed his trademark pussycat grin. Brett was her stylist and a co-owner of Root 66. A man who wore his hair bleached, spiked, and gelled. "Are you in need of a little more pampering? Should I send Krista over to do a French manicure?" He cast a slightly disapproving glance at Suzanne's blunt-cut nails.

"No thanks, I'm fine," Suzanne told him as she balled her hands into tight fists. What she wanted to tell Brett was that she had working-girl hands. Every day she muscled tables, swept floors, hauled in boxes of groceries, and wrangled two unruly dogs when she finally arrived home at night. In her free time, she stacked hay bales, mucked stalls, and guided her quarter horse, Mocha Gent, through his paces at barrel racing. Oh, and last week, on an egg run to Calico Farms, she'd manhandled a jack and changed a flat tire on her Ford Taurus. Lifestyles of the rich and famous? Here in small-town Kindred? Like . . . not.

Suzanne poked a finger at an annoying tendril of hair that tickled the back of her neck. *Ten more minutes*, she told herself. *Gotta white knuckle it for ten more minutes. Then I'm outta here.*

She knew she should relax and let herself be coddled, but there were things that needed to be done. Kit Kaslik's vintage wedding was tomorrow and she had to figure out what to wear. Toni was babbling about launching a new book club. Her horse, Mocha Gent, still wasn't ready for the Logan County Fair. And Petra was all freaked out about the dinner theater that was coming up fast. And what else? Oh man. She'd gone and invited her boyfriend, Sam, over for dinner next week. And hadn't he promised to bring a bottle of Cabernet if she grilled a steak for him? Yes, she was pretty sure they'd struck that particular deal.

Suzanne drummed her fingers. She wasn't high maintenance, but she was definitely a high-achieving type A. Even so, she projected a certain calm and sense of poise, looking polished but not prim today in a soft denim shirt that was casually knotted at the waist of her trim white jeans. But underneath that denim shirt beat the heart of a racehorse— a thoroughbred who was smart, kind, and the kind of crackerjack businesswoman who could drive a hard bargain or negotiate a sticky contract.

Suzanne shifted in her chair. She figured she had to be parboiled by now. After all, that wasn't her morning spritz of Miss Dior that was wafting through the air. In fact, it smelled more like . . . what?

A few inches of sludgy French roast burning in the back room's Mr. Coffee? A cranked-up curling iron? Someone's hair being fricasseed by hot rollers?

Suzanne peered around suspiciously. Maybe it was Mrs. Krauser, who was tucked under the hair dryer directly across from her. Mrs. Krauser with a swirl of blue hair that perfectly matched her light blue puffed-sleeve blouse.

Wait a minute. Now she really did smell smoke!

Suzanne wiggled her nose and sniffed suspiciously. Was it her? Was *her* hair getting singed?

Tentatively, she touched a hand to the back of her head.

She was warm but not overly done. So . . . okay. Peering around again, she felt a faint prickle of anxiety. It had to be Mrs. Krauser over there, blotting at her pink cheeks with a white lace hankie.

But wait, Suzanne told herself. There was something definitely going on. Something cooking. And it wasn't Brett's complimentary snickerdoodle cookies from his back-room oven.

So where on earth was that smell coming from?

Suzanne ducked her head out from beneath the behemoth hair dryer and gazed around the salon, where everything seemed copasetic.

Still . . . it really did smell like smoke. And were her eyes deceiving her, or did everything suddenly look slightly ethereal and hazy? Like she was peering through a gelled lens?

Holy crap on a cracker! That *was* smoke!

Suzanne scrambled to her feet so fast every pair of eyes in the place was suddenly focused on her.

"I think there's . . ." she said, and then hesitated. Standing in the middle of the beauty shop, with everyone staring at her, she felt a little unsure of herself now. No sense making a ruckus over nothing. But when she inhaled, she definitely detected a nasty, acrid burning scent. A scent that touched the limbic portion of her brain and sent a trickle of fear down her spine.

Smoke. I definitely smell smoke.

"Something's on fire!" Suzanne cried out, trying to make herself heard above the roar of the blow-dryers and the blare of show tunes playing over multiple sets of speakers.

Brett looked up from where he was shampooing a client. "What?" He sounded puzzled as bubbles dripped from his hands. "Something's what?"

But Suzanne had already crossed the linoleum floor in three decisive strides and was pushing her way out the front door. On the sidewalk, smack-dab in the middle of downtown Kindred, the summer breeze caught her. It ripped the foils from her hair and sent her purple cape swirling out around her as if she were some kind of superhero.

And as Suzanne stood there, arms akimbo, knowing something was horribly wrong, she heard a terrifying roar. A rumble like the 4:10 Burlington Northern Santa Fe freight train speed-balling its way through Kindred. Within moments, the roar intensified, building to such a furious pitch that it sounded as if a tornado was barreling down upon the entire town. And then, without any warning whatsoever, the windows in the redbrick building right next door to Root 66 suddenly exploded with an earsplitting, heart-stopping blast. And a molten blizzard of jagged glass, chunks of brick, and wooden splinters belched out into the street!

Suzanne ducked as shards of glass shot past her like arrows! She felt the intense heat as giant tongues of red and orange flames belched from the blown-out windows as if they'd been spewed by World War II flamethrowers.

Fearing for her life, her self-preservation instinct kicking in big-time, Suzanne dove behind a large blue metal sign that proudly proclaimed Logan County Historic Site. She buried her face in her hands to shield herself from flying debris, hunched her shoulders, and prayed for deliverance.

A few moments later, Suzanne peered out tentatively and was shocked to see that the entire building, the old brick building that housed the County Services Bureau, was completely engulfed in flames!

Like a scene out of a Bruce Willis action flick, people suddenly came streaming out of all the surrounding businesses. Realtors, bakers, bankers, and druggists, all screaming hysterically, waving their arms and pointing at what had become a roiling, broiling inferno right in the middle of Main Street. Everyone seemed hysterical, yet nobody was doing much of anything to help.

"Call 911!" Suzanne yelped to Jenny Probst, who ran the Kindred Bakery with her husband, Bill.

Jenny nodded frantically. "We called. We already called. Fire department's on its way."

Two minutes later, a fire engine roared to the scene. A dozen firemen jumped off the shiny red truck even as they struggled to pull on heavy protective coats and helmets.

"There are people in there!" Suzanne cried to the fireman who seemed to be in charge. She pointed desperately at the building that was now a wild torrent of flames. "You've got to get them out!"

"Stand back, ma'am," ordered one of the firemen, and Suzanne did. She retreated a few steps and took her place in the middle of the street along with the rapidly growing crowd.

A second fire truck arrived and a metal ladder was quickly cranked up to a second-floor window. To shouts of encouragement from the onlookers, a fireman gamely scrambled up. Then a siren blatted loudly directly behind Suzanne, giving its authoritative *whoop whoop*, and she was forced to move out of the way again. Sheriff Roy Doogie had arrived in his official maroon and tan cruiser, along with two nervous-looking deputies.

Sheriff Doogie, by no means a small man, hopped out and immediately began to bully the crowd back even farther.

"Get back! Give 'em room to work!" Doogie shouted as his khaki bulk quivered. "Get out of the way!"

Then a white ambulance came screaming into the fray and rocked to a stop directly next to Doogie's cruiser. Two grim-faced EMTs jumped out, pulling a metal gurney with them, ready to lend medical assistance.

Thank goodness, Suzanne thought.

When Suzanne glanced up again, she was thankful to see a terrified-looking woman and a small child clambering over a second-story window ledge and into the waiting arms of the fireman on the ladder.

"That's Annie Wolfson," said a voice behind her.

Suzanne turned around and found Ricky Wilcox, the young man who was the groom in tomorrow's big wedding, staring fixedly at the rescue that was taking place.

Good, Suzanne thought. *Annie and her child have been saved.* But what about the folks in the first-floor County Services Bureau? Bruce Winthrop, the county agent. And his longtime secretary, Hannah Venable. What about those poor souls? Were they still inside?

Suzanne's question was partially answered when Winthrop, looking bug-eyed and scared spitless, suddenly crashed through the crowd. Arms flailing, he caromed off her right shoulder and then continued to push his way toward the burning building.

"Hannah!" Winthrop cried, frantically trying to charge through the surging crowd. "Hannah!" He seemed ready to rush into the burning building and save her single-handedly.

"Whoa, whoa!" Suzanne cried out. She dashed forward a couple of steps, snagged Winthrop's arm, and tried to pull him back. But the man was in such a blind panic that he simply shook her off. Suzanne made a final frantic grasp at the back of his tweed sport coat, found some purchase, and fought to reel him in backward. "Wait," she cried. "You can't go in there. You've got to let the firemen do their jobs."

Winthrop spun around to look at her, but was in such an anguished state that he didn't display a shred of recognition. His face contorted with fear as he tried to jerk away. "Let me go!" he cried. Then, in a pleading tone, "I've got to go in and get her."

"No you don't," Suzanne told him. She grabbed Winthrop's arm and gave a sharp tug that made him suddenly wince. But at least she'd commanded his attention. "Better to alert Doogie," she said. "He'll send a couple of firemen in to rescue Hannah."

"Gotta hurry hurry hurry," Winthrop chattered.

Suzanne waved an arm over her head and cried out, "Doogie! Sheriff Doogie!"

Doogie heard his name called out above the roar of the fire and the nervous mutterings of the crowd. He swiveled his big head around, saw Suzanne, and frowned.

Suzanne pushed closer toward him, dragging Winthrop along with her. "Hannah Venable's still inside," she shouted. "You've got to send someone in to get her."

Doogie's eyes widened in surprise and he gave a sharp nod. Then, quick as a wink, he grabbed the fire chief and pulled him into a fast conversation.

"You see?" said Suzanne. She still had a firm grip on Winthrop's arm. "They'll get Hannah out. She'll be okay."

Winthrop just nodded woodenly as if in a sleepwalker's trance.

The firemen shot thick streams of water at the building now, trying to beat back the flames. As water gushed from fat, brown hoses that crisscrossed the street, the fire hissed with fury but seemed to slowly retreat.

"I think they're gaining on the fire," Suzanne said to Jenny, who'd taken up a spot in the front lines next to them.

"I hope so," she said.

Two firemen hastily donned protective gear—full breathing apparatus and special asbestos coats. Then, after a hasty conference with their fire chief, they plunged into the burning building to make the daring rescue.

They were the brave ones, Suzanne thought. They were the ones who risked their lives for others. God bless and keep them.

The firemen working the hoses were definitely gaining a foothold on the fire now. Flames were knocked back as charred beams and red-hot embers sizzled and hissed.

"Getting it under control now," said Darrel Fuhrman, a man Suzanne recognized as one of Kindred's firemen. He was tall with slicked-back dark hair and eyes that danced with wild excitement.

Suzanne wondered idly why Fuhrman wasn't in the fray lending a hand, as she continued to keep her eyes fixed on the front door of the building, waiting to see Hannah Venable come staggering out. Hannah was the sweet-natured clerk who had manned the front desk at the County Services Bureau for the past fifteen years. She answered phones, kept the books, and handed out brochures on how to grow snap peas, raise baby lambs, and put up fruit jams and jellies without giving your family ptomaine poisoning.

Antsy and nervous now, Suzanne moved forward. She could feel the heat from the fire practically scorching her face, like having a too-close encounter with Petra's industrial-strength broiler back at the Cackleberry Club. What must the firemen be feeling inside, she wondered? What must poor Hannah be going through?

Sheriff Doogie whirled around and saw Suzanne edging up to the barricade.

"Get back!" he yelled, waving a meaty arm. "Everybody, get back!"

Suzanne retreated two paces, and then, when Doogie turned around, when he wasn't looking anymore, she crept back to where she'd been standing.

"Watch out!" cried one of the firemen who was manning a hose and shooting water through one of the front windows. "They're coming out."

Everyone peered expectantly through the drift of smoke and ashes. And then, like an apparition slowly appearing from a dense fog, the two firemen who'd made the daring foray into the burning building came into view. Their faces were smudged, their eyes red, their respirators dangled around their necks. But they carried a stretcher between them.

"They got her," Suzanne whispered. Everyone in the

crowd behind her seemed to relax and heave a deep sigh of relief.

Sheriff Doogie, who'd been clutching a blue blanket, stepped forward and laid it gingerly over the stretcher.

Thrilled that the firemen had been able to make such a daring rescue, Suzanne pressed even closer. "Is it Hannah?" she asked Doogie. She crept forward expectantly, practically bumping up against his beefy shoulder now. Surely they were going to load Hannah into the waiting ambulance. They'd rush her, lights twirling and sirens blaring, to Mercy Hospital, where Dr. Sam Hazelet, Suzanne's *boyfriend*, Dr. Hazelet, would resuscitate Hannah and tell the old dear what an amazingly close call she'd had.

"Is it Hannah?" Suzanne asked again.

The brim of Doogie's modified Smokey Bear hat barely quivered. A muscle twitched in his tightly clenched jaw.

"Is she . . . ?" Suzanne was about to say *okay*.

Doogie turned to her, his eyes sorrowful, his hangdog face registering total dismay. And uttered the two fateful words that Suzanne had not expected to hear: "She's dead."

CHAPTER 2

By the time Suzanne got back to the Cackleberry Club on Friday afternoon, Toni and Petra had heard the news about the fire. They were standing in the kitchen, listening to the latest report on the radio, looking bewildered and shaken.

"The whole thing's been on the radio," Toni cried out. "Tom Wick, one of WLGN's DJs, was downtown when the fire started. So he called in to the *Afternoon Farm Report* and the station broadcast a kind of play-by-play." Toni was wild-eyed and skittish. Her roaring metabolism kept her sleek as a cat and today her frizzled blond hair was piled atop her head making her look like a show pony. Except that show ponies didn't wear scrunchies, false eyelashes, and coral lip gloss.

"Hearing the whole thing pretty much killed us," said Petra. She was big-boned and sorrowful in a pink shirt, khaki slacks, and bright green Crocs, clutching and twisting her red-checked apron in her hands as if it were a lifeline. "It was like watching one of those wars in the Middle East broadcast live on CNN."

"Did they say anything about Hannah?" said Suzanne.

Toni nodded solemnly and Petra, even with her natural stoicism, looked like she was about to cry. None of them were used to having a major disaster like this intrude into their daily lives. Kindred was a sleepy little Midwestern town where you shared coffee and sticky buns with your next-door neighbor, sang hymns in church on Sunday, grew bushel baskets of zucchini, and watched life chug along on a nice even keel.

Nestled in a river valley next to Catawba Creek, their town was, Suzanne often thought, reminiscent of Brigadoon, that wonderful, mythical Scottish village that disappeared into the Highland mist only to emerge every hundred years.

Petra continued to be dazed and more than a little angry. "How could this happen?" she choked out. "Hannah was a member of our *church*. She has grown children." Her placid, square-boned Scandinavian face shone with outrage.

Suzanne noticed that Petra was already speaking about poor Hannah Venable in the past tense.

"Maybe we should say a prayer or something," Toni mumbled. A self-proclaimed wild child who favored skin-tight cowboy shirts, she wasn't a regular churchgoer like Petra, but this occasion seemed to call for a certain degree of solemnity.

"Yes, let's," urged Petra.

Suzanne quickly glanced through the pass-through. There were three customers still sitting in the café. Two at a table, one at the marble counter. They were all working on their afternoon coffee and apple pie, looking perfectly content.

"Okay," said Suzanne. "Let's take a few minutes right now. But do it fast."

"Prayer should never be rushed," said Petra.

"I think she meant for us to keep it short but sweet," said Toni. "Really, I'm sure it will be heard."

"Dear Lord," said Petra as she bowed her head, "please accept dear Hannah Venable into your Kingdom. Please know that she was a truly good person, kind and gentle, and that she . . ." Petra halted abruptly as tears welled up in her eyes and streamed down her face. She bit her lip and shook her head, unable to go on.

"And know that Hannah made the best cherry pie in town," Toni finished.

"Amen," said Suzanne. She figured they really did have to wrap this up, since old Mr. Henderson was suddenly standing at the cash register, looking around, waiting to pay his bill. Not only that, she'd just caught a glint of Doogie's cruiser as it rolled into their front parking lot.

Now what? Suzanne wondered.

LIKE a rifle shot, the screen door whapped open hard against the wall and Sheriff Doogie strode into the practically deserted café. His leather utility belt creaked, his broad shoulders were hunched forward, and his gait seemed heavy and dragging. Only his sharp law enforcement eyes betrayed his high level of anger and intensity.

Toni, who was piling dirty dishes into a gray plastic tub, looked up and said to Suzanne, "I have a feeling we won't be closing none too early today."

Suzanne took one look at Doogie and figured the same thing.

Doogie made a beeline for the end stool at the marble counter. It was his favorite stool, the one that creaked when he sat down and, over the past couple of years, had assumed a distinct list.

Suzanne reached behind her and grabbed a pot of coffee from where it rested on the soda fountain backdrop they'd scrounged from an old drugstore. She filled a ceramic mug for Doogie and slid it across the counter to him. "How are things at the fire?" she asked. But she could tell by the look on his face that the situation wasn't good.

"Terrible," said Doogie. He took a quick gulp of coffee. "Real bad. The building's a complete disaster and—"

Petra came flying out of the kitchen, shoes clumping, hair sticking up in uncharacteristic spikiness, to interrupt. "Who *cares* about the stupid building?" she demanded. "We want to know about Hannah! Did the poor woman even have a chance?"

Doogie threw a sad, haunted look in her direction and shook his big head. "Probably not. I'm sorry . . ." His voice dropped off to a low mumble.

"Did Hannah burn to death?" Toni asked, edging closer to the group. Toni had a certain fascination with the macabre that wasn't always healthy.

"Toni!" cried Petra. "That's a terrible thought!"

But Doogie hastened to alleviate their fears.

"No, no," said Doogie, spreading his hands as if to make peace. "The fire chief was pretty sure that Hannah was overcome with smoke first."

"Which means she suffocated," said Petra. She gazed at them in horror. "That's a *terrible* way to go."

"Try not to think of it that way," said Suzanne. "Try to think of it as Hannah blacking out and not suffering much."

Petra sniffed and pulled a hankie from her apron pocket. "I can *try* to think about it that way, but it won't be easy."

"Do they know what caused the fire?" Suzanne asked.

"Was it faulty wiring?" asked Toni. "That was a pretty old building, after all."

"On the Historic Register," said Suzanne, recalling the sign she'd been so very lucky to duck behind.

Doogie sucked air through his front teeth and hesitated.

"Doogie, what?" said Suzanne. She knew the sheriff well

enough to know when he was stalling. Their battery of questions had caught him a little unprepared.

Doogie scratched at his chin with the back of his hand. "Ah, jeez." He looked like he was mulling something over in his head.

"What?" said Petra.

"Tell us," said Toni.

"Fire Chief Finley's working on a couple of things," said Doogie.

Suzanne cocked her head. "Such as?"

Doogie stared directly at her. "The fire started with a huge burst, right? I mean, you were there. Next door at that beauty salon."

"It felt like that's the way it happened," said Suzanne. Sure it had. She'd smelled smoke, run outside, and then, *boom*, the fire was suddenly raging.

"Did you hear a loud explosion first?" Doogie asked.

"Not really," said Suzanne.

"What are you thinking?" asked Toni. "That it was a gas main explosion?"

"Not exactly," said Doogie. He picked up his coffee cup and took a very deliberate sip. Watched out of the corner of his eye as the last customer got up and left.

"There's something else going on here, isn't there?" said Suzanne. "You're already working on a theory."

Doogie hesitated for a moment. "Fire Chief Finley thought there might have been an accelerant."

"An accident?" said Petra.

"No, an accelerant," Doogie repeated.

Toni frowned. "Oh, you mean like the fire accelerated and burned super fast? Like spontaneous combustion?"

"Not exactly," said Doogie. He looked around as if someone might be listening in. As if they weren't the only ones hunched around the counter at the Cackleberry Club at four in the afternoon. "You ladies have to keep what I tell you under your hats, okay? I mean, you can't be spreading this information all over town."

"What?" said Suzanne, her heart doing a little flip-flop. Then, when Doogie still seemed hesitant, she spoke the terrible words they'd all been thinking but hadn't wanted to voice. "Are you saying the fire was deliberately set? That it was arson?"

Doogie gave a kind of tight-lipped grimace. "It's looking that way, yes."

"How would you determine that for sure?" asked Toni.

Doogie frowned. "For one thing, Chief Finley is talking about bringing in an arson investigator."

"Oh my," said Toni. "This is serious."

"CRAZY things like fires and arson aren't supposed to happen in Kindred," declared Petra.

Sheriff Doogie had departed some fifteen minutes ago, a white bakery bag containing three sticky rolls clutched in his hand. Now the three of them were sitting in the Knitting Nest, trying to sort through and digest Doogie's words. Though he hadn't expanded on his arson theory, or said that he believed it was the absolute gospel truth, he'd certainly tap-danced around the idea.

"If it was arson," said Toni, "then it was . . ."

"Intentional," said Suzanne.

"Exactly," said Petra. "So who would . . . ?" She shook her head and dabbed a hankie to her eyes. For all of Petra's toughness, she was still pretty much in shock.

"Who indeed?" Suzanne murmured. She gazed about the Knitting Nest, the small shop that was adjacent to the café and right next door to their Book Nook. With hundreds of skeins of gorgeous yarn tucked into virtually every corner, and displays of knitting needles and quilt squares, it was a cheery little place. A kind of safe harbor. Women came from all over the tri-county area to settle into the comfy, rump-sprung chairs, work on their latest project, sip tea, and hang out. Generally, the Knitting Nest was Petra's domain. She taught knitting classes several nights a week, always encouraging her knitters with smiles and creative suggestions on new stitches and techniques. And the colorful shawls, wraps, and sweaters she'd whipped up herself were artfully displayed on the walls.

But today Petra's heart was truly broken. And no kind words would mend it, no pair of smooth bamboo knitting needles would soften the look of despair on her face.

"We have to do something," Petra said finally.

Toni hunched her shoulders. "Do what? That's easy to wish for from the cozy environs of the Knitting Nest, but how would we even begin to make things right?"

"Well, we probably can't do *that*," said Petra. "Since the damage has already been done and Hannah is dead. But we can certainly do something about finding her some justice."

"How about revenge?" said Toni. She prided herself on her feistiness. "That sounds good to me."

"You know what?" said Suzanne. "There *is* something we can do."

"Thank you, Suzanne," said Petra.

"Whatcha got in mind?" said Toni.

Suzanne held up a finger. "We can wait patiently until Doogie and Fire Chief Finley bring a professional arson investigator into town. An expert who can analyze the ashes and cinders and everything else and tell us what really happened. After all, it could have been an accident. We don't know for sure that it was arson. Doogie was really just . . . speculating."

"So we do nothing?" Petra sounded shocked. "But . . ."

"Arson just sounds awfully drastic," said Suzanne. "Especially for the County Services Bureau." She was suddenly pinning all her hopes on a logical explanation for today's fire.

"I don't know," said Toni. "Arson's not all that tricky to pull off. Any dunce can do it. Heck, Junior once stuffed some greasy old car rags in a coffee can and then lit up a Lucky Strike." Junior was Toni's estranged husband and not the brightest bulb in the box.

"Good heavens," said Petra. "What happened?"

"The dang rags pretty much exploded right in his face and the flames singed his eyebrows off is what happened," said Toni. "Burned those furry little caterpillars right off his face."

"I remember that particular mishap," said Suzanne. "Junior had to use an eyebrow pencil for months just to look normal."

"But he always used too much," said Toni. "And ended up looking like a Groucho Marx impersonator."

"Sometimes I think that husband of yours isn't quite right in the head," said Petra. She was sitting in a rocking chair, slowly picking nonexistent fuzz off her slacks.

"What do you expect?" said Toni. "The poor guy suffers from DDT."

"Don't you mean ADD?" said Suzanne.

"Yeah, that, too," said Toni.

"Petra," said Suzanne, glancing at her friend, who was slouching even deeper in her chair, "you look like you're headed into a deep blue funk."

"I think I am," said Petra. "Because I . . ." She seemed to want to say more, but stopped herself by tightly clenching her jaw.

Toni jumped up from her chair and scurried over to fling her arms around Petra. "Don't funk out on us, honey. Please try to think of something upbeat or happy."

"Like what?" said Petra. "When all I really want . . ."

"For one thing," said Toni, "tomorrow is Kit's big wedding day. I know you've been looking forward to that. We all have."

Kit Kaslik was a sometime Cackleberry Club employee

that Suzanne and Petra had rescued from her former job as an exotic dancer at Hoobly's Roadhouse, a disreputable bar out on County Road 18. Kit, now pregnant, was marrying her fiancé, Ricky Wilcox, tomorrow in an outdoor ceremony at Founder's Park. They'd all been looking forward to the wedding and, to celebrate the joyful event, Petra had even promised to bake a truly spectacular wedding cake.

"Yes," said Petra, still looking perturbed, "there is that."

"And remember," Toni went on, "Kit's having a *vintage* wedding. So the wedding party is going to be all duded up in vintage clothes from that funky little shop, Second Time Around, over in Jessup." She grinned. "I got a sneak peek at Kit's dress. It's all ruffled and romantic, very '60s earth mother."

"It sounds lovely," said Suzanne, chiming in.

"And it's nice and flowy," said Toni. "So you can't really tell that Kit's got a bun in the oven."

"Oh dear," said Petra, her brow furrowing. "I wish you hadn't brought *that* up." Petra wasn't thrilled that Kit was having what she euphemistically referred to as a shotgun wedding.

"Let's just let that go," said Suzanne. "It is what it is and we can't change things."

Toni looked thoughtful. "I just hope there isn't any fall-out from the fire and that it's not still smoky downtown. That burned building is awfully close to the park where Kit's wedding is gonna take place."

"I doubt the fire will upset her plans at all," said Suzanne. "That building's still a couple of blocks away. You can't even see it from where the bandstand is. There's a whole row of birch trees and a grove of oaks blocking the view."

"Petra," said Toni, "you're still going to bake Kit's wedding cake, aren't you?"

"Of course I am," said Petra. "I said I would and I never break my promises. I've got a design all sketched out and I plan to start baking first thing tomorrow so the cake's all nice and fresh."

"That'll for sure put you in a better mood," said Toni.

"I don't know," said Petra. She hoisted herself out of her chair with a huge sigh of resignation. "I can't stop thinking about Hannah and . . ." She stopped abruptly and shook her head.

"Petra," said Suzanne. "Is there something you want to tell us?" It felt like Petra was holding back.

"No," said Petra. "At least not until I get my mind in the right place."

CHAPTER 3

THEY locked up the Cackleberry Club then, getting ready to head for home. After Petra sped off in her car, still looking upset and out of sorts, Suzanne and Toni lingered in the back parking lot, talking.

With the late-summer sun lasering down through the oaks and pine trees that bordered the lot, the day felt warm and mellow. But the leaves on the sumac were starting to turn red and Suzanne had noticed a few tinges of gold and yellow among the poplars and white oaks.

Summer on the wane, autumn sneaking up on us, she thought. Where did the time go? Why did the seasons whip by as if you were riding a wildly spinning carrousel and leaning out to frantically grab the brass ring?

And then Suzanne remembered, she *had* grabbed the brass ring. After her husband, Walter, had died a year and a half ago, she hadn't been sure if she could ever be truly happy again. That worry had been one of the deciding factors, the impetus to open the Cackleberry Club. If you build it, they will come, she'd told herself. Plus it would give her mind a vacation from sorrow and sadness. And she had hoped that maybe, somewhere along the line, she might find peace and happiness again.

Well, customers had come. They poured in for morning breakfast, farm-to-table lunches, and afternoon tea and scones. And somewhere in that whole crazy, jumbled process of becoming an entrepreneur, negotiating contracts, building a customer base, and expanding into books and yarn, Suzanne found herself bouncing back. She found her happy. And then, wonder of wonders, she'd met Dr. Sam Hazelet, whose crooked grin, sense of humor, and steady optimism had *really* made her happy.

And wasn't that just the cherry on top of the hot fudge sundae.

Suzanne blinked, suddenly coming out of her reverie and realizing that Toni had just spoken to her.

"Excuse me, what did you say?"

"Have you got big plans for tonight?" By "big plans" Toni was asking if Suzanne had a date with Sam.

"No, nothing. What about you?"

"Aw, I'm just gonna go home and curl up with the latest issue of *OK!* magazine. See which stars are back in rehab."

"Ah," said Suzanne. She figured Toni had something on her mind. Sooner or later she'd spit it out.

Toni stuck the scuffed toe of one cowboy boot into the sand and shoved it around, creating a panorama of miniature hieroglyphics. "What if you and I went downtown and took a look at that burned-out building?"

"Why would we want to do that?"

Toni shook her head. "Dunno. It just feels like something we should do. Kind of for Hannah's sake. Look at the . . . remains."

Suzanne mulled this over for a few moments. "Okay. I guess I can see your point." Truth be told, she was a little curious, too. What was going on down there? Had any sort of arson investigation kicked into gear yet? Had the building been deemed an official crime scene? Maybe there were some answers to be gleaned. She pulled open the driver's side door of her Taurus. "See you there?"

"Sure," said Toni.

Just as Suzanne was pulling out, a blue BMW turned into her lot and cruised toward her. She rolled to a stop, grinned happily, and thought to herself, *Sam, how perfect.* She jumped from her car just as Sam came to a quick stop and jumped out of his car. He was wearing blue scrubs and a pair of New Balance shoes. With casually tousled brown hair and intelligent blue eyes, he had a slightly preppy, boy-next-door look to him.

They were in each other's arms in a heartbeat, kissing, hugging, cooing greetings to each other since it had been two whole days since they'd last seen each other.

"I was worried about you," Sam said, his words tumbling out. "I knew you were downtown today." His eyes mirrored his concern; his voice, generally smooth and mellow, conveyed a touch of worry.

"I witnessed the entire thing," said Suzanne. "The explosion, fire, everything. I was getting my hair, um, done at Root 66." She didn't want to go into too much detail. Sam was four years younger than she was, and didn't need to know all the sordid details about root touch-ups, foils, and hair color. Instead, she went on to tell him about the fire, the firemen showing up, and the tragedy of poor Hannah Venable.

"I knew it was bad," said Sam. "I was in a meeting at the hospital and heard the ambulance go screaming out of the ER bay."

"But they were too late."

"It's still a piece of luck that there was only one casualty."

"Sheriff Doogie's already talking arson," Suzanne blurted out.

"Is that a fact? Wow. I hadn't heard anything about that. That puts a whole 'nother spin on things."

"Why would someone intentionally set a fire?" Suzanne asked. "For the thrill of it? To cover something up? Or are they just . . . deviant?"

"I'm no psychiatrist," said Sam. "But I know that arson often has deep-seated roots that can stretch back to an unhappy childhood."

"Sounds awful," said Suzanne. "So a person does it just to gain attention?"

"Sometimes," said Sam. "Or they're acting out, crying for help, or . . ." He stopped.

"Or what?"

"Or they think their actions are perfectly normal."

Suzanne's brows knit together. "Normal? How would you deal with someone with that sort of mentality?"

Sam gazed at her. "Very carefully." Then his smile warmed up again. "Okay, gotta get back to work. You take care now."

"Always," said Suzanne.

"OH man," Toni cried when they met in the middle of Main Street some ten minutes later. "With the County Services Building destroyed, this block looks like a jack-o'-lantern with its front teeth knocked out."

Suzanne had to agree. The building, still smoldering, stood in total ruin. The front walls and windows were completely gone. So was the second floor, where a small apartment had been located. The only thing left of the roof was a web of blackened timber, open to the sky in most places. The brick wall that abutted Root 66 seemed relatively intact, but the opposite side and back walls had been reduced to rubble. The gutted, jagged remains reminded

Suzanne of old newsreels she'd seen of bombed-out buildings in Berlin at the end of World War II.

"And it's still all smoky," said Toni, wrinkling her nose.

"It's awful," Suzanne agreed. An acrid smell and faint haze hung over this entire block of downtown Kindred. And even though the rubble was black and charred—nothing really left to burn—the smaller of the town's two fire trucks was still parked at the curb with two uniformed firemen standing watch.

"I guess they think the fire might start up again," said Toni, gesturing at the fire truck.

"Or maybe that a gas line might have been disrupted and could spark another blaze," said Suzanne.

"They can do that?"

"I *think* so," said Suzanne. She noticed that Gene Gandle, the intrepid reporter from the *Bugle*, was dashing about, snapping pictures like crazy and scribbling in his notebook. With his skinny body and flapping suit, he reminded her of a scarecrow.

Toni glanced around at the crowd of two dozen or so folks who had gathered as a hazy twilight began to slowly descend upon their town. They all talked in low voices and seemed intrigued by the wreckage. "See, we weren't the only ones who felt compelled to come here. Lots of folks came out to take a gander."

"This is a major event for Kindred," said Suzanne. "In fact, I don't recall ever seeing a fire quite this destructive."

"There was that fire last year at the Pixie Quick," said Toni.

"I think some kids tossed firecrackers into the Dumpster out back. It just blew the top off and spread a bunch of rotten lettuce and oranges around."

"Oh . . . right," said Toni as she continued to scan the crowd. "Hey!" She brightened considerably when she suddenly spotted a familiar face. "Look who's here." She lifted an arm and pointed toward Ricky Wilcox.

"Back again," said Suzanne. "I ran into Ricky this afternoon right at the height of the fire. Well, him and just about everybody else in downtown Kindred."

"Hey, Ricky!" Toni called. She was waving like crazy now, all jacked up with excitement. "Howdy-do, fella!"

Ricky noticed Toni waving and lifted an arm in a shy return greeting. Then he ambled through the crowd to talk to them. Ricky had sandy brown hair that perfectly matched his eyes, a husky build, and a youthful face, sprinkled with freckles and tanned from a summer of outdoor work.

"What are *you* doing here?" said Toni. "Aren't you supposed to be attending some wild and crazy bachelor party and pouring Wild Turkey down your gullet? After all, this is your last night as a free man!"

Ricky ducked his head. "Ah, I was just checking on the arrangements over in the park."

"I hope everything's okay," said Suzanne. She hoped the smoke hadn't affected any of the wedding plans. To her, a wedding in the park, under a verdant bower of trees, seemed like a perfect idea. After all, what better cathedral to be married in than God's own?

"Everything looks pretty fantastic," said Ricky, a grin creasing his face. "The bandstand has been strung with garlands and little white twinkle lights, and the chairs go in first thing tomorrow."

"You must be all keyed up about this," said Toni. "I know we are."

"I just wish Kit and I had more time for a proper honeymoon," said Ricky.

"Oh no," said Suzanne. "Don't tell me your National Guard unit finally got called up?" She was afraid that was going to happen. Kit had been giving them constant updates on Ricky's unit and there'd been rumors all over town.

Ricky nodded. "Yup, looks like I'm off to Afghanistan. I was hoping it wouldn't happen until November, but our orders are to take off this coming Thursday. At least that's the plan." He furrowed his brow. "I had to give notice at work. Sure hate to give up twenty bucks an hour for what Uncle Sam is going to pay me."

"Only six days until you have to leave," said Toni. "That's an awfully short honeymoon." She gave a sly wink. "I trust you'll make the best of it."

Suzanne just smiled. With Kit three months pregnant, she figured the honeymoon had already come and gone. Now she just prayed that the two young people could manage the stress of a long-distance military marriage as well as the birth of their first child.

Toni clapped Ricky on the back. "Okay, Mr. Groom, we'll see you tomorrow!"

As Suzanne and Toni headed for their cars, they were suddenly accosted by another familiar character.

"Good evening, ladies," said Carmen Copeland. Carmen was a prominent romance author who lived in the neighboring town of Jessup. She was caustic, snooty, snotty, and exotic-looking—and the *New York Times* bestsellers she consistently churned out had made her rich. Which meant she indulged her taste in clothes and jewelry and always wrapped herself in the latest couture. Today her floral-print silk blouse and cream suede skirt were pure Givenchy, and the bright red soles on her four-inch-high alligator stilettos clearly proclaimed Louboutin.

Because Carmen considered herself a glittering fashionista and the undisputed arbiter in all matters of taste and style, she'd opened a clothing boutique called Alchemy in downtown Kindred. Suzanne always figured it was Carmen's fiendish scheme to impose fashion and flair on what Carmen considered the little brown wrens of Kindred. But to Suzanne's amazement, Carmen's boutique had proven quite successful. Women actually purchased the silk blouses, filmy scarves, leather moto jackets, statement rings, and Hudson jeans that Carmen stocked in her shop. And Suzanne's good friend Missy Langston, although she had been fired and rehired multiple times by Carmen, still worked as store manager.

Though Suzanne carried the entire backlist of Carmen's books in her Book Nook, the two women were basically oil and water. For whatever reason, they always seemed to argue or clash. Tonight, however, Suzanne made up her mind to be civil to Carmen. Correction, more than civil. She would shoot for cordial.

"How are things in the rarefied air of the *New York Times?*" Suzanne asked. Carmen's most recent release, *Blossom's Sweet Revenge*, had just landed at the number seven slot on the list.

"Holding my own," said Carmen. "But as far as rarefied air goes, isn't *this* a complete disaster?" She flapped one hand disdainfully at the hulking wreck of the burned building.

Suzanne bit down hard, the better to hold her tongue. "You know, Carmen, Hannah Venable was killed here today."

"You're right," said Carmen, "it's terribly sad." She didn't sound one bit sad. "But this horrendous odor . . . I'm terrified it's going to seep into my boutique and taint all our clothing. We just received an enormous shipment of Cavalli jeans this morning—a dozen boxes—and I'm debating whether to even unpack them." She waved a hand in front of her nose as if, through sheer force of will, she could eradicate the offensive odor.

"It's supposed to be nice and breezy tonight," said Toni. "Maybe this smoke will all get swept away." She gave a little snort. "Maybe all the way over to Jessup."

"I *live* in Jessup," Carmen said in a steely tone.

"Oh," said Toni. "Sorry."

"Are you coming to the big wedding tomorrow?" Suzanne asked.

"I'm afraid I had to decline," said Carmen. "As usual, I have a publishing deadline that's fraying my nerves and wrecking havoc with my beauty sleep."

"Be sure to stop by the Cackleberry Club when you get a chance," said Suzanne. "We'd love to have you sign a few copies of your new book. In fact, we've already sold nearly half our stock." Carmen gave a self-satisfied smile and Suzanne decided that Carmen reminded her of the evil queen in *Sleeping Beauty.* If Carmen ever offered her an apple wedge she'd for sure decline it.

"Your new book looks totally hot," Toni bubbled. "At least the guy on the cover does!"

"Aren't you sweet," said Carmen, "to offer such a learned literary critique." She gave Toni a withering glance that also seemed to convey pity.

"See you later," said Suzanne. She gave Toni's arm a good tug and pulled her away.

When they were out of earshot, Toni said, "Why is it I can start out feeling like a million bucks, and when I run into Carmen I get reduced to a lousy peso?"

"Don't pay the slightest bit of attention to her," said Suzanne. "She does that to everyone. Tries to intimidate or one-up you."

"With you, too?"

"Especially me," said Suzanne. "For whatever reason, Carmen never misses an opportunity to dis me."

"I think that's because Carmen used to have the hots for Sam," said Toni. "Especially when he first came to town." She grinned. "But *you* were the one who caught him."

"It's not exactly like reeling in a walleye," Suzanne chuckled.

"No, it's a lot better."

Suzanne hesitated. "Toni, would you like to come home with me and have dinner?" Since separating from Junior, Toni had been living in a cramped apartment that was basically just a couple of rooms. Her galley kitchen, which consisted of a two-burner stove and small refrigerator, was more suited to a college dorm room. Or a deer camp out in the sticks.

Toni grinned happily at the impromptu invitation. "Would I ever!"

CHAPTER 4

SUZANNE had two dogs, Baxter and Scruff. But when she and Toni walked through the front door, you'd have thought a pack of wild dogs from the Serengeti inhabited her house. The dogs whirled, twirled, howled, and barked, giving the impression of fierce guard dogs even as they wagged their tails furiously and pulled their mouths into happy little dog grins.

"Whoa, guys," said Suzanne, grabbing at collars and trying her best to get them settled. "Try to keep it down to a dull roar, okay?"

But Toni had already dropped to her knees and was administering expansive hugs and pets. "Baxter, you handsome hunk of dog, gimme five." Baxter, an Irish setter and Lab mix, lifted his paw and placed it in Toni's outstretched hand.

"That's funny," said Suzanne, observing them. "I never taught him that particular trick."

Toni was busy chucking Baxter under the chin. "That's because he doesn't do cheap tricks. Baxter is his own dawg."

She turned to Scruff, a black-and-white mongrel that Suzanne had found wounded and wandering down a dark country road. "And you, Mr. Scruff. Lookin' good as usual."

"Are you sure you never studied to be a dog trainer?" Suzanne asked. Toni seemed to have them eating out of her hand. "Or a dog whisperer?"

Toni popped up and wiped her hands on her jeans. "Nope, I just have a natural affinity with animals." She grinned. "Maybe that's why I still get along so well with Junior. He's kind of a mangy critter himself."

Suzanne headed into her kitchen, Toni and the dogs following along behind. "I thought you were going to file for divorce." She turned on the faucet and washed her hands. "It's high time, you know."

Toni and Junior had gotten hitched in Las Vegas and their marriage had lasted about as long as it took for the return flight to touch down on the tarmac. Toni talked a good game about divorcing Junior Garrett, but so far there hadn't been any serious forward progress.

Toni scrunched her face into an expression of mock concern. "I know you and Petra think I should dump Junior for good. But the thing about him is . . . he kind of grows on you."

"You could say the same thing about mildew or dry rot," said Suzanne.

"Seriously," said Toni, "Junior's been trying very hard to make things up to me. You remember a couple of months ago when he spray-painted my name on that overpass? In Day-Glo silver?"

"How could I forget? The state police came calling and wanted to issue you a citation. If we hadn't asked Doogie to step in . . ."

"Yeah, I know," said Toni. "But don't you see, it was proof that Junior cares about me, that deep down he really loves me."

"You think?"

"Oh yeah. I mean, dangling over a couple lanes of traffic like that, he could have fallen and broken his fool neck. But he risked it anyway. He did it for love."

"Dear Lord," muttered Suzanne. She wondered when coming just inches from being encased in a full-body cast constituted true love.

WHILE Suzanne chopped tomatoes and fresh herbs for her salad, Toni sat at the counter playing with a set of wooden spoons, drumming them against the counter.

"I love this kitchen," Toni said with a quick *rat-a-tat-tat*. "If I ever won the Publishers Clearing House sweepstakes, I would take all the money and design a kitchen just like this. This has gotta be my dream kitchen."

"If you win your million, maybe you should build a house first," said Suzanne.

"I get that. But this kitchen, this is a real *cook's* kitchen."

Suzanne smiled, because she knew it really was. Their old kitchen (hers and Walter's) had been your basic '60s-style kitchen installed in a 1930s vintage Cape Cod home. It had sported so-so linoleum, harvest green appliances, and crappy cupboards. But a few months of planning, dealing with contractors, and living amidst Sheetrock and throat-clogging dust had resulted in the kitchen she enjoyed today. It was a bright, modern space complete with granite countertops, an area to hang her collection of copper pots and pans, a Wolf gas range, and a Sub-Zero refrigerator.

"Whatcha planning to do with that chicken you've been whacking into submission?" Toni asked.

"Do a stir-fry with some onions, ginger, red peppers, bok choy, and water chestnuts," said Suzanne. "And then add some sweet-and-sour sauce."

"Yum. Do you want me to help? I feel like a useless blob just sitting here."

"Why don't you grab a bottle of wine out of the fridge and pour us a little liquid refreshment?"

"Now there's a grand idea," said Toni. She reached overhead and grabbed two wineglasses from a hanging rack. "Have ourselves a nice relaxing TGI Friday drink."

"If not now, when?" said Suzanne.

While Suzanne chopped her veggies, Toni took care of the wine.

"Here you go, cookie," she said, handing Suzanne a glass of Chablis.

Suzanne took a sip just as the phone shrilled.

"Hmm," said Toni. "I hope it's not more trouble."

It wasn't trouble at all, it was Sam. He was anxious to hear if Suzanne had picked up any more information about today's big fire.

"Not really," she told him. "But the building is still smoldering and there's a bunch of looky-loos wandering around."

"Including you."

"Including me and Toni. Are you still at the hospital?"

"Yup, but I'm leaving in . . . oh, another hour or two. Three at the most."

"Take care," said Suzanne.

"I wish I could be there with you," said Sam. "I hope you're not lonesome or anything." He sounded kind of wistful.

"I'm good. Toni's here for dinner."

"Have fun then." Now he really did sound wistful.

When Suzanne hung up the phone, she said, "Sam says we should have fun."

"That means we should probably refill our wineglasses, right?"

"Sounds right to me," said Suzanne. She took off the ring she was wearing, set it on the counter next to the stove, and started her stir-fry in earnest.

"That ring you have," said Toni. "The mother-of-pearl?"

"Hmm?"

"I've always wondered. If there's mother-of-pearl is there also father-of-pearl?"

"You pose an interesting question," said Suzanne as she dumped her diced chicken into the sizzling wok.

"The thing is," said Toni, really getting into it now, "I'm always confused when there isn't an opposite. Take, for example, the term 'starter house.' Does that imply there's also an 'ender house'? Or what about feeling overwhelmed. If you're not all that upset can you just be whelmed?"

"Toni," said Suzanne, "your mind works in very strange ways."

"Suspicious ways, too," said Toni.

BECAUSE she enjoyed homemaking and setting a nice table, Suzanne placed linen place mats on the table, added a couple of tall white tapers in silver candlesticks, then placed sets of chopsticks next to their plates.

"Yikes," said Toni as Suzanne lit the candles and dimmed the lights. "It's not enough that we have to dine like we're in a fancy restaurant? Now I gotta use chopsticks, too?"

"I've seen you use chopsticks before."

"Sure, when I pick up an order of sweet-and-sour chicken at Mr. Chang's Golden Foo Foo Palace. But not like this." She picked them up. "What are these . . . ivory?"

"I don't think you're allowed to import ivory anymore, I'm pretty sure these are just acrylic."

"Excellent," said Toni. "No acrylics were harmed in the making of this meal."

They sat down and ate, enjoying the stir-fry chicken, sipping their wine, talking again about today's big fire.

"I bet once Doogie brings in a state arson investigator," said Toni, "all his questions will get answered fairly quickly."

"You think so?"

"Oh yeah. I once watched a show on the Discovery Channel that was all about arson. Turns out those investigators are real cagey guys. They can run precise chemical tests that'll determine exactly what kind of gas or kerosene or lighter fluid was used. They can almost pinpoint it down to the exact gas station where it was purchased."

"What good would that do?"

"Then the police can go through surveillance videos of all the area gas stations." Toni shrugged. "Pretty much every gas station and convenience store has cameras these days. Because of, you know, all the stickups and stuff."

"You know a lot about this forensics business, don't you?"

"It's all I watch on TV. Well, that and *Dancing with the Stars* and the medical mysteries shows. But not the really gross stuff, like poisonous snake bites and sixty-pound tumors."

"You might be right about arson investigators figuring this out fairly quickly," said Suzanne. "But when we talked to Doogie, he seemed a little . . . what would you call it? Stumped."

"Still," said Toni. "He can be smart when he wants to."

They had just finished dinner when the doorbell sounded. *Bing bang bong.* Which of course set off a cacophony of barks and the dogs' mad rush to the door.

"Who do you suppose that is?" asked Toni. "Were you expecting somebody to drop by? Maybe Sam?"

"Nope," Suzanne said over her shoulder as she hurried to the front door. "Not tonight anyway."

"Maybe he changed his mind," Toni called after her. "In which case I should probably skedaddle. Leave you two lovebirds to . . ."

"Petra!" came Suzanne's surprised voice.

Toni did a double take. "Petra? She's here?"

Not two seconds later, Suzanne and Petra came strolling into the dining room followed by the pair of dancing dogs.

"Hey," said Toni, her voice sounding buoyant after two glasses of wine. "Long time no see." Then she registered the look of grim determination on Petra's broad face and said, "Uh-oh, did something happen?"

"Petra wants to talk to us," Suzanne said to Toni.

"I *need* to talk to you," said Petra. She hesitated for a moment, and then said, "Actually, it's more like a group think. But it can wait until you've finished eating."

Toni popped up from her chair like an excited gopher. "We're done. Really. What's on your mind?"

"Let's move into the living room," said Suzanne. She picked up her wineglass and said, "Petra, would you like a glass of Chablis?"

"Um . . . sure," said Petra.

"Make yourself comfortable and I'll get you one," said Suzanne.

"No need," said Toni. "I'll just run and grab the bottle."

They all finally settled down, Suzanne and Petra on the cushy sofa, Toni sitting cross-legged on the floor. Petra shrugged out of her nubby sweater and set her purse down in the middle of the coffee table. Her bag was a big old black leather thing, square and clunky, like the ones that the queen of England carried. Only Petra's was about twenty years old, since she prided herself on frugality and was always loath to quit on a good thing.

"What's up?" Suzanne asked. For whatever reason, Petra was clearly on edge and reluctant to begin.

Petra cleared her throat and said, "I've been thinking."

"About what?" said Toni.

"Petra, what's bothering you?" said Suzanne. Petra looked frightened and her pent-up emotion had subtly changed the atmosphere in the room, making it feel almost electrically charged.

"I think somebody set that fire on purpose," said Petra.

Suzanne was watching her friend closely. "Well, I think

we all pretty much agree on that. That's what Sheriff Doogie was alluding to with his talk about accelerants and bringing in an arson investigator." So why exactly was Petra here? she wondered. Just to confirm their suspicions and talk it out—try to ease her mind about Hannah? Or was something else going on?

Toni suddenly jumped in. "Yeah, we get that, honey. Of course, the big question is, *why* would somebody set fire to that building? I mean, it was the County Services Building where Hannah and Bruce worked. So what would be the purpose, anyway? To burn all the little printed pamphlets and stuff? That doesn't make sense to me."

"Okay," said Petra, her posture suddenly stiffening. "How about this? What if Hannah Venable's husband was cheating on her?"

"What!" said Toni. She reacted so violently, jerking her arm back, that she splashed wine onto Suzanne's carpet. "You mean Jack?"

Petra's words had pretty much dropped a big fat bombshell right in the middle of their cozy little confab.

"Whoa, whoa, whoa," said Toni even as she grabbed a napkin to sop up the spill. "Do you know this for sure?"

"Trust me," said Petra, her gaze hardening, "I pretty much know."

"Hannah told you?" said Suzanne. She looked at Petra in alarm, deciding this piece of information might be crucial to Doogie's arson investigation.

"Well, Hannah didn't tell me in so many words," said Petra.

Toni looked curious. "Then what'd she say?" Having been estranged from Junior for the past couple of years, Toni was well versed in the intricacies of dealing with cheating spouses. After all, when Junior had cheated on her, the *first* time Junior had cheated on her, it was with the floozy bartender at the VFW who wore hot pink extensions in her hair. Since then, he'd moved on to a few trailer park babes.

"Petra," said Suzanne, "I think you need to explain yourself a little more clearly. Was Hannah's husband cheating on her or wasn't he? And I hate to ask this, but had Jack threatened her in some way? Was she . . . was Hannah afraid for her life?"

There was a sharp intake of breath from Toni.

"Not that I know of," said Petra.

"Whew," said Toni. "But, please, tell us what's going on!"

"This whole idea has been gnawing at me for the past couple of hours," said Petra. "Really tearing me up inside. I mean, I know Jack, he goes to our church. He's always seemed like a fairly respectable guy."

"Except that he's cavorting with another woman," said Toni. "Who is she? A waitress at Hoobly's? Or one of the dancers?"

"Is there a difference?" said Suzanne.

"There's a minor technicality," said Toni.

"I don't know the exact details," said Petra. "Hannah just confided to me one day that Jack wanted out."

"Out of their marriage?" said Suzanne.

Petra nodded. "That's right."

"So Hannah figured he was having an affair," said Suzanne.

"That's right," said Petra. She still hadn't touched her glass of wine, just kept twisting her hands together, over and over.

"You're sure Jack wasn't just having a fling?" asked Toni. "A one-shot passing fancy? Some guys edge into their fifties or sixties and they go a little nuts. 'Middle-age crazy' I think they call it."

"I think Jack Venable was pretty serious," said Petra. "I think he was ready to walk out the door."

Suzanne thought about this. "Let me get this straight. I

think what you're really saying is that Hannah didn't want Jack to leave. She didn't want a divorce."

Petra was near tears. "That's it exactly. She still loved Jack, human frailties and all."

"But Jack wanted out," said Toni.

"Yes," Petra whispered. "I think he did. I'm pretty sure he did."

"Hannah told you this?" said Suzanne.

"Yes," said Petra. "A couple of weeks ago, Hannah pretty much broke down. It was right after church services, after our social hour. When we were cleaning up the coffee cups and cookie crumbs and things."

Suzanne took a sip of wine and locked eyes with Toni, who gave a kind of grimace. She knew exactly what was running through Toni's mind, so she let her say it.

"Jeez," said Toni. "If Jack Venable had something to do with that fire, it would make him suspect number one."

"Worse than that," said Suzanne, "it would make him a monster."

Petra nodded. "I . . . I think so, too. I guess that's why I'm here."

"So what do you guys think we should *do* with this information?" said Toni.

"Much as I'd like to, we can't exactly go cowboying over to Jack Venable's house and make a citizen's arrest," said Suzanne.

"Then what?" said Petra.

Suzanne grimaced. "What we're going to have to do is share this information with Sheriff Doogie."

"Ah," said Petra. She leaned back against the sofa and sighed. "I was afraid you were going to say that."

CHAPTER 5

CHICKEN sausage and chopped red peppers sizzled in cast-iron frying pans. The tantalizing aromas of sour cream coffee cake and cinnamon muffins wafted from the oven. Saturday-morning service at the Cackleberry Club was going to be short and sweet. Just breakfast as usual and then a limited luncheon menu served until one-thirty.

"I feel all nervous and fumbling this morning," Petra told Suzanne, who was standing at the butcher-block table, slicing ripe peaches. It was the last good fruit of the season. Until the apple harvest got fully under way.

"You're doing just fine," Suzanne assured her. The truth of the matter was they were crazy busy. And all three of them, including Toni, who was out in the café taking orders like mad, didn't seem to be performing at the top of their game.

"I've got everything measured out for my cake batter," said Petra. "As soon as my coffee cake and muffins come out of the oven . . . as soon as I have five minutes to breathe . . .

as soon as I finish these pancakes . . . I'm going to whip up my batter and start baking cake layers."

"How many layers for Kit's wedding cake?"

"Five," said Petra, grabbing her bowl of pancake batter and giving it a quick stir.

"Sounds good to me," said Suzanne. Kit and Ricky were having a smaller wedding, maybe forty or fifty guests, so that size cake should be just about right.

Petra diced a Vidalia onion and tossed it into a pan of hashed brown potatoes. "You think Doogie really will stop by today?"

"He'll be here," said Suzanne. "When I called him earlier, I made it crystal clear that we needed to talk to him. As soon as was humanly possible."

Petra looked nervous. "You said 'we.' That means you and I? You're going to stand toe-to-toe with me on this, right?" She plunged a ladle into her pancake batter and dropped perfect little circles of batter onto her griddle.

"Of course, I will," said Suzanne. "But it would be much better if the information—the explanation—came directly from you."

Petra gave a mock shiver. "What if I'm butting in and doing the wrong thing? I mean, I don't really *know* what went on between Hannah and Jack Venable."

"Sure you do," said Suzanne. "You know it in your bones. And, believe me, you've got good bones."

Toni came slaloming through the swinging door, carrying a handful of orders. "Hey, Davey Holzer is asking for an order of Canadian bacon. Do we have any of that left?"

"No," said Petra. "There's nothing left. The pantry is empty."

"Huh?" said Toni, frowning and looking around. "But you've got sausage and taters sizzling in your frying pans. And you're doing silver dollar pancakes, right?" She tiptoed over and peered at the grill. "I see bubbles popping up. You'd better hurry up and flip those puppies."

Petra grabbed her spatula and flipped her pancakes just in the nick of time.

"Our Petra's feeling a bit frazzled this morning," Suzanne explained to Toni. "She's nervous about talking to Doogie."

"I can understand why," said Toni. "That's a mighty big, red-hot, heartburn-inducing breakfast burrito that you're gonna lay on him."

Petra looked even more upset. "I'm not making any accusations, per se. I'm just going to tell Doogie what I *know*."

"And what you suspect," said Toni.

"Toni," said Suzanne. She knew she'd better stop this little back-and-forth between them. "You're just making things more tense."

"I didn't mean to," said Toni. She made a comical downturned face. "Jeez, Petra, I'm sorry if I upset you."

Petra waved her big metal spatula as if to clear the air. "Oh, foo. Don't worry about me. I've been upset before. I'll get over it."

Suzanne spread out a half dozen white plates and watched as Petra doled out sausages and hash browns.

"Great," said Toni. "Thanks. I'll run these orders right out."

"And these peaches are ready for the pancake orders," said Suzanne.

"Got it," said Petra. She placed four pancakes on each plate, then stepped back while Suzanne added sliced peaches and a dollop of whipped cream. She carried the plates to the pass-through slot and tapped a small silver bell, her signal to Toni that more orders were up.

Another sharp *ding* meant the oven timer had just gone off.

"Perfect," said Petra, pulling her coffee cake and muffins from the oven.

"Gorgeously golden brown," said Suzanne. "Now you can get on with baking your wedding cake."

While Suzanne took over at the stove and filled orders for the next twenty minutes, Petra quickly mixed up her batter, filled five cake pans, and stuck them in the oven.

"You still look worried," Suzanne observed.

"That's because I *am* worried," said Petra.

"Think about the cake-decorating part. You always do such a wonderful job." It was true. Petra's skill for baking made-from-scratch cakes, plus her ability to spin ordinary sugar-based frosting into intricate flowers, rosettes, and spirals, had convinced more and more customers that the Cackleberry Club was the perfect place to special order cakes for weddings, graduation parties, and birthdays.

Petra forced a smile. "I just have to stay positive today, especially for Kit's sake. I don't want to spoil her wedding after all."

"Honey," said Suzanne, "you could never do that."

JUST as Suzanne was writing their abbreviated luncheon menu on the chalkboard, Sheriff Doogie walked in. Actually, it was more like a swagger. Doogie's hat was pulled low, he wore mirrored sunglasses, the kind state troopers favored, and his walk was distinctly jaunty. With a jingle of keys and a flap of his holstered gun, he took his customary seat at the counter.

Suzanne grabbed a cup of coffee for Doogie and set it in front of him, along with a knife, fork, spoon, and sugar bowl. Doogie had a ferocious sweet tooth and loved his sugar. Not just one or two lumps for him, it was more like three or four.

"Would you like a sweet roll, too?" Suzanne asked.

The brim on Doogie's hat dipped.

"And are you looking for a late breakfast or an early lunch?" Suzanne asked.

Doogie reached a big paw up and slid his hat off. He placed it on the stool next to him in a territorial manner, then ran a hand over his thinning gray hair.

"Depends on what you've got for lunch," he growled.

"Well, it's a short day today, because of the wedding," Suzanne told him. "So it's a short menu. We've got pita bread stuffed with grilled vegetables, ham and Swiss on rye, tomato soup, and tuna melties."

"That's it? No cheeseburger?"

"If that's what your little heart desires, I'm sure we can rustle up a cheeseburger."

"Naw," said Doogie, squinting at the chalkboard. "I'll just go with the ham and cheese. But maybe make it cheddar cheese?"

"You got it," said Suzanne. She printed out her order slip and slid it through the pass-through slot to the kitchen.

Petra leaned down and caught her eye, then made a little face. She was clearly nervous and getting cold feet.

Meanwhile, Doogie was surveying the café, which was almost half filled. Toni continued to scurry around, a coffeepot in each hand, pouring refills and joking with the customers. She could, Suzanne observed, charm the stitches off a baseball.

"I suppose people are still talking about yesterday's big fire," said Doogie.

"That's pretty much all they're talking about," said Suzanne. She hesitated. "Are you still going to pursue that arson angle?"

"I think we pretty much have to," said Doogie. "Fire Chief Finley is pretty firm about it."

"He's the expert," said Suzanne.

"Actually," said Doogie, "we've gone ahead and contacted

some real experts, from the state crime lab. They should be hitting town later today."

"I know you're busy," said Suzanne. "So I want to thank you for coming in."

"That's okay." Doogie patted his ample belly. "A man's gotta eat."

"I know, and I apologize for being a little vague on the phone with you first thing this morning. About asking you to come in and talk to Petra."

"You were very mysterioso," agreed Doogie. He took a sip of coffee. "So . . . what's up?"

"You're not going to believe this . . . and maybe it doesn't amount to anything, but . . ."

The front door to the café suddenly flew open and a tall, red-faced man appeared in the doorway. His blue-and-white-checkered shirt was half un-tucked from his jeans, his boots were only half laced, and waves of anger seemed to radiate off him like gamma rays.

"What on earth?" said Suzanne. She wasn't the only one staring at this strange man. Now pretty much everyone in the café had turned to look, too.

The man lifted a hand and pointed in Suzanne's direction. "You!" he thundered.

"Me?" she said, her heart catching in her throat. Who was this man? And what had she done to get him so riled up?

And then Doogie turned and slipped off his stool in one fluid motion. He anchored himself in place, feet apart, hands on his belt, and said, "He means me, don't you?"

"Who is he?" Suzanne hissed.

"Marty Wolfson," said Doogie, keeping his voice low. "The husband of the woman who was rescued from that second-floor apartment yesterday. The *estranged* husband."

"Oh," said Suzanne as Wolfson clomped across the floor toward Doogie, and all her customers watched with growing curiosity.

"What do you want, Wolfson?" asked Doogie. His meaty face wore the bored look of a duly elected sheriff who'd seen it all. Or at least most of it.

But Marty Wolfson had worked up a giant head of steam and wasn't about to be put off by Doogie's calm yet authoritative demeanor.

"You're investigating *me*?" Wolfson shouted. "Are you serious?"

"I'm the one who generally asks the questions around here," said Doogie.

"And you've been asking them behind my back!" snarled Wolfson. "How dare you!"

Suzanne's eyes bounced from Doogie to Wolfson and then back to Doogie, as if she were following a championship tennis match instead of a raging argument. She couldn't believe that the normally excitable Doogie was keeping his cool. And she couldn't believe how angry Marty Wolfson was. Every time he started in on a new rant, drops of spittle exploded from his mouth. She made a note to wipe down the entire marble counter with a good dose of Lysol.

"Back off, Wolfson," Doogie warned. His voice carried a flinty edge as he held up a hand.

But Wolfson was overwrought and seething with indignation. "How *dare* you!" His right hand was clenched in a fist and his entire arm seemed to be spasming. "If you weren't—"

"Gentlemen," said Suzanne, suddenly finding her voice. "I think you need to take this outside." She was well aware that her customers were hanging on every single word. She didn't doubt that they were itching to see a physical confrontation, too.

"She's right," said Doogie. "Outside with you." Doogie made a shooing motion with his hand. "Now."

"You arrogant blowhard!" Wolfson shouted. "You've got nothin' on me!" He spun fast and his shoulder caught the edge of an antique wooden cupboard that stood next to the kitchen door. The cupboard shook, the colorful flock of ceramic chickens that perched on the shelves rattled precariously, and then one little hen, a Speckled Sussex chicken, suddenly toppled over and plunged to her death. Hitting the floor, she shattered into a dozen pieces.

Wolfson clumped out, with Doogie close on his heels.

"Great gobs of gook!" cried Toni. She'd been watching the whole messy encounter with saucer-sized eyes. "That jerk just broke one of our chickens."

"It's okay," said Suzanne, though she knew it really wasn't. Anytime a precious memento got broken it was like a dagger to the heart.

Showtime being over, their customers turned back to their breakfasts. But Toni knelt down and carefully gathered up the broken pieces in her apron.

"Poor little chickie," said Toni, cradling the largest part. "Broke its little neck clean off."

"What are you people *doing* out there?" Petra called through the pass-through. "If this cake falls while it's in the oven, somebody's going to pay dearly!"

FIVE minutes later, Sheriff Doogie strode back into the Cackleberry Club. He sat down and rested his elbows heavily on the counter.

"Is my sandwich ready yet?" he asked.

"Coming right up," said Suzanne. She turned, grabbed a platter, and set the whole thing in front of Doogie. "Petra grilled it and added some hash browns, too."

Too bad she didn't slip a Xanax in there.

"Good," said Doogie. He picked up a half sandwich and started eating with gusto. "Arguing with jackholes always works up my appetite," he said, between bites.

"I can see that," said Suzanne. "So . . . that guy Wolfson. I take it he's one of your arson suspects?"

"One of them," Doogie said in a noncommittal tone.

"He seems like a real hothead."

Doogie stabbed at his hash browns. "Now we just need to find out if he's a firebug, too."

"Why do you think he would be?" asked Suzanne. She couldn't imagine that a husband, even one who was estranged, would try to kill his wife and child. Or set fire to the entire building.

"I talked to Mrs. Wolfson," said Doogie. "Annie. Even though they're separated, she acts like she's afraid of him."

"Really?"

Doogie nodded. "Annie also told me that her husband's name is still on her parents' will and all their joint insurance policies."

"So he would be the one to inherit if something happened to her?" said Suzanne.

"Substantially inherit," said Doogie.

"It seems to me," said Suzanne, "that a father wouldn't put his own child in that kind of danger."

Doogie looked up at her. "The kid wasn't supposed to be there. He was supposed to be in nursery school, but he stayed home because of a cold."

"That does change things," said Suzanne.

SUZANNE left Doogie to finish his ham and cheese. She and Toni did their whirling, twirling ballet, setting tables, readying the café for lunch, and seating a few early customers.

Once everyone had been escorted to a table and Toni was busy taking orders, Suzanne grabbed Petra. She dragged her out into the café and shoved her into the Knitting Nest with Doogie.

Five minutes later, as Suzanne was grilling onions and red peppers at the stove, Petra returned. She looked nervous but relieved.

"All done with your talk?" Suzanne asked.

Petra gave a weak smile. "For now anyway. Doogie said he might have to ask me some more questions later."

"Everything went okay? I mean, he didn't rush you or pressure you or put words in your mouth?"

"He was a little brusque at first," said Petra. "But when he saw I was on the verge of tears, he kind of eased up."

"Tears," said Suzanne. "One of those weapons in our female arsenal that usually works. Well, at least ninety percent of the time anyway."

Toni pushed into the kitchen with a handful of orders. "Not anymore it doesn't. I'd put our odds at about fifty percent now. In case you haven't noticed, men have changed."

"You think?" said Petra.

"Oh yeah," said Toni. "They're onto us big-time."

SUZANNE cut a whopping slice of pecan pie and carried it out to Doogie.

When he saw it, his eyes danced with happiness. "Now that's what I call getting a piece of the pie," he enthused.

She laid down a clean fork and gingham napkin and said, "So? What do you think? About what Petra told you about Jack Venable, I mean."

"It's an angle," said Doogie.

"Isn't the husband often the guilty party in the death of a spouse?"

Doogie shifted uncomfortably on his stool. "That's sometimes the case."

"Does that mean you're going to take a careful look at him?"

"If you're asking me if I'm going to question Jack Venable,

the answer is yes," said Doogie. "But I was going to do that anyway."

"Really?" said Suzanne. And then, because her curiosity had been piqued, she said, "Why?"

"If it was arson," said Doogie, "and it's looking like it is, I need to ask Jack if he knew anyone who might have had a beef with Hannah. Or with him, for that matter."

"So just the usual run-of-the-mill questions?"

"Yeah, except now there's a different aspect to it."

"The possible divorce aspect."

"The operant word being 'possible,'" said Doogie. "Since we don't really know what went on between them."

"But you heard what Petra said. And you saw that she was genuinely upset, so she wasn't just making her story up."

Doogie leaned back and loosened his belt. Suzanne suspected he let loose a suppressed belch, too.

"When you've got your domestic-type situation," said Doogie, "you never know what to expect. Most of the time it's fairly cut-and-dried. Somebody gets angry and calls the cops. But once in a while, a woman will call 911 and claim that her man is beating on her. Then, when we show up, she does a total switcheroo and is ready to claw *our* eyes out if we make a move to haul him away."

"That's crazy," said Suzanne.

"Welcome to the wonderful world of law enforcement."

"Do you have anyone else you're looking at?" asked Suzanne. "Besides that Wolfson guy and, now, Jack Venable?"

Doogie took another bite of pie and chewed thoughtfully.

Suzanne knew him well enough to read his body language. "So there is someone else."

"Ah . . ."

"Come on," said Suzanne. "I'm hip-deep in this thing already. You can tell me."

"There's this other guy. I don't think you know him. Darrel Fuhrman."

"I do kind of know him."

"Good-looking guy," said Doogie. "Tools around town in that candy apple red Jeep Grand Cherokee."

Suzanne nodded. She'd seen him at the fire yesterday.

"Well, Fuhrman got let go from the fire department a couple of months ago."

"Why?"

"What they call disciplinary measures."

"I get that," said Suzanne. "But why exactly?"

"I don't know the full story, that's why I'm meeting with Chief Finley in a couple of hours. Who knows? Fuhrman might have had a bone to pick."

"If he intentionally set yesterday's fire that would have been an awfully big bone," said Suzanne. She paused. "You know he was at the fire yesterday, watching the whole thing."

"Fuhrman was?"

"Kind of interesting, huh? At the time I wondered why he wasn't suited up with the other guys."

"Now you know," said Doogie.

"Maybe there's more to know." She reached for his plate and said, "So now you've got three people to investigate."

Doogie lifted a shoulder. "Looks like."

Something in his tone made Suzanne hesitate. "Dear Lord, don't tell me there's someone else? *Another* suspect?"

Doogie's gray eyes grew hard as steel pennies. "Maybe, maybe not. But we had a kind of strange tip called in. So I've got to check on a couple of things."

CHAPTER 6

By noon, the café was almost full, with just one single table left.

"We're selling those pita sandwiches like crazy," Toni said as she buzzed past Suzanne.

"Good," said Suzanne. "Maybe we'll run out soon and we can get out of here at a reasonable hour."

"Gotta start our beauty routine. Hair, nails, makeup, the works."

"Listen," said Suzanne. "Are you planning to wear a real fancy dress?"

"I thought I'd wear that peach-colored sheath that you told me you liked," said Toni. "The one that makes me look like a morning anchorwoman for a Southern TV station."

"Sounds perfect. You think I'm okay with my black dress?"

"Sure. Why wouldn't you be? You worried that it's too witchy?"

"No, it's just . . ."

The café door opened and Suzanne saw Mayor Mobley's face peep around it. She quickly put a smile on her face, ready to greet him. Mobley wasn't her most favorite person in the whole world—he was a little too greasy, a little too artless in his dealings, and way too slick for a politician. But he was a customer, nevertheless.

Then Suzanne's smile turned to stunned surprise when she saw the man who was with Mobley.

Bruce Winthrop! The same Bruce Winthrop who'd served as county agent all these years. The same Bruce Winthrop who, just yesterday afternoon, had tried to run in and rescue Hannah Venable. And then had been stunned beyond words as he stood helplessly by and watched the tragic ending along with everyone else.

Suzanne's heart immediately went out to Winthrop. Here he was, looking beyond middle-aged and shaky, as if he'd aged ten years overnight. And the sad expression on his face pretty much announced that he'd lost someone very dear to him.

"Good morning, Mayor," said Suzanne.

Mayor Mobley responded with a perfunctory, "Morning, Suzanne."

"Bruce," said Suzanne, gazing up into Winthrop's hangdog face, seeing his watery blue eyes looking sad and mournful, "I'm so sorry about Hannah. I know you two worked together for a long time."

Winthrop managed a faint smile. "Six years," he said in a papery voice. "And thank you, Suzanne. Your words mean a lot to me."

Suzanne led them to the last available table and, as Winthrop dropped heavily into his chair, she said, "How are you doing, really? How are you holding up?"

"To be perfectly honest, Suzanne, it's been difficult," said Winthrop. "This is about the worst thing I've ever experienced. To have poor Hannah killed and our building completely gutted and burned to the ground . . ." He hesitated, looking utterly bereft.

"I'm so sorry," said Suzanne. She patted Winthrop on the shoulder and he gave her an appreciative nod. "If there's anything I can do to help . . ."

"You could start by getting us some coffee," said Mobley.

"Of course," said Suzanne. She hastened over to the counter, grabbed a pot of her best French roast, and headed back to their table.

"Thank you," said Winthrop as Suzanne poured his coffee. "You're awfully kind."

But Mobley seemed vexed. With his burgundy golf shirt stretched tight across his stomach and his chubby face with deep-set, piggy eyes, he seemed mostly immune to Winthrop's sadness.

"Don't you worry," said Mobley. "We'll find the culprit. All of us in government are anxious to get this sorted out." He ran a pudgy hand across his bad comb-over. "A situation like this is bad for the town. Bad for bidness." The word "bidness" rolled off his tongue as if he'd just watched the latest Jay-Z rap video.

"I know Sheriff Doogie's doing his best," put in Suzanne.

"We *all* are," said Mobley.

"The thing is," said Winthrop, still looking bereft, "all our records were lost. Everything's completely gone. It's . . . incomprehensible."

"You didn't have your paperwork backed up on computer?" said Suzanne.

"Everything *was* backed up on the computers," said Winthrop. "But the doggone computers are fried. We haven't been able to salvage a single one."

"No cloud computing?" said Suzanne.

Winthrop just shook his head sadly. "I kept putting in requests for additional funding, but . . ." He shrugged.

"With the old technology we were working with, we were lucky to have Windows 95."

Mobley glanced sharply at Suzanne. "I'll have the tuna melt."

"And you, Bruce?" said Suzanne. "What can I bring you?"

"Just a bowl of soup," said Winthrop.

Suzanne went into the kitchen and said, "I need one more tuna and a soup. And I think that's going to be the last of the orders. Toni wants to lock the front door in about twenty minutes and put up our Closed sign."

"Sounds good to me," said Petra. She smeared tuna salad on two slices of bread, added cheese, and popped them under the broiler. Then she ladled out a bowl of tomato soup.

"How's your cake coming?"

"See for yourself," said Petra. She stepped aside and there, sitting on the back counter, were three layers, stacked up and iced with white frosting. They glistened and gleamed in the light, holding the promise of a beautiful wedding cake, the kind of cake that dreams are made of.

"Wow!" said Suzanne. "So far, so good. I can't wait to see what you do with the other two layers. I guess that's the tricky decorating part."

"Huh, with my trusty pastry bag I can squirt out two dozen roses in under ten minutes."

"Is that what you're going to do? Roses?"

"That and a few other things," said Petra. "I'll use my star tips and leaf tips. Maybe do some ruffled fondant and edge each layer with beading."

"Amazing," said Suzanne. She picked up the two orders and hurried out to deliver them.

Five minutes later found Suzanne in the Book Nook. She was hunched over the counter, tallying up the price of three books that Cheryl Tanner, one of their regulars, had picked out.

"You're going to like this book on tea parties," Suzanne told Cheryl.

"I was thinking of trying to do a tea party on my own," she said. "Not that I'm trying to go into competition with you, of course," she hastened to explain.

"If you did, it wouldn't bother me a bit." Once they'd been open for a few months, Suzanne had introduced the idea—and the decorum—of afternoon tea. After the detritus from lunch was cleared away, the Cackleberry Club was transformed into a cozy little tearoom that looked like it might have been airlifted in from the Cotswolds in England. White linen tablecloths decorated the battered wood tables. A crazy quilt of cups and saucers, small plates, silver spoons, and butter knives was laid out. Tiny vigil lights were placed inside glass tea warmers and topped with chintz-decorated teapots.

And the women of Kindred had willingly embraced the notion of afternoon tea, loving the bone china cups, finger sandwiches, and Old World gentility à la *Downton Abbey*. Sometimes their afternoon tea offerings were as simple as Chinese black tea and a scone with Devonshire cream. But when they catered an event, Petra created three-tiered trays overflowing with tiny triangle sandwiches that boasted fillings such as crab salad, dilled egg salad, and basil-pesto cream cheese.

"Suzanne?"

Suzanne had just handed the books and change to Cheryl when Bruce Winthrop walked in. He smiled sadly as Cheryl scurried past him.

"Bruce," said Suzanne. "You look absolutely beat."

Winthrop nodded. "I am, but I'm trying to stay positive. I've been getting a lot of support from the community . . ." He favored her with a grateful smile. "Especially from friends like you."

"I meant what I said before. If there's anything I can do."

Bruce seemed to hesitate, then made up his mind to go ahead.

"Maybe there is, Suzanne," said Winthrop. "I know you're awfully friendly with Sheriff Doogie."

"I think he mostly drops by for Petra's sticky buns and chocolate donuts."

Winthrop moved a step closer to her. "And I know you're in a unique position to hear things. Heck, half the people in Kindred pass through your doors every week." He was stammering a little now.

"Are you asking me to keep my eyes and ears open?" said Suzanne.

He smiled gratefully. "Could you? Would you?"

"You know I will," Suzanne said without hesitation. "If I hear anything, anything at all, I'll be sure to let you know. And the sheriff, too."

Winthrop let loose a long sigh of relief. "Thank you, Suzanne. I wasn't sure if I should talk to you about this or not. But I remembered how instrumental you were in helping Sheriff Doogie figure out that awful thing up in the cemetery."

"Luck," said Suzanne.

"Smarts," said Winthrop. He looked profoundly relieved, and his shoulders seemed to relax some. "So thank you. I appreciate *any* help you're able to lend."

"I haven't done anything yet," said Suzanne, her heart going out to him again. "But I'm going to try. And just so you feel better, you're not the first one to ask for my help."

Bruce Winthrop held up his right hand. His middle finger was crossed over his index finger. "Good to know," he said. "And thanks." Then he gave a wan smile and disappeared.

WHAT *a sad state of affairs*, Suzanne thought to herself. She was poking a broom under one of the tables, trying to snag a few errant crumbs. Poor Hannah was dead, Bruce was all bent out of shape and maybe even dealing with a case of survivor's remorse, and Sheriff Doogie was trying to track down any number of so-so suspects and question them. At this moment in time, even though she and her partners were doing the odious task of cleaning up, she felt quite happy and satisfied to be the proprietor of the Cackleberry Club. In fact, she thanked her lucky stars that she wasn't one of the town's politicos or first responders. That she hadn't had to deal with the fire—or the aftermath of the fire—knowing that Hannah hadn't survived.

No, indeed, running the Cackleberry Club suited her just fine. And even with the downturn in the economy, they'd managed to hold their own rather well, thank you very much. She wasn't sure if their continued prosperity was due to their breakfasts and lunches, afternoon tea, the Book Nook, or the Knitting Nest. Whatever the magic formula was, everything seemed to be working in sync.

Suzanne straightened up, looked around, and smiled.

There, almost done.

A knock at the front door caused her smile to fade just a little. She walked over and called through the lace curtains, "I'm sorry, but we're closed."

The knock sounded again.

Is Doogie my persistent visitor? Has he come back for some reason?

Suzanne swept the lace curtains aside only to find Gene Gandle staring in at her. Gandle not only wrote feature stories for the *Bugle*, he also handled ad sales, classifieds, sports, and obituaries, not necessarily in that order. His last feature story had been about a bull that had escaped from a pen and trapped a farmer inside his barn for nearly two days.

Gandle held up a hand and made a spinning gesture. "Gotta talk to you, Suzanne." His voice sounded hollow through the door. He also sounded upset.

Reluctantly, knowing she probably shouldn't, Suzanne unlatched the door and let Gandle in.

"What?" she said.

"And a fine afternoon to you, too," said Gandle. He looked skinnier and goofier than usual and acted as if he was all jacked up.

"What do you want, Gene?" Since it was too late for lunch, Suzanne figured Gandle was here to pump her for a few newsworthy tidbits.

"The big fire," Gandle spit out.

"Tragic."

"What else do you know about it?" He pulled out a pad and pen.

"That Hannah Venable was killed and the entire building was destroyed," said Suzanne.

Gandle tapped a pen against his spiral notepad. "Well, I already know that."

"Gene, what do you want?" Suzanne was fast losing her good humor. Actually, she'd left it in the dirt two minutes ago.

"I understand that Sheriff Doogie was in here earlier."

"Doogie is always in here," said Suzanne. She pointed at their old-fashioned, '20s-era soda fountain counter, stools, and backdrop. "You see that stool at the end of the counter? I'm having a brass plate engraved. It's going to say Property of the Sheriff's Department."

"I understand Doogie has already found himself a couple of suspects," said Gandle.

"You'd have to ask him," said Suzanne.

"I did ask him. Now I'm asking you."

"I don't know why you think I know anything more."

"Come on, Suzanne," Gandle said in his trademark wheedle. "Don't tell me you're not getting involved in this arson case. I know you were there. I *saw* you there."

"Me and half the town," said Suzanne.

"What can you tell me about Marty Wolfson?"

"I really don't know the man," said Suzanne. "Except that he came storming into the café a few hours ago and tried to give the sheriff what for."

"I need more than just your folksy take on this, Suzanne, I need facts. I'm on deadline!" Gandle always acted like he was the third man on the Woodward and Bernstein team.

"It's Saturday, Gene. Relax. The *Bugle* doesn't come out until Thursday."

"It's about getting a jump on the other media," said Gandle.

"By 'other media' you mean our local radio station? I understand they broadcast live from the scene of the fire."

"But radio is so fleeting," said Gandle, gesturing with his pen. "They do two minutes of news, five minutes of crappy commercials, then play a song. Nobody takes them seriously. Radio is so . . . disposable."

Suzanne thought about making a nasty crack about sticking a newspaper in the bottom of a birdcage. But she was a friend of Laura Benchley, the editor and publisher of the *Bugle*, so instead she said, "I don't have anything for you, Gene. I don't *know* anything."

Disappointed, Gandle began slouching his way back toward the door. Then he turned and called back at her, "When you figure something out, I expect a call from you. You owe me one!"

"I don't owe you anything," said Suzanne as Gandle slammed the door.

"Who was that?" asked Toni. She'd slid through the swinging door so quietly she might have been a cat on the prowl.

"Gene Gandle. Sniffing around for news on the fire."

"More like skulking," said Toni, glancing out into the parking lot. "What a putz." She paused, squinted, and said, "Uh-oh."

Suzanne tensed. "Don't tell me Gandle's coming back in?"

"Naw," said Toni. "Junior just drove up."

Junior Garrett, Toni's estranged husband, was a character in and of himself. He barely held down his job at Shelby's Auto, lived in a secondhand trailer home that was parked illegally out by the town dump, and had never seen a junker car that he didn't fall in love with. He was your basic sixteen-year-old juvenile delinquent in a forty-three-year-old man's body.

The door rattled loudly, then Junior strolled in, carrying a large amber bottle. Dressed in his typical black leather jacket and saggy jeans, a silver wallet chain dangling from his belt, Junior took his own sweet time, as if he didn't have a care in the world.

Toni put her hands on her hips in a gesture of confrontation. "What are you doing here?" she asked.

"Got something to show you ladies," said Junior, a smirk on his dark face.

"What's that?" said Suzanne.

Junior thrust his bottle forward with all the excitement of someone who's just stolen a quart of water from the fountain of youth. "This here!" he said excitedly.

"It's beer," said Toni, peering at the bottle, definitely not impressed.

"But not just *any* beer," said Junior, undaunted. "It's *craft* beer."

"Craft beer," Suzanne repeated. God help her, but she found this man's chutzpah and constant stream of crazy ideas absolutely mesmerizing. Once again, she felt like a charmed mongoose drawn to a dangerous cobra.

"It's my own brand," said Junior, angling the bottle to show off a scruffy-looking brown label. "Hubba Bubba beer. Pretty neat, huh?"

"Where'd you get it?" said Toni.

Junior grinned stupidly, then waggled his head and did a little jig in place. "Hah, hah, I *made* it!"

"You. Brewed. Beer?" said Suzanne.

"Seriously?" said Toni. And then, "Where?"

"In my bathtub," said Junior. "Like I said, it's *craft* beer. That means you brew it in real small batches until it catches on and develops a cult following."

"You think some swill you cooked up in your dirty bathtub will draw a following?" said Toni. She did everything but let loose a loud, derisive hoot.

"Sure," said Junior. "This beer thing is a huge trend. Don't you get it? Haven't you heard of microbrewing?"

"I have heard of it," said Suzanne. In fact, she had a feeling that every beer aficionado and his brother-in-law were brewing micro beers and dreaming up wacky names like Hound Doggie and Red Demon and Buster Boy Beer.

"Have you made any sales yet?" asked Toni.

"Ah," said Junior. "Now you're talking about distribution, a critical component of my marketing effort."

"What *is* your marketing effort?" Suzanne asked.

"I was thinking about doing a Facebook page or putting a video on YouTube. Hope it all goes viral."

"Social media," said Toni.

"Yeah," said Junior. "I gotta do some of that, too."

Suzanne shook her head. She really didn't want to hear any more. Better, she decided, to change the subject entirely. "Are you coming to the wedding this afternoon?" she asked.

"Heck, yes," said Junior, his eyes lighting up like a pinball machine. "I wouldn't miss it for the world. Ricky's a great kid. I once helped him install a Hemi in his '88 Camaro. I tried to talk him into letting me race it over at Golden Springs Speedway, but he said no way."

"Smart kid," said Suzanne.

"Heh heh." Junior was dancing his little jig again.

"Now what?" said Toni. "Why are you cackling like a rabid turkey?"

"We got major plans for Ricky's car!"

"Who's got major plans?" Petra called out. She was

scrunched down, gazing out at them through the pass-through.

"Me and some of the guys from Shelby's Auto," Junior told her. "We're gonna tie a bunch of tin cans to his back bumper. And then shoot Silly String all over the hood and windows."

"That's very mature of you, Junior," said Suzanne.

Junior's shoulders slumped. "Oh, come on, Suzanne. It's a *wedding*. That's what people do. It's considered . . . romantic."

"Scraping Silly String off your windshield is romantic?" said Petra.

"Okay, look at it this way," said Junior. "It's traditional."

"So is throwing salt over your shoulder to ward off the devil, but you don't catch me doing that," said Petra. "I rely on good old-fashioned prayer."

But Toni was starting to see the humor in Junior's Silly String décor. "Something old, something new," she chuckled. "Something sticky with pink goo."

"Good one!" said Junior, shooting an index finger at her.

ONCE Junior had been hustled out of the Cackleberry Club, they all convened in the kitchen to gaze in wonderment at Petra's cake.

"Gorgeous," said Suzanne. Petra had stacked three round twelve-inch layer cakes straight up, then carefully tilted two more eight-inch layers on top of that. The upshot was that the cake looked like two frilly hatboxes, the smaller hatbox set at an artful angle. Each hatbox was decorated with fondant roses, ferns, and daisies, and strung with strands of fondant pearls. At the very tippy-top she'd placed a sugary bride and groom.

"Kit's gonna go crazy for this," said Toni. "It's perfect!" She glanced over at a piece of paper that was stuck to Petra's corkboard. "Oh, you guys already put together the menu for our big shindig next Friday?" Next Friday evening, the Cackleberry Club was hosting a dinner theater, the first ever done in Kindred. They'd been approached by the Kindred Community Players and asked to put together a British-themed dinner, while the actors staged Noël Coward's *Blithe Spirit.* Tickets were priced at $25 each, with proceeds going to the local library. Needless to say, all of the tickets had already been sold.

"I've got the menu," said Petra. "I just don't know if I have the energy for one more big project."

"Come on," said Toni, "it's almost a week away. You'll be fine."

"I hope so," said Petra. She touched a finger to the cake, pressing one of her fondant ferns a little tighter into the frosting.

"How are you planning to get your cake to the reception hall?" asked Suzanne. "Is somebody from the wedding party going to drop by and pick it up?"

Petra glanced at her watch. "Joey promised to come by at two." Joey was their slacker busboy who worked for them on occasion. Joey's major avocations in life were skateboarding, snowboarding, wearing rapper chain jewelry, and trying to keep his baggy M.C. Hammer pants from sliding down and puddling around his ankles.

"Wait a minute," said Suzanne. "You said pick it up. That means he's driving?"

"Joey's going to borrow his mom's station wagon," said Petra.

"And he's going to deliver the wedding cake to Schmitt's Bar?" said Suzanne. That was where the reception was taking place. At Schmitt's Bar in their newly remodeled Boom Boom Room.

"Jeez, I hope they remember to move the Pac-Man machine out of the way," Toni fretted.

"I just hope Joey's got a legitimate driver's license," said Suzanne.

CHAPTER 7

SUZANNE sat at her dressing table in her upstairs bedroom, gazing into the mirror. She was dressed and almost ready, but concerned with her hair, which she thought looked a little too fluffy. As if that wasn't enough, she was thinking she might have spackled on a little too much eye shadow. On the other hand, she was wearing a black dress, which had a slight cocktail feel to it. So . . . what was her look today? Sophisticate or strumpet?

Stop that ridiculous negative talk this instant, she chided herself. *You look good. In fact, you look elegant. Kind of like . . .*

She tilted her head. Maybe a touch of Michelle Pfeiffer? Hmm. No, not really. But maybe, with her hair poufed up, she looked a little like Linda Evans? In the *Dynasty* years anyway.

Sam Hazelet emerged from the bathroom and stood behind her, fussing with his cuff links. He'd come directly from the Westvale Clinic, his suit packed up nice and neat in a black plastic carry-on bag. Now, standing there in his navy blue suit with his pale blue shirt and red rep tie, he looked very dapper and elegant.

"Hey, you look great," Sam told her.

Suzanne gazed into the mirror at his reflection. "You do, too," she replied. Did he know she was devouring him with her eyes? Or should she try to be a little more subtle? But, yee gads, the man was handsome. Plus, he was four years younger than she was. Which somehow struck her as being awfully neat. A lady in her mid-forties attracting a guy who was young enough to be her . . . boyfriend.

"So what kind of wedding is this, anyway?" Sam asked. He was trying to keep the very affectionate and nosy Baxter from rubbing up against him and laying down a carpet of silver dog hair on his newly dry-cleaned slacks.

"I think you could characterize it as a nondenominational-outdoorsy-Edwardian-slash-vintage wedding."

Sam looked puzzled. "Women are really into that kind of stuff, aren't they?"

Suzanne held up a strand of pearls and smiled at him. "Whatever do you mean?"

"You know, specific *theme* weddings. Like beach weddings, Renaissance fair weddings, Victorian weddings . . ."

"You seem to know a lot about this." Suzanne fastened the pearls around her neck and adjusted them carefully.

"Nah, we just have umpteen dog-eared copies of *Modern Bride* piled up in the waiting room." Sam paused, looking down at his slacks. "Hey, do you have one of those lint roller things?"

Suzanne reached into a drawer, poked past a tangle of panty hose, combs, and perfume samples, and pulled one out for him. "I guess women just enjoy weddings," she said. "All the parties, planning, and pageantry. To say nothing of the romance." She turned slightly in her chair and gazed sideways at him. "I don't think that's necessarily a bad thing, do you?"

Sam was diligently working the lint roller up and down his slacks. "I guess not," he replied.

SWEET strains of harp music greeted Suzanne, Sam, and the other guests as they strolled down a grassy lane edged with birch trees. The leaves rustled lightly in the afternoon breeze; the sun shone down brightly from a powder blue sky. Then, as they rounded a small tree, where white ribbons fluttered from its branches, they found themselves in a secluded woodsy bower. Now a violin and keyboard joined in and the strains of Bach's Sinfonia from Cantata 29 echoed through the oaks and poplars where the octagonal-shaped wedding gazebo was located.

As Suzanne gazed at the décor, she couldn't help but gasp in wonderment. The old-fashioned gazebo was trimmed with tiny white lights and garlands of pink and white roses. Leafy green vines woven with daisies were strung overhead from tree to tree. White candles flickered from their perches in trees and in dozens of hanging candle holders. Fifty white wooden folding chairs were arranged in a semicircle. Flanking the chairs were enormous bouquets of gladiolas and zinnias. A center aisle of dark green moss was lined with white candles flickering in mason jars.

"This is amazing," said Sam, looking around. "I've never seen anything like it. All that's missing are elves and a flock of white doves."

"It's truly magical, isn't it?" said Suzanne.

"Really gorgeous. The décor conveys wedding, but it's not the stuffy kind of wedding that men tend to shy away from. There's this feeling of openness and nature and . . . of everything being fresh and green."

"God's own cathedral," Suzanne murmured to herself, loving how the flora and fauna had turned this small piece of parkland into a glorious intimate space, wondering at the same time if something like this might ever be in her own future.

As guests continued to stream in, Suzanne quickly spotted Toni and Petra.

"Let's go join the ladies, shall we?" Suzanne said to Sam.

He followed after her, clasping her hand tightly, as they edged their way along a row of chairs, nodding and smiling at friends, stopping every few feet to talk.

"I feel like I just got picked up by some crazy tornado and dropped into a magical kingdom," were Toni's first words once they all met up.

"This really is spectacular," Suzanne agreed.

"Never seen anything like it," said Sam, who kept gazing in awe at the vines strung overhead.

"You know who arranged all this, don't you?" said Petra.

"Who?" they all asked at once, sounding like a chorus of owls.

"Brett and Greg's little side business," said Petra. "Party Animal."

"I always knew they had a flair for the dramatic," said Suzanne. "I mean, they helped set up that spa tea for us last year . . . but this. This kind of blows my mind."

"Look at the programs," said Petra, picking one up off a chair. "Sepia-toned ink printed on vintage-looking paper. And look at the edges." The edges of the program had been cut in such a way that they formed a lace border.

"Oh sure," said Suzanne. "They used one of those special deckle-edge scissors, like you find in scrapbook shops."

"I'm gonna get me a pair of those scissors," said Toni. "Maybe I can learn to make cards and programs like this. It could be a sort of sideline business."

"Here's your sideline," Petra said under her breath. "Or would you call him more of a sideshow?"

Junior, wearing blue jeans, scuffed black motorcycle boots, and an '80s-style black suit jacket with shoulders that were two sizes too large, was heading directly toward them.

"How goes it?" asked Junior, giving a hearty wave. He joined the group, leaned in, and curled an arm possessively around Toni's waist. "You look great!" He planted a lopsided kiss on her cheek. "Grrrr, you smell good, too. What's that you're wearing? Perfume?"

"No, it's my flea and tick collar," said Toni. "Yes, it's perfume." She pulled away. "And please stop jerking my dress up."

"Nag, nag, nag," said Junior, grinning stupidly. He glanced at Sam. "You see why Toni and I get along so well?"

"Looks like a marriage made in Heaven to me," said Sam.

Suzanne gave him a subtle sideways kick in the ankle.

"Ooh," said Sam. "Or some other prime location in the afterlife."

"You oughta see what we did to Ricky's car," said Junior. "It's so cool, even the sheriff stopped by to take a look."

"Yeah, right," said Toni.

"Maybe we should all take our seats?" said Petra. She was the churchiest one of the bunch, always concerned with decorum and proper etiquette. Toni generally winged it, while Suzanne played it slightly close to the edge.

They took their places in the third row of chairs from the front. Sam, Suzanne, Toni, Junior, and Petra, in that order.

Toni leaned forward to talk to Petra. "You're wearing slacks. I thought you were going to wear your pink lace dress."

Petra stared stolidly at her. "The only time I wear a dress is when all my fat pants are in the laundry."

Junior gave a snort, which was immediately quashed by Petra's cold, dead-on gaze.

Toni punched Junior in the arm, then whispered, "Sorry," to Petra. "Didn't mean to hit a nerve." She turned the other way to face Suzanne and grasped for her hand. "Isn't this one of the prettiest weddings you've ever seen?"

"I had no idea you could take a slice of a city park and make it look this stunning," said Suzanne.

"Makes me want to get married all over again," said Toni.

"No," Suzanne whispered. "Take a deep breath and wipe that thought from your sweet little head."

Toni chuckled, and then nodded at Sam, who was busy talking to a man in the row behind him. "What about you two?" she whispered. "Any plans?"

"When there are," said Suzanne, "you'll be the first to know."

As the musicians struck up another tune, a hush fell over the crowd. Everyone turned in their seats or crooked their heads around, the better to see.

Ricky Wilcox and his best man, a fellow Suzanne recognized as the bag boy from Dill's Supermarket, came walking down the aisle. Both wore lavender tuxedos with frilly shirts. In any other situation, they might have looked like they were all decked out for the junior prom, but when they climbed the steps to the white wooden gazebo and took their places, the tuxes suddenly looked appropriate.

The two men were followed by Reverend Judith Wilson, wearing a long black robe. Reverend Wilson was the new minister at the Unitarian Church and also brand-new to Kindred. She seemed friendly and nice, and had agreed to perform Kit and Ricky's wedding ceremony even though they both claimed it was nondenominational.

Suzanne figured that with church attendance on the wane these days, you had to get your audience wherever you could.

Kit's matron of honor, her older sister, Cara, was next. She walked slowly down the aisle, followed by two small girls, flower girls, who dipped their hands into little baskets and scattered white petals along the way.

"Aren't they adorable?" Toni said under her breath.

Suzanne had to agree.

There was a short pause. Then the trio broke into the opening strains of Pachelbel's Canon in D Major and Kit suddenly appeared. As the music swelled in sweetness and intensity, she hesitated for a moment, glancing around with a smile, knowing all eyes were upon her. Then she walked slowly down the center aisle of emerald green moss. Another hush fell across the guests and then a few whispers started up, because she really did look stunning.

Kit's Empire-waist wedding gown was cream colored with a long, lacy train. It fluttered and flowed as she walked, making her look like a ripe earth mother, almost a throwback to the '60s. She wore a wreath of woven leaves and flowers in her long, blond hair and she carried three white calla lilies with trailing ribbons. As she walked down the aisle, her almond-shaped eyes, tipped with luxurious lashes, shone with happiness.

She looks radiant, Suzanne thought to herself.

"Wow," said Toni. And then in a whisper to Suzanne, "See? You can't even tell she has a bun in the oven."

"Shhh!" Suzanne put an index finger to her lips. This wasn't the time or place for that. This was Kit's big day, her glorious wedding day, and nothing could or should take away from that.

As Kit walked past them, Sam reached down and gently twined his fingers with Suzanne's. She'd been thinking back to her own wedding day, some ten years ago with Walter. Now Sam's touch brought her back to the here and now.

No looking back, Suzanne told herself. *Live for today. Make every second count.*

And then Kit was mounting the three steps that led to the gazebo's platform and Ricky took her by the arm, pulling her close to his side as if he never wanted to let her go.

Reverend Wilson began by reading a poem. And then the trio played a soft melody that Suzanne recognized as the English folk song "Greensleeves." Soon it was time for the exchange of vows.

Kit and Ricky had written their own vows. Ricky spoke first, promising to love, protect, and respect Kit. Telling her that she was the love and the light of his life.

And then it was Kit's turn. With every eye (many of them damp) focused upon her, she spoke slowly and clearly in a melodious voice.

"I love you with all my heart," Kit told Ricky. "I was lost until you came into my life and found me. Now, I feel complete. Ricky, I promise always to respect you, take care of you, and give you comfort, long into our old age."

"So sweet," said Toni, dabbing at her eyes with a hankie.

"And now the exchange of rings," said Reverend Wilson.

Ricky's best man dug in his vest pocket and pulled out two thin gold bands.

"Ricky," said Reverend Wilson, "place your ring on Kit's hand and repeat after me. With this ring . . ."

"With this ring," Ricky repeated.

"I thee . . ." began Reverend Wilson.

And that's when Kit's picture-perfect wedding erupted into a complete nightmare.

"Stop!" commanded a loud, authoritative voice.

"What?" said Suzanne, shocked. What was going on here? There was the loud tromp of boots and what seemed like a kind of shoving match at the entrance to the clearing. Suzanne stood up halfway, and was stunned to see Sheriff Doogie and two of his deputies thundering down the aisle, looking grim-faced and determined.

"Excuse me!" said Reverend Wilson with all the outrage she could muster. "There's a solemn wedding ceremony being . . ."

Doogie held up a meaty hand. "Sorry, but it's going to

have to wait." Taking two steps at a time, he leapt up onto the gazebo and dropped a heavy hand on Ricky's shoulder. "I'm sorry to tell you this, son, but you're under arrest on suspicion of arson and probable murder."

The cries of outrage from the crowd seemed to drown out everything else.

But Suzanne had heard Doogie's words loud and clear. Arson. And murder. *That couldn't be right, could it?* she thought to herself. *I mean . . . Ricky Wilcox?*

Deputy Driscoll produced a set of gleaming silver handcuffs that clicked around Ricky's wrists as fast and neat as a snapping turtle's bite.

"But . . . but . . . we're not even married yet!" cried Kit. Her voice, the expression on her face, conveyed shock, outrage, numbing fear.

It didn't matter. Ricky was hauled away before anyone had a chance to say, "I do"! Or even . . .

"What on earth is going on?" Suzanne cried out. "What's Doogie saying?"

"Arrested?" said Sam.

"This is cuckoo!" said Junior. Even he was upset.

Toni was hopping mad. "Did you guys see that? Did you *see* that?" she sputtered, as if she were the only one who'd witnessed this outrage. "Doogie grabbed Ricky and . . ." She was tripping over her own words, fighting to catch her breath. "And . . . and he's been arrested and hauled away!"

Petra was the only one who wasn't completely unnerved. "I hate to say this," she said, looking tight-lipped and solemn, "but maybe stopping this ceremony was a good thing."

"No way," cried Toni.

"Maybe it's a form of divine intervention," Petra whispered.

"This is *Doogie's* intervention," said Suzanne. Honestly, did he and his deputies really have to come galloping in like a pack of Nazi storm troopers and ruin Kit's wedding? It was completely unacceptable! In fact . . .

Suzanne was so enraged that she suddenly leapt from her seat and pushed her way to the center aisle.

"Where are you going?" Sam called after her.

"Suzanne, stop," said Petra. "Don't interfere!"

But Suzanne had a mind of her own. She rushed down the aisle and elbowed her way through the confusion and chaos of upset guests.

"Doogie!" she yelled out. She was twenty feet behind him now and catching up as fast as her shiny black stilettos would allow. "What's going on? How could you *do* that?"

As Suzanne spun her way past a stand of aspens, she saw Deputy Driscoll's hand on top of Ricky's head as the hapless groom was pushed into the backseat of a maroon and tan cruiser.

"You just embarrassed Kit and Ricky in front of all their guests," Suzanne cried, rushing up on Doogie's heels. "And ruined their wedding ceremony!"

Doogie turned a flat gaze on her and gave a warning motion with his hand for her to stay back. "Keep out of this, Suzanne."

"No," she cried, coming closer. "I'm *not* going to stay out of this. What possible reason could you have for arresting Ricky Wilcox? I mean . . . no way is he connected to yesterday's fire."

"Do you know where Ricky Wilcox works?" Doogie asked, glaring at her. His face was as red as a Roma tomato. His Smokey Bear hat was on crooked, giving him a strange, lopsided look.

Suzanne frowned. What did that have to do with anything? She shrugged. "I don't know. The post office?"

Doogie shook his head vehemently. "Not since a couple of months ago. Now he works at Salazar Mining."

"So what?" said Suzanne. Her heart was beating so fast it felt like a timpani drum run amok. Surely she could straighten this out. Surely she could help save the day. Kit's wedding day!

"Do you know what they *do* out there?" asked Doogie.

Why is Doogie peppering me with all these stupid questions? she wondered.

"Um . . . it's some kind of silica sand mine, right?"

"Correct. And do you know *how* they get the silica sand out of the ground?" Doogie hooked his thumbs in his gun belt and advanced on her.

"Bulldozers," said Suzanne. "Shovels." She had no idea. Nor did she care at this point.

Doogie pushed his face closer to hers. "They *blast* it out of the ground. With nasty combustibles like dynamite and plastic explosives."

That stopped Suzanne for all of five seconds. "Wait a minute, this is totally absurd. You don't really think that Ricky . . ."

"There were blasting caps missing from the mine," said Doogie. "Do you know what blasting caps *do*?"

Suzanne shook her head. No. But she had a pretty good idea that Doogie was about to tell her.

"They're used as a primary explosive device to detonate a much larger explosive."

Oh dear Lord, Suzanne thought. *Doogie really is pointing a finger at Ricky for the fire. And for Hannah's death.*

"Just because Ricky is an employee at that mine doesn't necessarily mean that he stole them," said Suzanne. "It could have been anyone."

"Oh yeah?" said Doogie. "Then how come we found blasting caps in the trunk of Ricky's car?"

"What?" Suzanne cried. She could hardly believe this.

"That's right," said Doogie. "When Deputy Driscoll and I showed up looking for Ricky, just wanting to ask him a couple of routine questions, your buddy Junior happened to spring the trunk of Ricky's car open. And there they were. In plain sight." He paused dramatically. "So tell me, please, just what am I supposed to surmise from that kind of hard evidence? Just why do you think Judge Carlson signed a warrant for Ricky's arrest?"

Suzanne opened her mouth to protest, and then closed it. She couldn't think of anything to say. In fact, she couldn't think of any reasonable explanation at all.

CHAPTER 8

THEY all trudged the couple of blocks over to Schmitt's Bar anyway. It was late Saturday afternoon, everybody was in need of a stiff drink, and, of course, there was cake.

But it was a sad, desultory party that seated themselves at one of the round tables in the Boom Boom Room.

"Drinks," said Junior. He'd somehow taken it upon himself to play maître d'. "A show of hands for whoever wants a drink."

"I suppose a watermelon daiquiri is out of the question?" said Petra.

"You'll have better luck with beer and a bump," advised Junior.

"Junior," said Suzanne, rapping her knuckles on the table to get his attention. "Why on earth did you open the trunk of Ricky's car for Sheriff Doogie? What was *that* all about?"

Junior blinked at her. "Why? Because the sheriff was interested." He folded his arms across his chest, causing his too-large jacket to billow up around his scrawny neck. "Don't you get it, Suzanne? Men *like* cars, it's a male bonding thing. They like cylinder heads and differentials, and chrome wheels, and . . ."

"Car trunks," said Suzanne. "Do you know that Doogie spotted some missing—or maybe even stolen—blasting caps in Ricky's trunk? That's why he came storming into the wedding and hauled him away!"

"*That's* why?" Junior gaped at her.

"You got it," said Suzanne. She wasn't really mad at Junior, just upset with the situation, complicated as it might be.

"So it was all *your* fault," said Toni, balling up a fist and giving Junior a sharp punch in the arm.

"Owww," moaned Junior, cradling his arm and pretending to be seriously injured. "Why is it *my* fault?"

Petra held up a hand. "Wait a minute. So there really *were* blasting caps in the trunk of Ricky's car?"

"Apparently so," said Suzanne. *Exhibit A: blasting caps. Situation not looking good for Ricky.*

"And Sheriff Doogie thinks Ricky used them to set off that fire?" said Petra.

"That's his basic reasoning, yes," said Suzanne.

"Case closed," said Sam. He'd been quiet until now, listening to everyone argue back and forth, but now he said his piece. "Having possession of blasting caps, especially ones that were stolen, is awfully damning evidence."

"Not so fast," said Suzanne. "We don't *know* for sure that they were stolen. They could have been planted, and they could have come from anywhere. Think about it, what possible reason would Ricky Wilcox have for wanting to burn down the County Services Building?"

"What reason would anyone have?" asked Sam. "The whole thing is fluky and nonsensical. I mean, there's no clear *motive*." His eyes fastened on Suzanne. "Aren't you always telling me that all crimes have to have a basic motive? And that, in order to solve a crime, you need to figure out the motive?"

Me and my big mouth, Suzanne thought.

"Maybe Ricky had a grudge against Hannah?" said Petra. "Or against Bruce Winthrop?"

"The mild-mannered county agent and his capable assistant," Suzanne said slowly. "They don't strike me as being *anyone's* adversary."

"I do see your point," said Petra.

Everyone was silent for a few moments and then Junior stood up and, once again, said, "Drinks?"

This time everyone put in an order.

SUZANNE had barely taken a sip from her lemon drop when Kit came barreling in with her sister, Cara, in tow. She stopped suddenly at the entrance to the back room and gazed around at the white streamers, silver wedding bells, and bouquets of flowers on the tables. Then she looked pointedly at the wedding cake that occupied its own table, the cake Petra had so painstakingly baked and decorated. And her lower lip began to quiver.

"Honey . . . no," said Suzanne. She jumped from her chair and swept Kit into her arms. "Please don't cry. This is all going to be sorted out, I promise you. I'm sure this is all a . . . a huge mistake." At least she hoped it was.

But Kit did cry. Tears streamed down her face and great sobs tore from her. And Cara, feeling upset or maybe just left out of the action, began crying, too.

"Oh jeez," said Junior. "Here come the waterworks."

"You keep quiet," warned Toni. "You've caused enough trouble for one day."

"Sorry, turtledove," he muttered. "I didn't mean to."

"Kit," said Cara, fighting to get her emotions under control and plucking at her sister's sleeve, "let's go back into the front room. We'll sit in a booth, order a nice stiff drink, and try to calm down. Okay?"

"Okay," said Kit. She squeezed Suzanne's hand and murmured a strangled "Thank you." Then she turned and headed into the front bar, as the train of her beautiful wedding dress dragged through the detritus of peanut shells and cigarette butts.

SUZANNE managed to enjoy a couple more sips of her drink before Doogie showed up.

"Oh no," said Toni, wrinkling her nose when she spotted him. "You. How can you even dare show your face here?"

"Because I'm upholding the law, that's why," said Doogie. He wasn't about to take any crap from Toni or anyone else. "And I need to speak to Junior."

"Me?" said Junior, jerking like he'd been touched with a hot poker and practically spilling his glass of beer. "What'd I do?"

"You're an accessory to the crime," Toni told him.

"I don't want to be no accessory to the crime!" Junior whined.

"You're not an accessory," said Doogie. "You're a witness."

"There's a difference?" said Junior.

"I guess the poor boy never did finish law school," Petra said in a droll voice.

"Take a chill pill, Junior," said Doogie. "I just want to talk to you about Ricky's car."

"Heh, heh," Junior said, jittering in his chair. "About the tin cans and Silly String and stuff?"

"About the blasting caps," said Doogie.

"I didn't put them there!" Junior cried. "No, sir, it wasn't me."

"Can you stop by my office tomorrow afternoon around three?" Doogie asked.

"What for?" asked Junior, still on the defensive.

"Just to talk. To answer a few questions."

"I won't be arrested?"

This time Doogie's mouth twitched and he couldn't help but smile. "No, Junior, you're not going to be arrested."

Junior's hand did a mock swipe across his brow. "Whew. You had me scared there."

Doogie hitched up his utility belt and turned to leave. But two seconds later, he found himself facing a very angry Kit Kaslik.

"What are *you* doing here?" Kit demanded. She was so angry she was practically spitting at him.

"Funny," said Doogie. "People keep asking me that." He ran the back of his hand down the side of his cheek. "I'm trying to solve a case of arson and what looks like murder, and folks keep asking me what I'm doing." He took a step closer to Kit and his voice dropped a few chilly degrees. "I'm doing my job, that's what I'm doing. And anybody who doesn't like it can get the heck out of my way!"

Doogie lumbered off, leaving Kit looking astonished.

"You can't talk to me like that!" Kit hurled after him. She turned and threw a pleading look at Suzanne. "He can't talk to me like that, can he?"

"Clearly he just did," said Sam.

Suzanne pushed her drink away and stood up. She went over to Kit, hooked an arm around her, and hauled her down a narrow corridor toward the ladies' room. "We need to talk," she told her.

They stood in the hallway under a tin sign that read, Beer—It's Not Just for Breakfast Anymore. Kit dropped her head and sobbed quietly and defeatedly for a few minutes. Suzanne let her. She figured it was good for Kit to get it all out.

Finally, Kit pulled a hankie from her purse, blew her nose, and focused red-rimmed eyes upon Suzanne. "Can you help me?" she asked in a hoarse whisper.

"Honey, I can try," said Suzanne. "But you're going to have to hold it together." She placed her hands on Kit's shoulders and squeezed. "Do you think you can do that?"

Kit nodded. "I'll try."

"Good," said Suzanne. "First things first. Ricky's going to need a lawyer."

"Okay."

"Can you handle that or do you want me to make some calls?"

"I can do that," said Kit. "I want to do that." She hesitated and gave a loud sniffle. "But I really do need *your* help, too."

"With . . . ?" said Suzanne. She was pretty sure she knew what was coming.

"You're close to Doogie," said Kit. "And you're good at figuring things out."

"Not really."

"Yes, you are!" said Kit. "You're clever and you've got good instincts and a real knack for unraveling tough cases." Her words tumbled out fast.

"Don't let Doogie hear you say that," said Suzanne.

"I don't care if he *does* hear me," said Kit.

"What's going on?" said a voice at their elbows. It was Toni. She'd crept quietly down the hallway to see what kind of confab they were having.

"I'm asking Suzanne for help," said Kit.

"Good," said Toni.

"Not good," said Suzanne.

"C'mon, girlfriend," said Toni. "You're a first-class ama-teur sleuth. A regular Nancy Drew."

"I wish you wouldn't say that," said Suzanne.

Toni snapped her fingers. "Okay, how about that lady in *Murder, She Wrote*? You're kind of a younger version of her."

"I'm not sure what I can do," Suzanne hedged. She wanted to help, she really did. As much as she tried to resist it, Suzanne was a champion of underdogs, a fighter for lost causes. No wonder she could never say no when dog rescue groups, women's shelters, and veterans' groups called on her to volunteer her time or services. But this . . . this was a thousand times trickier. And dangerous, too.

Now Toni and Kit were both looking at Suzanne with hopeful, pleading expressions on their faces.

Oh man. How can I say no to this poor girl? Suzanne thought. *The fact is, I can't. I just can't. Not on what was supposed to be her wedding day. Not with her being three months pregnant.*

"Okay," said Suzanne. She held up an index finger. "I'm not promising anything here, but I'll do what I can."

"Thank you," said Kit.

"Atta girl," said Toni.

SUZANNE and Toni drifted back to their table, where Petra seemed to be caught up in a serious discussion with Sam. Junior watched from the sidelines, one eye on Petra and Sam, one eye on the cake.

"The thing is," said Petra. Her brow was furrowed and she'd developed a deep set of 11's between her eyes. "What if Ricky *did* set that fire? I mean, what do we really know about him?"

"Wait a minute," said Suzanne, sitting down next to Sam and gazing at Petra. "Not so long ago you had us practically convinced that Jack Venable was the arsonist and killer. Now you've gone all Chutes and Ladders with a *different* theory, thinking that Ricky might be the guilty one. Which is it, Petra? Because you can't have it both ways."

"I don't *know*," said Petra, getting red in the face. "None of us do. It's a mystery."

"A murder mystery," said Junior. He looked across the table at Suzanne and winked.

Suzanne tried her best to ignore him.

"We have to try to figure out motive," said Sam. Now he was gazing at Suzanne.

Motive, thought Suzanne. She had to start somewhere and maybe the best place was to try to figure out who Jack Venable was having an affair with. That might lead somewhere . . .

"Did Kit just ask you for help?" Petra asked.

"She sure did," said Toni.

"And you said yes?" Petra asked. Now *she* was gazing at Suzanne, too.

Suzanne tried to avoid everyone's eyes. "I said I'd try," she mumbled. "I said I'd try."

"Jeez," said Junior, "are we ever gonna cut that cake?"

THEIR little party broke up some ten minutes later. Except that Sam wanted to stay at Schmitt's Bar and have something to eat. And Toni and Junior wanted to sit at the bar and enjoy two-for-one Happy Hour drinks. Double Bubble, they called it here.

"Are you sure you want to stay?" Suzanne asked as they slid into one of the battered wooden booths in the front section of the bar. "Because I can fix us something at home."

"Nah," said Sam. "This is fine. Why not make it easy on ourselves?"

"Probably because nothing is easy," Suzanne said under her breath.

Freddy, the aging hippie bartender/owner, was at their booth in a heartbeat. "Here are your menus, folks," he said, handing them grease-stained, floppy menus that everyone pretty much knew by heart. Freddy's goatee was braided and fastened with a tiny gold ring and he wore blue jeans, red suspenders, and a T-shirt that said You Had Me at Bacon.

"Burger basket," said Sam. He generally stuck to a heart-healthy diet of chicken, fish, veggies, and fruit, but when it came to Freddy's grilled hamburgers all bets were off. Sizzled on an old-fashioned, grease-encrusted grill that looked like it had been dug from the embers of Hell, the burgers came out pink and juicy on the inside, nicely charred on the outside.

"Cheese?" said Freddy. "I got some special Maytag blue in the cooler."

"Sold," said Sam.

Freddy smiled at Suzanne. "How about you, ma'am?"

Suzanne felt like an arrow had pierced her heart. She'd been ma'amed. No woman, even if she was just a hair over forty, wanted to be ma'amed.

"I'll have the same thing," Suzanne told him.

"How about a tasty basket of onion strings to accompany those burgers?" Freddy asked. He was always skillful at pimping the extras.

"Sure," said Sam.

Freddy wrote down their orders in his crooked, back-slanted handwriting, then looked up at Suzanne and said, "I'm really sorry about the wedding reception. I heard what happened over at the park." He shook his head gravely. "It wasn't right, the sheriff charging in like that. He should have at least waited for that young couple to say their I do's."

"I hear you," said Suzanne.

"I ain't going to charge them for use of the back room, neither," said Freddy. "It wouldn't be right."

"That's very sweet of you," said Suzanne. For some reason, Freddy's small kindness made her feel like crying. Up to this point she'd been shocked, angry, amazed, and befuddled, but certainly not tearful. Now, everything seemed to boil up inside of her, and her emotions felt like they were ready to pour out.

Sensing Suzanne's inner turmoil, Sam stretched an arm across the table and gently touched her hand. *Take it easy*, he seemed to be saying. Then he very carefully and deliberately mouthed the words *I love you*.

ONE hamburger, two handfuls of onion strings, and a glass of white wine later, Suzanne was feeling a whole lot better. Someone had cranked up the jukebox and now it was pumping out Little Richard's "Good Golly Miss Molly."

The Saturday night crowd had arrived in full force and the proverbial joint was jumping. The decibel level rivaled that of a jet engine, harried waitresses delivered foaming mugs of beer, the grill sizzled and popped nonstop, and there was the faint sound of pool balls being racked in the far corner.

"Hey, you guys are still here," said Toni.

She and Junior had relinquished their stools at the bar and eased over to Suzanne and Sam's booth, looking relaxed after more than a couple of $2 beers. Sam was studying the check and peeling off bills to pay for supper.

"Not for long," said Suzanne. "We were just leaving."

"You oughta stick around," said Junior. "There's gonna be a meat raffle later on. To benefit the Jaycees."

"Sounds like fun," said Sam. He glanced sideways at Suzanne and the corners of his eyes crinkled.

"It's a fifteen-pound chuck roast from Pekarna's Meats," said Toni.

"Put that baby in your freezer and you can eat for a month!" exclaimed Junior.

"Only if you defrost it first," said Suzanne. She gathered up her purse, glanced over at the bar, and registered that a slight commotion was going on. And there, right in the center of things, wearing a red plaid shirt and faded denim jeans, and looking as if he'd been dropped there by the hand of God, was Darrel Fuhrman. He was leaning forward, elbows on the bar, looking belligerent and shaking his finger at someone, obviously trying to drive home a point.

Suzanne nudged Toni. "Isn't that Darrel Fuhrman at the bar?"

Toni twisted her head and looked around. "Oh yeah," she said. "I guess it is."

"Who's Darrel Fuhrman?" asked Sam.

"Believe it or not," said Suzanne, keeping her voice low, "he's one of Doogie's suspects."

"What?" Sam and Junior said together in a rush.

"Well, maybe he's not one of Doogie's suspects anymore," Suzanne amended. "Now that the situation has changed somewhat."

"Hold everything," said Sam. "Where did you get this information?"

"From Doogie," said Suzanne. "He told me this morning that they were taking a hard look at Fuhrman."

"And why would they do that?" said Sam.

"Because he was let go from the fire department by Chief Finley," said Suzanne.

"Why was he let go?" asked Junior.

Suzanne shrugged. "I don't know, I guess you'd have to ask Chief Finley."

"Maybe I'll do that," said Junior.

"Don't get involved," Toni warned.

"Seriously, Suzanne," said Sam. "Why on earth would Doogie suspect this guy Fuhrman?"

"I'm not sure exactly," said Suzanne. "He just kind of mentioned it in passing."

"I've heard stories," said Junior, "about firemen who really enjoy the excitement of a fire. The flames, the heat, the destruction. In fact, they get to liking it so much that they sometimes go out and set fires themselves." Junior's eyes practically bulged during the telling.

"That's very creepy," said Toni. "But is it true?"

"I've read a few case studies that confirmed that," said Sam.

They all looked over at Fuhrman, who seemed to be holding court now at the bar. He was listing on his barstool, obviously drunk, and still talking way too loud.

Then, as if their collective gaze had alerted him, Fuhrman looked over at the group and said, "You people lookin' at something?"

"Uh-oh," said Sam. They all turned their eyes back on one another.

"You hear me talkin' over here?" Fuhrman demanded. He sounded cocky and confrontational. Like he might be itching for a fight.

Again, nobody breathed or moved a muscle.

"I guess you heard the rumor, too, huh?" Fuhrman said loudly. "That it was me who set that fire?" He giggled drunkenly as he swayed on his barstool. "Now you all know that I'm innocent because Sheriff Doogie just *arrested* some other poor sap!"

"Come on," said Sam. "Let's get out of here."

Toni made the mistake of glancing over at Fuhrman as they passed by him.

Fuhrman cocked a murderous eye at her and bellowed, "Or maybe a *woman* set that fire. These days you never know." Then he turned back to the bar and cackled like a hyena.

CHAPTER 9

SUZANNE creaked a single eye open and looked around her bedroom. The light was dim and the clock on her nightstand said six-fifteen. Ooh . . . still early. Way too early to make any pretense of the old rise and shine. Yet, the space next to her was unoccupied. Not only that, but the pillow had been punched up and smoothed, and the patchwork quilt had been pulled up so everything was all neat and tidy.

Dr. Hazelet, where did you slip off to?

Suzanne rolled back over and thought for a few moments. She'd been vaguely aware of Sam's cell phone going off around five o'clock this morning, and him mumbling something about a possible emergency appendectomy. Or maybe it had been a tracheotomy?

Whatever. She was feeling woozy and confused and suddenly worried that she might have overcommitted herself to Kit last night. Could she really talk to Doogie and get things straightened out? After all, Ricky couldn't be guilty, could he?

Taking a deep breath, Suzanne sat up in bed and tried to focus. She swung her legs around and scuffed her bare toes against the furry flokati rug on the floor.

There . . . better. Her head was starting to clear.

After a minute or two of wake-up time, a few more cogent thoughts rumbled through Suzanne's brain. She thought about how Kit had begged for her help. And Bruce Winthrop, too. Winthrop was crazed with grief over Hannah, and Kit was terrified that Ricky was going to be tried for murder.

What a nasty situation. For everyone involved.

And Doogie . . . how many suspects did he have now? Suzanne tallied them up on her fingers. There was Hannah's husband, Jack Venable. Ricky Wilcox. Darrel Fuhrman, the ex-fireman. And Marty Wolfson, the estranged husband of the rescued woman. He was still in the picture, right? Sure he was, he had to be.

If Doogie was on the right track, and he'd certainly proved to be a smart, tenacious investigator, one of those men must have committed arson. The problem was, which one?

Suzanne dropped her head into her hands and rubbed her eyes. Then she let her hands wander to the back of her neck, where a couple of overnight kinks seemed to have lodged. She massaged her neck gently and, when she looked up, two pairs of limpid brown eyes were staring at her. Baxter and Scruff.

"What?" she said. Then, "Yeah, I know you're hungry. Give me ten minutes to brush my teeth, comb my hair, and jump into my T-shirt and a pair of leggings. Then I'll feed you guys a nice bowl of kibbles and we'll all go for a lovely walk. Okay? Everybody like that idea?"

By the wide doggy grins and thumping of tails, she could tell they liked it just fine.

A bright red cardinal, with a sunflower seed clutched in its beak, flitted from one cedar tree to another as Suzanne headed out the back door. Baxter watched the bird with little interest; Scruff wagged his tail. They walked across the backyard and, once again, Suzanne wondered how she was ever going to get her lawn back in shape. Not only was it a crossword puzzle of brown and yellow patches, but several large holes had been recently excavated. She didn't know if the dogs dug holes for recreational purposes or if they had found inspiration in watching *The Great Escape*. Thank goodness they'd stayed well away from her herb garden, where her chives, rosemary, basil, and parsley were growing.

The herb garden had been a struggle. First it had been unseasonably cold and rainy. Then, once the plants had poked their tender heads up, the rabbits had invaded. A couple of rolls of chicken wire had settled that score. Then the bugs had taken more than a casual interest. Little crawly green caterpillars that chewed holes in the leaves and deposited tiny white dots that she assumed were larvae. It had been an ongoing conflict between her respect for nature, and her God-given right to grow a meager crop of herbs. Pesticides were out, of course. And though the dogs now kept the rabbits at bay, they'd never quite got the hang of chasing caterpillars. Maybe she should have chanted and burned sage?

Out the gate and down the back alley the three of them charged. The dogs strutting their stuff out in front of Suzanne while she clung to their leashes like a Roman chariot driver. It was still early morning and it looked as if nobody in the neighborhood was even awake yet. So a good time to sniff along the boulevards, stray into a yard or two, and maybe even discreetly lift a leg.

Even though it was the tail end of August, warm weather had been holding on during the daylight hours. A few flowers were still in bloom, but the bumblebees were starting to get logy and the deciduous trees looked as if they'd already peaked and wanted to start shedding their leaves any day now. And mornings, especially this particular morning, had a crispness in the air that was a distinct harbinger of autumn.

As Suzanne cruised along with the dogs, she felt her muscles warming and fell into a nice rhythm. Because it felt so good to get out and move, she continued walking, block after block, past the little Cape Cods and modified Queen Anne homes in her neighborhood, past homes with porch swings and window boxes, and one enormous American Gothic home with a tabby cat sneaking around the front yard.

Until, suddenly, with more than a dozen blocks behind her, Suzanne found herself a short distance from the park, gazing at its expanse of trees and green grass.

The park. Oh no. I wonder if the decorated gazebo and garlands are still in place?

Curiosity pulled Suzanne across the street and down the same lane of trees she'd strolled just yesterday afternoon with Sam.

Had it only been yesterday? Really, just sixteen hours ago? It feels like a month has transpired.

With a tinge of sadness and a little trepidation, Suzanne stopped and gazed at the little glen where the wedding was supposed to have taken place. The chairs were gone, but the garlands and vines were still hanging there. Up in the tree, she saw it wasn't just little bows that had been tied in the branches as she'd first thought. There were little pieces of paper attached.

Wedding wishes.

Suzanne reached up and pulled one down. Written in gold ink on a small circle of parchment were the words *Forever Happy*. She folded the paper carefully and tucked it in the pocket of her hoodie.

Would Kit and Ricky ever find themselves forever

happy, she wondered? Or would circumstances take them down a different path, a darker path?

Tugging at the dogs' leashes, Suzanne wheeled around and retraced her footsteps. She cut across the playground, where teeter-totters sat expectantly and swings dangled in the breeze. Passing Kuyper's Hardware Store now, she turned at the corner and, on impulse, hung a quick left. And found herself strolling slowly down the alley behind the burned-out building.

It still reeked of smoke back here and yellow crime scene tape fluttered from where it was still attached to the adjacent buildings. But the tape had been broken in several places, so she assumed any number of curious folks had driven or walked down this same alley and poked around.

To find what? Probably nothing. Probably the arson investigator had cowboyed in and found whatever there was to be found. He'd taken his little samples, sent them back to the lab for analysis, and then . . . Then, she didn't know what might happen.

The dogs stayed in the middle of the alley, acting bored, but Suzanne was walking as close as she dared to piles of ashes and timbers and rubble. In one spot, where the ash was light gray, she could see large footprints that looked like they'd been made by a Vibram-soled hunting boot. Someone had walked in there, dodging fallen timbers and leaning columns of scorched bricks, to take a serious look around.

Not me, though. This whole scene looks way too dangerous.

In fact, Suzanne wondered why Doogie or Chief Finley hadn't stretched some plastic fencing around the entire area just to keep things safe. To keep the kids out.

Pausing now, Suzanne studied the scene. She wondered what the fire's point of origin had been, what torturous thoughts had gone through poor Hannah's mind in the last few moments of her life. A soft scratching sound behind her suddenly made Suzanne stiffen. She whirled around. Was someone there, watching her? Or had Baxter been taking care of an itch?

But, no, he was standing there practically motionless, watching her. Wary now, Suzanne glanced up and down the alley. But all she saw were debris, trash cans, and a random pile of fallen, scorched bricks.

Nothing, she told herself. *Nothing there.*

She let loose a sigh and was about to move on, when something caught her eye.

Hmm?

She squinted at the ground and saw, under a pile of half-burned paper or shingles or whatever, a tiny hint of red. What could it be?

Suzanne glanced around, grabbed a stick, and stirred the pile of ashes, unearthing the little bit of red.

Then she bent down and picked it up.

It was some type of token. Like a game token or an old-fashioned streetcar token. She wasn't exactly sure what it was, but it was interesting. A little bit of something salvaged from all that damage.

Not thinking twice about it, Suzanne dropped it in her pocket.

At eleven o'clock, Suzanne was in her kitchen, rattling pots and pans, trying to decide whether to make herself a cheese omelet or whip up a batch of pancake batter. She pulled open her refrigerator, grabbed a carton of cream and a few other choice ingredients. Just as she lifted a knee and pushed the refrigerator door shut, she heard a soft knock at her front door. Then a distinct click of the latch.

"Hello?" It was Sam's voice calling to her. He'd come back from the hospital.

"In here," she called back. "Kitchen."

He padded in, looking tired, slightly bedraggled, and totally adorable in a faded red Henley shirt and blue jeans.

"You're back," Suzanne said.

"I told you that I would be."

"You did, really?" She gave a distracted smile. "Because I don't remember you saying that."

"I didn't think you were quite awake."

"Well, I am now," said Suzanne. "In fact, I've been up for a while. I even considered jumping on the old Learjet and heading off to Maui for a day at the beach, but then I thought, *What if Sam drops by? What if the poor guy's hungry?*"

"I am hungry," Sam said. He eased himself onto a stool at the counter and gave her a hopeful look. "Starved, in fact."

"Don't like the Jell-O they serve at the hospital commissary?"

"Nope."

"How about their powdered eggs?"

"Pass."

She smiled. "Then I'm happy to inform you that my kitchen is open for business."

Sam looked suddenly relieved. "I was hoping . . ."

"You realize, however, that on Sunday mornings I function as more of a short-order cook than a full-service chef. So what might your little heart desire? Eggs? Pancakes?"

"Pancakes would be wonderful," said Sam.

"How about a short stack of my trademark blue velvet pancakes?" Suzanne said.

Sam's eyes lit up with anticipation. "I don't know what they are, but I'm pretty sure I want them."

As they were enjoying brunch in the dining room—Suzanne had fixed a couple slices of Canadian bacon to go with her blueberry pancakes—Sam said, "What are you going to do today?"

Suzanne was about to reply, *Investigate a murder.* Instead, she caught herself and said, "I thought I'd take Mocha Gent over to the field by the City Works Garage and work him for a little while." Her quarter horse was a barrel racer. He'd been schooled as one when she bought him, and, over the past couple of years, she'd tried to maintain his barrel racing skills. Which basically meant riding hell-bent for leather around a cloverleaf of metal barrels, hanging on tight, and hoping Mocha didn't rip her leg off when they spun too hard and fast around a barrel.

Though Suzanne knew she was kapow crazy for even considering it, she was thinking about entering the barrel racing contest at the Logan County Fair this coming week.

"When does the county fair start?" Sam asked. He knew about her secret hankering for a barrel racing win, even if she had to settle for fifth or sixth place.

"Ah . . . I think this Thursday. Yes, Thursday night. That's when the parade is scheduled to go through downtown."

"And when is your barrel racing event?"

"Friday afternoon. But I still haven't decided if I'm even going to enter."

"Sure you are, you've been practicing like crazy."

"I don't know," said Suzanne. "The thing is . . . I've got a lot of other fish to fry, too."

Sam glanced sideways at her. "You mean like shadowing Sheriff Doogie? Trying to figure out who set that fire?"

"Noooo. I was thinking about the tea group that's coming in on Tuesday, attending Hannah's funeral on Wednesday, and getting the Cackleberry Club spruced up and ready for the dinner theater we're hosting on Friday night."

Sam lifted an eyebrow. "So no more chasing crooks and solving crimes?"

"I'm really more concerned about what's happening at work this week," Suzanne said, trying to ease her way out of his line of questioning. "In fact, I'm wondering if you've even memorized your lines for the play." Sam had recently been recruited by the Kindred Community Players and given a role in this Friday night's production.

"Excuse me," he said. "Did you not realize I have Shake-spearean training?"

Suzanne gazed at him. "I suppose you're referring to the summer stock you did at the Globe Theatre, in between your medical internship and residency?"

"That's it," said Sam. He reached out and took her hand. " 'Now is the winter of our discontent, made glorious summer by this sun of York.' "

"That's all very well and good," said Suzanne. "But I hope you realize that instead of dueling with a rapier and playing Richard III, you're going to be duded up in Victorian garb. Because the play you signed on for happens to be *Blithe Spirit*."

THE farm that sat across the enormous expanse of fields behind the Cackleberry Club was Suzanne's. She and Walter had purchased it as a sort of investment and, for the past few years, she had rented it to a farmer by the name of Reed Ducovny. He lived on the farm with his wife, Martha, and worked the land diligently, raising bumper crops of soybeans and Jubilee corn.

Where once dairy cows had chewed and mooed in the large, hip-roof barn, Suzanne now stabled her two horses. Correction, one horse named Mocha Gent and a mule named Grommet.

The two were best buddies and Suzanne was pleased that they kept each other company so well.

Mocha Gent was either keenly attuned to her scent or genuinely psychic. Because he let out a low whinny just as Suzanne walked past the row of empty cow stanchions and approached his box stall.

"Hey, fella." Suzanne reached out as Mocha pressed his chest up against the gate of his stall. She scratched him behind the ears, then ran the flat of her hand down his fine Roman nose and under his bristly chin. As an extra gesture of goodwill, she leaned forward and blew out a small puff of air. Horses liked this sharing of breath and scent. It told them you were friendly and trustworthy. Or at least that's what horse whisperers had divined.

In the stall next to Mocha, Grommet shuffled about anxiously and thrust his large black head out. Suzanne stepped sideways and gave him a pat behind his enormous ears.

"Hey, nobody's leaving you out in the cold," Suzanne told him. She sometimes rode Grommet, just to keep the old boy in shape and prove that she wasn't playing favorites. But his shuffling mule gait was a little hard to take.

"So what we're going to do," Suzanne said, turning back to Mocha, "is do a few practice rounds today. Just in case we decide to go to that fair." Mocha's ears shot forward as she swung open the stall gate. "You up for that?" He shifted sideways as she tossed a red and black buffalo plaid saddle blanket onto his broad back. Then she walked back out to the tack area and grabbed a brown Western saddle. She tossed it on his back, tightened the cinch, waited a few moments, and then poked him in the belly with her knee. When Mocha let out the air he'd surreptitiously gulped, she snugged the cinch again.

Three miles away, next to the City Works Garage, the Circle K Riders, a local riding club, had set up practice courses for barrel racing, keyhole racing, and pole bending.

Suzanne cut across a couple of fields, wandered down a blacktop road, and then turned in at the garage. It was your basic enormous cinder-block building painted flat gray. Inside were the large trucks that served as snowplows, road graders, and sanders when winter's ice compacted the roads. Which, throughout winter, was pretty much every day.

Suzanne and Mocha rounded the building at a brisk trot and Suzanne was pleased to see that she was the first one to arrive.

Excellent. She could practice to her heart's content. At least until a few other riders showed up and the place turned into an impromptu rodeo ring.

The barrel racing course consisted of three barrels set up in a triangle. The object of the race was to successfully maneuver your horse through a sort of cloverleaf pattern, galloping as fast as possible as you rounded the three barrels. It was a timed trial and the horse and rider who completed the course the fastest was the winner.

Suzanne aimed Mocha at the marked entrance to the course, gave him a sharp kick, and took off. They flew across the entrance, heading for the first barrel on their right. They whipped around this barrel in a half circle and headed for the second barrel. This was a left turn and Suzanne had to shift her weight to make sure Mocha went into the turn with the correct lead. Then they flew down the course, circled the back barrel, and headed for the finish line.

They did it four, five, six times. Suzanne worked on keeping her legs securely along the girth, hugging the barrels tightly, and sprinting like crazy down the homestretch.

When she thought they had it, she walked Mocha slowly in a circle for ten minutes to cool him down, then she took him back to the start. Over on the cement apron, in front of the garage, a car was parked. She wondered if they were watching her, or if it was just a maintenance worker who'd come to grab some tools. Either way, she gave a friendly wave and then turned back toward the course.

One more time, Suzanne told herself. *And this time we'll go for broke.*

As they dashed across the starting line, Suzanne glanced at her watch and registered the time. Then she gritted her teeth, focused all her energy on her horse, scrunched down in the saddle, and tried to be the best rider possible.

The barrels flew by in a blur. A right turn, a left turn, and then another left.

As they crossed the finish line, she looked down at her watch. The time was good. Eighteen seconds. It wasn't exact, of course, but she figured she just might be in the ball game.

Maybe they did have a chance this Friday. Maybe.

"You did great," she told Mocha as she walked him over to a water trough. She sat on his back as he sucked in water, stomped in the dust, then took in a little more water.

As they turned for home, Suzanne noticed the parked car, but nobody was in it. Lucky, she thought. Lucky she had this course all to herself. Lucky she had this horse and a healthy dose of chutzpah. She knew there were cowgirls younger and more experienced than herself. Tough rodeo veterans in their twenties who chewed gum like it was a wad of tobacco, and were fearless about spurring their horses around the barrels to take home another blue ribbon.

We'll see, she told herself. *We'll try to squeeze in one or two more practice sessions, and then we'll see.* Better to err on the side of caution.

Instead of riding down the blacktop road again, Suzanne cut across a hay meadow and ducked into a nearby woods. This trail was a little rocky, a little steep, but it would probably cut a half mile off her return trip.

And it was pretty in the woods as they jounced along a faint trail.

Whenever the breeze picked up, yellow and gold leaves fluttered in the air, raining down in the sunlight like butterflies on the wing.

The day had gotten warmer, too, and it felt good. Winter would be here soon enough and then riding would be curtailed to just short jaunts around the barnyard.

They crossed over a narrow streambed, the water

burbling over round, humpy rocks. Mocha, sure-footed and as careful as a trail horse, was picking his way gingerly, when something whizzed past Suzanne's head.

Shweeek!

Suzanne flinched instinctively.

What on earth?

Her heart nearly thumping out of her chest, her body pumping out a hot shot of adrenaline, Suzanne suddenly realized what had happened.

It had been a rifle shot. A very close call with live ammo.

Suzanne's head spun one way, then the other, as her eyes searched frantically through the woods, trying to spot who-ever had fired at her.

"Whoa, whoa!" she shouted out. "Don't shoot! I'm riding here."

No sound came back to her save the whisper of wind through the poplars and aspens.

Was someone out doing target practice? Although she really had experienced the feeling of live ammo.

So, a hunter?

Suzanne dug her heels into Mocha's flanks and spurred him forward. She knew the smartest thing, the safest thing, would be to get out of there as fast as possible.

But as she galloped down the trail, her mind whirring and her leather saddle creaking, she remembered that hunt-ing season didn't open for another month.

CHAPTER 10

RINGS of red peppers sizzled in Petra's cast-iron frying pan, giving off a sweet, pungent aroma. Once they were crispy on one side, she edged a spatula underneath each one and flipped it over. Then she cracked a farm-fresh egg inside each pepper ring and let them fry. Voilà. There you had it—eggs in a frame.

Of course, Petra had another version, too. That was when she toasted a nice thick chunk of sourdough bread, used a biscuit cutter to make a hole in the center, tossed the bread in the pan, and dropped an egg in to fry. That was version two of eggs in a frame.

"Holy baloney," said Toni, as she slewed her way through the swinging door and into the kitchen. "The joint's really jumpin' out there."

"It's Monday," said Petra as she cracked eggs one-handed into a speckled ceramic bowl. "We're always jam-packed on Monday."

"Aw, we're busy almost every day," said Toni. She handed

Petra a bunch of orders and turned to Suzanne, who was busy making toast. "Aren't we?"

"And thank goodness for it," said Suzanne. The Cackleberry Club was a business, after all. And Suzanne was well aware that making a profit was a far cry from just eking out a break-even living. What she liked to think of as her diversification—the café, Book Nook, Knitting Nest, and special event hosting—had proven to be a fairly dynamic business combination. When other small businesses were struggling or even shutting their doors, the Cackleberry Club just seemed to keep steaming full speed ahead.

"I suppose our customers are still buzzing about the fire?" said Petra as she tossed a handful of chicken and rice sausages onto her grill.

"That and Ricky Wilcox's arrest," said Toni. "That's mighty big news, too." She grabbed a strawberry, tossed it into the air, and caught it in her mouth. "I still can't believe that wedding scene," she said, chewing. "Just awful."

"So was Hannah's death," Petra said with grim determination.

"Somehow," said Suzanne, "I just don't see a connection between Ricky Wilcox and Hannah's death."

"Blasting caps," said Petra.

"But Ricky didn't have anything against Hannah, did he?" said Suzanne.

"Those blasting caps could have been planted in Ricky's car trunk," said Toni. "Easy as pie."

"By who?" Petra demanded.

Toni shrugged. "Don't know. Somebody who wanted to frame Ricky? Or smoke-screen the police investigation?"

"Really," said Suzanne, "it could have been anybody who works out at that mine." She wondered if Doogie had taken a hard look at all the people who had access to blasting caps. There were highway crews who did blasting, too, right? She'd have to ask him when he came in. And she figured

Doogie was sure to come in fairly soon. Monday was when Petra always baked her famous cranberry-nut bread.

"I feel really awful about Hannah," said Toni, "but I'm also bummed that Kit's wedding never took place." She accepted the side order of toast that Suzanne had just buttered and placed it on her serving tray. "On the other hand, I ended up having a fairly decent time at Schmitt's Bar after all."

"Because you were with Junior?" said Suzanne.

"Yeah, I guess he still melts my butter," said Toni.

Petra gave a little shudder. "I knew there was a reason I didn't stay very long."

"It got a little wild after you left," said Toni. "Lots of partying and—well, it wouldn't hurt you none, Petra, if you let go and danced yourself silly to a Beyoncé power ballad once in a while."

"No thanks," said Petra.

SUZANNE trailed Toni out into the café and kicked it into high gear. While Toni distributed steaming plates of food and took orders from newly arrived customers, Suzanne got busy brewing pots of Sumatran roast coffee and English breakfast tea. Then, looking around the Cackleberry Club and noting three empty tables, she made a few last-minute adjustments to table settings before the rest of their morning customers came tumbling in.

By ten o'clock there was a pleasant hum in the place. Though all the tables were filled, most of their customers had finished breakfast. Now they were just kicking back and enjoying a final cup of coffee, having neighborly chats, and planning their week.

"I think that's going to be it," Suzanne said to Petra as she slid into the kitchen. "Probably no more breakfast orders." If there was a pleasant hum in the café, there was an even more pleasant aroma in the kitchen. "Mmn, what smells so good?"

"I've got two loaves of cranberry-nut bread in the oven and now I'm working on my pumpkin bread," said Petra. She turned a large lump of dough onto a floured board. Then, as an afterthought, she pulled off her wedding ring. Petra was married, but her husband, Donny, lived in the Center City Nursing Home. Donny had Alzheimer's and barely recognized Petra anymore. Still, three or four nights a week, Petra made the trip over, taking cookies and lemon bars to Donny, talking to him, holding his hand while she watched TV with him. The fact that she had to introduce herself to Donny every time didn't seem to deter her. For Petra, marriage really did mean for better or worse, till death do you part.

"I love watching your hands when you knead bread dough," said Suzanne. "They always look so strong and confident."

"People get freaked out about making bread," said Petra. "But it's not really that difficult. Of course, you have to use the very best ingredients and know what you're doing." She stopped kneading for a moment and looked pointedly at her wedding ring, which rested on the nearby counter. "You know what?"

"What?" Suzanne said. Petra's face had assumed a strange, almost frightened look. "What's wrong?"

"Just now, when I took off my ring to knead the bread, I remembered something that Hannah mentioned to me . . . oh, two or three weeks ago."

"What's that?"

"That she misplaced her wedding ring," said Petra.

"And you think that's significant . . . why?"

"I don't know. I just find it strange. Like maybe her husband, Jack, took the ring and did something with it. Like it might be symbolic in some weird way . . . that he didn't want to be with Hannah anymore."

"Or *she* could have simply misplaced it," said Suzanne.

"There is that," agreed Petra.

"Wait a minute, did she mention the ring before she told you about Jack? When she said he might be having an affair?"

"I think it was before," Petra said slowly.

"Then it's probably nothing."

"Probably," said Petra. "Still, it seems a little strange."

"Maybe." Suzanne knew that Petra was still jumpy about Hannah's death, so she figured her mind might be a little muddled, too. She couldn't blame Petra for trying to make sense out of a tragedy.

Petra continued to knead her dough with great gusto, punching and rolling it, adding a pinch or two of flour as she went along.

Suzanne pointed at their overflowing trash can. "Do you want me to take the trash out and dump it? It's awfully full."

"And stinky, too," said Petra. "I was trimming out a couple of baked chickens for our chicken salad. And . . . well, there's a reason chicken is also called fowl, or in this case, foul."

"Then I'll run the garbage outside," said Suzanne.

"Oh," said Petra. "Do you think any bittersweet has popped up in the back woods yet? I was thinking a few sprigs of those little red berries would look really great nestled among the crocks of cattails and milk pods that Toni put on the tables."

"I'll be sure to take a look."

Suzanne gathered up the black plastic bag of trash, wrapped a twist tie around the opening, and hauled it out the back door. The sun was shining down in a deep cerulean blue sky and the temperature was edging up to around sixty. By mid-afternoon it was going to be a perfect day.

After tossing the bag of trash in their Dumpster, Suzanne was careful to latch it. Bands of marauding raccoons and clever coyotes roamed the countryside. And those animals would like nothing better than to do a little Dumpster diving and rustle up a tasty meal of bread crusts, day-old donuts, and chicken parts.

Suzanne crossed the packed-earth parking lot and stepped into the woodlot at the back of the property. It was thick with poplars, cedar trees, and wild buckthorn. Her own little bit of the north woods wild country. Vines snaked out to grab her feet as she moved along, trying to find a sprig or two of bittersweet growing among the underbrush.

Click click . . . cheeee.

Suzanne stopped abruptly in her tracks.

What?

She stiffened. After the potshot somebody had taken at her yesterday, either real or imagined, she suddenly felt jumpy and on edge.

Click . . . cheeee.

There was that sound again.

Suzanne studied the thicket of trees that surrounded her. Nothing. No squirrels, raccoons, or even people. So what was it? She moved stealthily forward as the grass just ahead of her stirred gently. She stopped, leaned forward, and peered down. And there, huddled no more than two feet away from her, was a tiny blob of fur.

At first she thought it might be a baby bunny.

But there were no floppy ears or cotton tail, just a tiny, puffy creature.

She knelt down and stared at it more carefully. Not fur, but downy feathers. And when big eyes, enormous eyes stared back at her, she knew it was a baby owl.

Oh no. What should she do?

Suzanne knew there were feral cats that prowled the neighborhood. When Baxter and Scruff came to work with her and were tied out back, the cats wisely stayed away. But when the dogs weren't around, she was pretty sure that Petra, kindhearted soul that she was, put out scraps of left-over food for the cats.

No way could she let a cat pounce on this unsuspecting little owl.

Pulling off her apron, Suzanne wrapped it gently around the little owl and gathered it up. Then slowly, carefully, she carried the owl back to the Cackleberry Club. Outside the back door, she found an empty cardboard box. She bunched the apron into the bottom of the box and set the little owl on top of it.

"Look at this," said Suzanne as she eased her way in the back door. "Look what I found."

Petra took a peek. "Jeepers. What is it?"

"A baby owl."

"Where'd the little thing come from?"

"Out back," said Suzanne. "I think it must have fallen out of its nest."

"Well, can you put it back?"

"I don't know. Maybe. Unless the mother has already rejected it."

"Your mother rejected you?" said Toni as she barged into the kitchen. Then she saw Suzanne standing there, holding the cardboard box in her arms. "What have you got there? Some kind of special delivery?"

Click click.

"Huh?" said Toni. "What the heck is that? A rattlesnake?"

"Hardly," said Suzanne. "It's a baby owl."

"Technically an owlet," said Petra. "Suzanne found it out back. Poor little critter must have fallen out of its nest."

Toni looked at both of them as if they were crazy. "What are you gonna do with it?"

"I don't know," said Suzanne. "Maybe try to get it into the witness protection program?"

Toni tiptoed closer to the box and peered in. "Hmm, it's actually kind of cute. Like a little hair ball with eyes."

"What I'm going to do," said Suzanne, "is call the Department of Natural Resources and see if they've got any bright ideas."

"But first you gotta do the menu," said Petra. "Menu first, owl later."

"Owlet," said Toni.

EVERY day, Suzanne wrote Petra's luncheon menu on the chalkboard in the café, and today was no different. She scanned the index card Petra had given her, nodded to herself at the delicious selections, and then picked up a piece of bright yellow chalk and began printing.

There was chicken salad on cranberry-nut bread, chicken paprikash, squash and fennel soup with a cheese popover, a pita bread vegetarian pizza, and a wrap with Brie cheese and honey-glazed ham.

There was also a Ritz cracker and strawberry pie. So Suzanne used a piece of pink chalk to make a cartoon drawing of a wedge of pie and printed under it, *Strawberry pie, $2.95 a slice.*

Suzanne never bothered to list the rest of their goodies, because most of the customers knew there was always a fresh assortment of sticky buns, cookies, lemon bars, muffins, and scones to be had. In fact, most of their enticing baked goods were on display in the circular glass pastry case that sat atop the marble counter.

Because there was still a good thirty minutes before the luncheon crowd began easing their way in, Suzanne went over to the sputtering old cooler in the corner and checked the shelves. She had wheels of Mike Mullen's cheese, a good supply of homemade banana bread, jars of sweet pickles, canned jellies and jams, and cardboard trays filled with zucchini squash. These were items that local producers brought in to the Cackleberry Club to sell. It was really a win-win situation for everyone. Suzanne took a small percentage of retail sales and the growers and producers got the lion's share.

She knew one woman who paid for her daughter's ballet lessons just on what she earned from selling her potato rolls and pickles.

As Suzanne's eyes scanned the shelves, she was suddenly aware of a pouf of cool air as the front door opened, and then someone creeping up slowly behind her. She wheeled around to find Kit Kaslik regarding her with a shy smile on her face.

"Kit!" she said, startled by what was obviously a huge change in mood.

"Suzanne." Kit seemed as happy as the proverbial Cheshire cat. "How can I thank you?"

"I don't know," said Suzanne. "Maybe you should tell me what I did."

"You must have really worked your magic on Sheriff Doogie."

"Not really. Why? What's going on?"

Kit's grin grew even broader. "Ricky's being arraigned this afternoon and our attorney is positive that he's going to make bail and then be remanded into the custody of his mother."

"That's great news," said Suzanne. "You must have hired a really good attorney."

"Ricky's mom hired a lady lawyer from over in Jessup. Susan Atkins," said Kit.

"I've heard of her," said Suzanne. "And she is good. I know she even did some pro bono work for that women's shelter, Harmony House." She hesitated. "So what exactly are you saying? That Ricky's no longer a suspect?"

"Oh, he's still a suspect," said Kit. "But his fingerprints

were definitely not on those blasting caps, and Sheriff Doogie is now looking at several other suspects." She seemed almost breathless with the news. "Isn't that great?"

"I knew this would eventually get straightened out."

Kit was silent for a few moments, and then she said, "Would it be okay if I hung out here for a while? Or better yet, if I helped out?"

"We'd love to have you," said Suzanne. "But . . . you sure you're up to it?" She was also wondering how Petra would feel about Kit being here.

"My outlook is lots better now. Really hopeful, you know?"

"I can just imagine," said Suzanne. "Well, come on, let's go in the kitchen and find you an apron. Tell Petra that you're going to be on board for the rest of the day."

Surprise, surprise, Petra was delighted to see Kit. "We could use some help today," she said. "It was busy for breakfast and I can just imagine what lunch will be like."

"Probably insane," put in Toni. "But hey! It's great to have you back, Kit. So Ricky's out on bail?"

"He will be this afternoon," said Kit. "They can only hold a person for forty-eight hours. Then they either have to charge him or not." She seemed pleased with her newfound grasp of the law.

"So they never did formally charge him?" said Suzanne.

"No, and I don't think they will," said Kit. She grabbed a long black Parisian waiter's apron and draped it around her neck. "Since there isn't a shred of evidence."

Not yet, there isn't, thought Suzanne. But knowing Doogie, he was still out there sifting and digging.

WHILE Toni, Petra, and Kit fussed about the kitchen, Suzanne put in a quick call to the nearest DNR office. The fellow she talked to, a man by the name of Irv Humphries, was moderately helpful.

"A baby owl, huh?" said Humphries. "How old do you think it is?"

"I don't know," said Suzanne. "Maybe a couple of weeks?"

"Well, you could drive it to the nearest Wildlife Rehabilitation Center and let them take care of it."

"Where would that be?"

"You're calling from Kindred?"

"That's right."

"The nearest center's about two hundred miles from you," Humphries told her.

"Mnn, is there something else I can do?" *Aside from sending the owl in a cab? Or FedExing it?*

"You could feed the owlet and keep it warm," said Humphries. "Kind of rehabilitate it yourself. Then try to reunite it with its mother."

"So I would feed it what?"

"Probably a ground-up mouse."

"No. I can't do that."

"Well then, just try some boiled hamburger and rice."

"That'll work?" said Suzanne. "Just hamburger and rice?"

"Suzanne," called Petra. "Stop exchanging recipes and get over here and help us!"

CHAPTER 11

RIGHT when Suzanne was serving a ham and Brie wrap to Burt Gundelson, right in the middle of a busy lunch service, Sheriff Doogie came tromping in accompanied by two men she'd never seen before. But she could venture a guess. They were probably his arson experts.

Suzanne hustled over to greet Doogie and escorted him and his guests to the table by the window. After a fair amount of chair squeaking, feet shuffling, and glancing about, Doogie finally said, "Suzanne, these two guys were brought in because of the fire."

"Arson experts," she said.

"That's right," Doogie said. "This is Norm Allman and this other guy here is Bob Deek."

"Nice to meet you, gentlemen," said Suzanne. "Welcome to the Cackleberry Club."

Doogie stabbed a thumb in Suzanne's direction. "That's Suzanne. She owns this place and was one of the first ones to sound the alarm on the fire."

"It's nice to meet you," said Deek. He had close-cropped silver hair and an almost military bearing. He was in his mid-thirties and good-looking, too.

"How's the food here?" Allman asked, cutting directly to the chase. He was older and a little paunchy with round, wire-rimmed glasses that made him look like an accountant.

"You came on the right day," said Suzanne, cranking up the dial on her charm. "We just happen to have a terrific menu." She figured she could catch more flies with honey than vinegar, right?

"Suzanne's right about that," echoed Doogie. "They've got the best food in town." He patted his ample stomach. "I should know, I'm living proof."

Suzanne went through the menu with them, wrote down their orders, and then hustled into the kitchen.

"Doogie's brought a couple arson guys to lunch," she told Petra. "Make sure everything is extra good, because I intend to pump them like an old rubber tire and try to get as much information as possible."

"Our food's always extra good," said Petra.

"Then make it extra extra good."

"THE younger one's kinda cute," Toni said, sneaking a peek through the pass-through at Sheriff Doogie's luncheon companions.

"Not bad," Kit agreed.

"You two gals are twittering around like you're passing notes in study hall," Petra grumped. "One of you is married and the other is . . . well . . . almost . . ."

"Almost only counts in horseshoes and hand grenades," said Toni. "Besides, there's nothing wrong with looking. It's not against the law or anything."

"Your orders are up, Suzanne," Petra said. She placed all

the food on a large silver tray, then carefully sprinkled candied pumpkin seeds atop a steaming bowl of squash and fennel soup.

Suzanne grabbed the tray and hurried back out into the café. Deek, the object of Toni's and Kit's interest, had chosen the ham and Brie wrap. Allman showed a little more restraint with his bowl of soup. And Doogie had chosen the wrap with brie cheese and ham.

Suzanne placed the men's orders in front of them and stepped back. "Is there anything else I can get you?"

"No," said Deek. "But thank you. This food looks amazing."

"Wait until you taste it," said Suzanne. "Our chef, Petra, is quite talented."

"It sure is a pleasure to find good food like this in a small town," said Allman. "I was expecting some kind of greasy spoon diner, but this is a nice surprise."

Suzanne continued to beam at them. "I'm sure you men are famished for a good meal after . . . what's it been now? A couple days of work?"

"It hasn't been easy," agreed Doogie. "We've been at it almost nonstop."

Suzanne continued to hover at their table even as the men dug into their lunches. "And I'm guessing you've been combing through the wreckage, looking for evidence of blasting caps?"

"That's part of what we've been doing, yes," said Deek. "Plus, we finally received an aerial photograph of the building."

"That's key," said Allman.

"And now we're going to search police records for any accounts of vandalism in the area, as well as interview local gas station owners," said Deek.

"There ain't much in the records," Doogie said with his mouth full.

"Still," said Deek, "when we have a potential homicide we follow a carefully set protocol, even reviewing coroner's reports and the like. Once we've amassed our evidence, we try to work out a few possible theories on what happened."

"Deek does most of the chemical analysis—the geeky stuff—while I dig through bank records, insurance information, and tax stuff," Allman told her.

"Fascinating," said Suzanne, because it was. She leaned toward Deek and said, "So you're the one who'll determine if there's a connection between the fire and the blasting caps found in Ricky Wilcox's car?"

"That's right," Deek mumbled around a mouthful of ham and Brie.

"This all sounds very tricky," said Suzanne. "Have you been able to figure out where this particular fire started?"

"Pretty much," said Deek. "The area with the greatest burn is generally the incendiary point. So we start there and look for burn holes in walls or floors to determine which way the fire moved. It sounds strange, but fire's almost like a living, breathing thing."

Suzanne continued her line of questioning. "And it's possible to determine if an accelerant was used?"

"Definitely," said Deek. "Spontaneous combustion is pretty rare unless you're the drummer for Spinal Tap."

As Suzanne laughed politely, Doogie gave her a hard stare. He was getting a little annoyed with all her questions.

But Deek was warmed up and clearly a talker. "As far as accelerants go," he said, "it's often as simple as looking at patterns on a wall or floor. Your V-shaped pattern means a pool of liquid, and what we call a trailer pattern means the liquid was spread from one location to another. In this case, it's certainly plausible that our suspect could have used blasting caps to ignite some type of accelerant like acetone, lacquer, or gasoline."

"Do you think they were blasting caps from Salazar Mining?" Suzanne asked. "Or from some highway road crew?"

"Fire seldom destroys all evidence of arson," said Deek. "So if we find evidence of blasting caps, we can use chemical signatures and serial numbers to . . ." Deek stopped abruptly and gazed across the room.

Suzanne's head swiveled to see what Deek was staring at. Then she chuckled. It was Toni. She had popped the top pearl button on her embroidered pink skintight cowboy shirt and was slinking toward them like a panther on the prowl, carrying a pot of fresh coffee.

"Hellllllooo," Toni purred.

"This is Toni," said Suzanne. "She's one of the partners here. Although sometimes we just keep her around 'cause she looks so darned cute."

Both Deek and Allman hastily stood up to greet Toni and shake her hand. Only Doogie remained seated, his attention focused on his lunch.

"Please, gentlemen, sit," said Toni.

"This place just gets better and better," Deek said with a wide grin.

"Aren't you the sweet one," said Toni. She stretched forward, brushing up against his shoulder as she refilled his coffee cup.

"Thank you," said Deek. He could barely take his eyes off her now.

"I could use a splash, too," said Doogie, but Toni was focused solely on Deek.

Suzanne noted that the electricity generated between Toni and the arson investigator was fairly crackling. If Petra could plug into it, she could power her electric mixer all day long.

"Suzanne," said Toni, never taking her eyes off Deek, "I think Petra needs you in the kitchen."

"Really?" said Suzanne.

Toni pursed her lips. "Absolutely. Besides, I've got this under control, hon. I really do."

"That's what I'm afraid of," Suzanne mumbled as she walked away.

LUNCH might have been over, but Toni still remained seated at the table with Doogie, Deek, and Allman. Her chin rested in her palm as her eyes remained glued on the very chatty investigator. Suzanne surmised by Toni's nods, smiles, and giggles that she was drawing additional information out of them. Would it do any good? Who knew? In any case, it surely couldn't hurt.

"Is Toni still hosting her salon out there?" Petra asked.

Kit gave a cursory glance through the pass-through. "She sure is. In fact, she's got them all sort of . . . mesmerized."

"That girl," said Petra. "She does seem imbued with a special something."

"More like well-endowed," said Suzanne.

Then they heard the front door creak open and Petra said, "Did somebody else just come in? Do we have a late customer for lunch or an early customer for afternoon tea?"

"It's that awful reporter," said Kit, still looking out into the café. She sounded nervous.

"Gene Gandle?" said Petra. "Now what does *he* want?"

"Probably to pester me," said Suzanne as she hustled out to the café.

Gene Gandle strode across the café, hurled an angry glance at Doogie and company, then seated himself at the counter just as Suzanne slid in behind it.

"Gene," she said, "I'm afraid you're a little late for lunch. We stopped serving fifteen minutes ago."

Gandle flipped open his spiral-bound notebook and said, "No problem, Suzanne. I'm just here to ask a couple quick questions."

"Let me guess," said Suzanne. "You're still working on your fire story."

His head bobbed on his stalklike neck. "Of course."

Suzanne aimed a finger at the table where Doogie, Deek, and Allman still lingered with Toni. "Those are the people you should be talking to."

"I *tried* to interview them this morning," said Gandle, looking peeved. "But they wouldn't say a word to me. Shagged me away like some kind of mongrel dog. Can you believe it?"

"You reporters do have it tough."

"It's an insult," said Gandle. "Here we are . . . trying to educate and enlighten the public. But those guys . . ." His eyes fixed on Doogie and the arson investigators again. "They won't give me a single snippet of information."

Suzanne almost laughed out loud. Here they'd already given her a torrent of information. And Toni had probably pulled out a whole lot more.

"Life sucks," said Gandle. "And then you die."

"Hold on, Gene," said Suzanne. "It's not *that* bad." She watched as Doogie stood up from the table, stretched languidly, and threw down three $10 bills. The other two men stood up and said a few more friendly words to Toni. Then they all headed out the door, probably back to the scene of the crime.

Toni came back behind the counter and said, "Hi, Gene," in a syrupy voice. Then she slipped two of the tens into the cash drawer and popped the third ten into their glass tip jar. "Got some good information. Not bad for twenty minutes' work, huh?"

"Jeez," said Gandle. "Did you ever think of becoming a reporter?"

"Naw," said Toni. "I'd rather make the news."

* * *

BUT the excitement didn't end there. Because just as Gandle picked up pen and paper, another person strolled into the Cackleberry Club.

Young, good-looking, with a smile that hinted at arrogance, the man strolled over to the counter, where Suzanne and Gandle were talking. Or, in Suzanne's case, not talking.

When Gandle caught sight of their new visitor, he screamed, "You! Again!" He sounded, Suzanne thought, like a scalded cat.

The young man basically ignored Gandle's outburst and said to Suzanne. "Ms. Dietz? I'm Bobby Boerger from the *Jessup Independent.* I was wondering if I could ask you a couple of questions?"

"Another reporter?" said Suzanne. That was all she needed. Double trouble.

But Gandle wasn't nearly finished with his burst of outrage and indignation. In fact, he was just getting wound up. "What are *you* doing here?" he demanded of Boerger. "This is *my* turf. How do you have the gall to come over to Kindred and start asking questions?"

"Turf?" Boerger snorted. "Come on, Gene, what are we—the Sharks and the Jets? You want to have a gang war over this?"

Gandle was so worked up he was starting to sweat through his pale blue golf shirt. "There is something known as professional, journalistic courtesy," he sputtered. Then he hopped off his stool, aimed his index finger at Boerger, and jabbed it hard into the man's solar plexus.

"Hey," Boerger protested, while Gandle looked sublimely pleased with himself.

"That's it!" said Suzanne as she flew around the counter. "I've had enough from you two." Like an angry schoolmarm herding two recalcitrant boys to detention, she grabbed Gandle firmly by the arm and dragged him into the Book Nook. Turning back to Boerger, she said, "You. You come along, too."

Safely in the Book Nook now, Suzanne let her displeasure show. "The two of you come strolling into my nice respectable café, throw down the gauntlet, and want to have it out with pistols at high noon? This isn't Dodge City, and I'm sure not Miss Kitty!"

"But he . . ." Gandle began.

"Enough," said Suzanne. "This is over. But if you still want to shuffle out into the parking lot and club each other like barbarians, I'm sure I can get Sheriff Doogie to come back and referee. And then he'll provide each of you with overnight accommodations while you cool off." She glowered at each man. "So . . . are we done here?"

Each man grumped a barely audible "Yes."

Then Gandle hissed something that Suzanne couldn't quite decipher and huffed his way back into the café and out the front door.

Suzanne looked at Boerger. "Do you have something nasty to say, too?"

"May I have a cup of coffee, please?"

Suzanne stared at him for a few seconds. "Yes, you can. Provided you remain on your best behavior."

Boerger put up his right hand like a Boy Scout taking an oath, and a crooked grin creased his face. "I promise."

BOERGER perched at the lunch counter while a few customers began filing in for tea and scones, and a few men in overalls arrived for coffee and pie. It was what they always referred to as their change of shift. Which also meant the pace was a lot more relaxed.

True to his word, Boerger remained on his best behavior.

Suzanne poured him a cup of coffee, gave him a bowl of peach cobbler, and then said, "Now what was it you wanted to ask me?"

"Just a few things about the fire that took place last Friday."

"That's what I figured."

"But first, may I say . . . this peach cobbler is outstanding. Did you by any chance bake it yourself?"

"No," said Suzanne. "Petra did. But I'll be sure to pass along your compliments." She folded her arms across her chest, waiting for the inevitable onslaught of questions.

"So," said Boerger, "I understand the sheriff found a number of blasting caps in the trunk of Ricky Wilcox's car? And then he rushed in and actually stopped the poor guy's wedding? I guess you don't see that sort of thing every day, huh?"

"Thank goodness, no."

"So what's your take on all of this? Do you believe Wilcox is a legitimate suspect?"

"What does my opinion matter?" Suzanne asked.

Boerger favored her with a winning smile. "You helped sound the alarm, you're one of the people who's in the know and fairly close to Sheriff Doogie . . ."

"You've been asking around about me," said Suzanne. She wasn't sure if she should be flattered or unnerved.

Boerger shrugged. "I try to be a good reporter and cover all the bases."

"So you're asking me if I think Ricky Wilcox was responsible for the fire?" said Suzanne.

"Yes."

"No," said Suzanne.

"No what? No, you won't answer my question or no, you don't think he had anything to do with it?"

"I think," said Suzanne, "and this is complete conjecture on my part . . . that Ricky Wilcox might have been set up." Suzanne noticed that, where Gandle was fond of spiral notebooks, Boerger used an iPad. She hadn't seen him type on it yet, so she was pretty sure he was recording their conversation.

"Sounds like you're pretty sure of yourself," said Boerger.

"I'm friendly with Ricky's fiancée and, knowing her as I do, trust her judgment. If she had any hesitation about Ricky's character she never would have agreed to marry him." *Other than the fact that she was pregnant*, Suzanne thought to herself.

"Not the most quantitative way to measure guilt," said Boerger, "but I'll take it." He cocked his head and said, "You know, I've heard a few things about you."

"Such as?"

"Oh, that you're blessed with excellent people smarts and a kind of sixth sense. And that you've worked with Sheriff Doogie several times before in solving local crimes."

He gave her a shy, almost boyish smile and Suzanne suddenly realized that this young, good-looking reporter was flirting with her.

"How old are you?" Suzanne asked.

Boerger's eyes crinkled. "Twenty-seven. Why? How old are you?"

Suzanne put her elbows on the counter and leaned forward. "Old enough to know better. Old enough to know when I'm being played."

BY four o'clock, Toni and Kit were clearing the last of the tables while Suzanne sat at a table by the window, scratching ideas into her notebook. Sunlight streamed through the filmy curtains, imparting a late-afternoon glow. Even their Greek chorus of ceramic chickens, perched high up on the wooden shelves, looked happy and content.

When the door from the kitchen creaked open, they all turned to look.

"I am dog tired," Petra declared. "And feeling as creaky as this old door."

"Nothing a shot of WD-40 won't fix," said Toni. "For the door, I mean."

"You deserve to be tired," said Suzanne. "It was a hectic day."

Still wearing her signature Crocs, Petra squished her way across the café and dropped into the chair next to Suzanne. "You're working on the dinner theater menu?"

Suzanne nodded. "Sort of. Mostly just going over the menu card you gave me and seeing what else we can add in."

"I still like the idea of mini meat pies for appetizers," said Petra.

"Agreed," said Suzanne.

"And I'd love to take advantage of some of the lovely brussels sprouts I've been seeing at farm stands around town," said Petra. "So I'm definitely thinking a bubble and squeak."

"What's that?" said Toni, who was pushing a broom nearby.

"A bubble and squeak is a kind of traditional English vegetable casserole," Petra explained. "With carrots, broccoli, potatoes, brussels sprouts . . ."

"Weird name," said Toni.

"And then roast beef with Yorkshire pudding," said Suzanne. "With some good old-fashioned soda bread."

"And we can't forget the scorched eggs," said Petra.

"Scorched?" Toni made a face. "You mean burned? Yuck."

"Oh, you'll like them," said Petra. "Scorched eggs is just the old Scottish term for eggs that were originally cooked on the hearth. They're basically hard-boiled eggs wrapped in meat and a tasty batter. Now they mostly go by the name Scotch eggs."

"That does sound a lot better," agreed Toni.

"And for dessert?" said Suzanne.

"What else but a trifle?" said Petra. "I'll do a heavy sponge cake diced and mixed with fresh fruit, walnuts, and pudding."

"A pudding cake," said Toni, liking the idea.

"And some British-inspired tea," said Suzanne. "Black tea, like a Darjeeling or an oolong."

Toni drifted closer to their table. "Have you thought about how we should arrange the café?" she asked. "So everyone gets a clear view of the stage?"

"Since the Book Nook and Knitting Nest are going to serve as backstage changing rooms," said Suzanne, "we should hang curtains across those doorways. And then another larger curtain in front to serve as the main stage curtain."

"Who's going to engineer all that?" asked Toni. "Not Junior, he'll just screw it up."

"I can get Ricky to do it," said Kit.

Three pairs of eyes were suddenly focused on her.

"Really?" said Suzanne.

"Sure," said Kit. "He's very handy when it comes to that kind of thing."

"Well . . . okay," said Petra. She flapped a hand. "The stage will be at the far end of the café, with the fortune-telling table . . ."

"Good thing *Blithe Spirit* has a fairly small set," put in Toni.

"That's the exact reason we steered the Kindred Community Players toward that play," said Suzanne.

"So," Petra continued, "we'll borrow that big blue velvet curtain from the church basement and Ricky will hang it across the end of the café."

"Perfect," said Toni.

"Wait," said Suzanne. "We forgot one thing." She gave Petra a sly conspiratorial wink.

"What?" said Toni, not knowing she was being set up.

"You're right," said Petra, trying hard not to crack up. "We forgot all about the kidney pie."

"What?" Toni's voice rose in a tremulous squawk. "That's not dessert, that's a medical experiment!"

CHAPTER 12

It had been a hectic day so far. But Suzanne was energized after her discussion with Doogie and the arson investigators, and quickly formulated a plan to visit Bill and Jenny Probst at the Kindred Bakery. With their bakery directly across the street from the crime scene, they had a unique perspective. Plus they'd been the very first ones to report the fire. Suzanne decided she'd chat them up and see what they knew.

But first things first. Petra was hosting a late-afternoon knitting group today. Suzanne knew that Petra was having a difficult time dealing with Hannah Venable's death and was kind of dreading Hannah's candlelight memorial tonight. That, coupled with the fact that she'd been slaving over a hot stove all day, meant she surely deserved a couple of hours of quiet relaxation with her knitting friends. So Suzanne had volunteered to straighten up the Knitting Nest.

It wasn't tricky, just a simple matter of arranging a semi-circle of chairs, making sure their colorful yarns were enticingly displayed in baskets, and readying the knitting needles and felting pads. Suzanne enjoyed her work and hummed as she went along. It was peaceful and quiet in here and the little craft area gave off a reassuring vibe.

Ten minutes later, Suzanne waved good-bye and was out the door and on her way to the Kindred Bakery. That was the nice thing about living in a small town—everything was within a quick drive or a pleasant walk. With the late afternoon still bright and sunny, Suzanne cranked her windows down and reveled in the warmth. It was the exact kind of day that answered everyone's question when they inevitably cried, "Why do we live here?" when they were hip-deep in snow and shivering from twenty-below windchill in mid-January.

The ring-ding of a bell announced Suzanne's entry into the bakery, where she was suddenly surrounded by the sweet aromas of sugar, cinnamon, ginger, and nutmeg.

Bill Probst poked his head up from behind the donut counter and said, "Hey, Suzanne. What can I get you? We've got some chive and onion rolls if you're interested."

"I'll take a dozen," said Suzanne.

"I'll give you two dozen," said Bill. "Take a bag to Petra, she might want to order some for the café."

While Bill packaged up the rolls, Suzanne said, "I was wondering if I could ask you and Jenny a couple of questions about the fire."

"Sure," said Bill. "I don't know what we can . . . Jenny! Can you come out here for a minute?"

Jenny Probst came dashing out from the back, a white baker's apron and cap covering her paisley shirt and head of reddish blond curls.

"Suzanne," Jenny said. She darted toward one of the cases, grabbed a roll, and placed it on a paper plate. "You've got to sample one of our maple-glazed pumpkin swirls." She rolled her eyes. "To die for."

"Suzanne wants to ask us about the fire," Bill said.

Suzanne took a bite of roll. "Good," she said. Then, "I was just wondering if you guys noticed anything unusual last Friday."

Jenny and Bill exchanged glances. Then Bill said, "Not really."

"We didn't see much," said Jenny.

"I smelled smoke," said Bill. "At first I thought it was from *our* ovens, but when I looked out the front window I saw there was a boil of smoke coming from the County Services Bureau."

"Bill yelled at me to call 911," said Jenny. "So I did."

"That's when I looked out and saw you running out of Root 66," said Bill.

"And I heard the big explosion while I was on the phone with the dispatcher," said Jenny.

Bill shook his head at Suzanne. "Never seen anything like that . . . hope to never see anything like it again. Praise the Lord *you* were okay."

"I jumped out of the way pretty fast," said Suzanne. "But . . . you didn't see anything out of the ordinary? People hanging around the building earlier? Maybe Ricky Wilcox or somebody else?"

"Nope," said Bill. "The Wilcox kid has been in here, sure, but I never saw him hanging around that particular building."

"What about Jack Venable?" said Suzanne.

Bill's eyes slid over to meet Jenny's.

"What?" said Suzanne.

"Tell her," said Jenny.

"I don't want to be a tattletale," said Bill. "But I have seen Jack Venable driving by here quite a few times in the last couple of weeks."

"We told Sheriff Doogie the same thing," Jenny volunteered.

"I think Jack was checking to see if Hannah's car was parked outside," said Bill. "For what reason, I don't know."

"Tell her about the argument," said Jenny, her eyes widening.

"Oh, Jack and Hannah had a kind of shouting match one morning," said Bill. "About a week ago. I don't know what it was about, but it was over pretty quick."

"Interesting," said Suzanne.

"It is," said Jenny. "But from what we've been hearing, from the rumors around town, there are quite a few suspects."

"That's my understanding, too," said Suzanne.

"You know who you could talk to," said Bill, "is Joe Dodd next door. He's kind of gossipy and he's got cameras. Because of the type of merchandise he deals in."

"Thanks," said Suzanne. "I'll do that." She dug in her purse for her wallet, but Bill held up a hand.

"Compliments of the house," he told her.

DODD'S Pawn Shop couldn't have looked more out of place in quaint downtown Kindred. Next door to the blue-shingled bakery, the pawn shop, with its cinder-block construction and barred windows, seemed like it would be more at home in a run-down industrial zone.

There was no tinkling bell on the dented steel door to announce Suzanne's arrival, just an annoying, computerized beep. She followed the line of metal shelves that held stacks of used electronics, sporting goods, CDs, musical instruments, and snow tires, thinking this was a business that thrived on human misfortune. Desperation caused good people to come here and sell their possessions.

Rounding a bright yellow plastic kayak, Suzanne headed for a glass counter where the owner, Joe Dodd, was standing. He was polishing a pair of silver candlesticks and humming a tuneless song.

"Excuse me?" said Suzanne.

Dodd looked up. "Help you?" he said. He was rail thin with a narrow face and dark pools of eyes. A faint scar showed at the corner of his mouth. Suzanne had heard something about a hunting knife accident. Then again, you never know.

"Looking for something special?" Dodd asked. He would have been downright creepy if his voice hadn't sounded so friendly.

"I hope so," said Suzanne. "I'm Suzanne Dietz and I . . ."

"The Cackleberry Club," said Dodd, pointing a smudged finger at her. "You serve those nice maraschino cherry scones."

"Only on Thursday," said Suzanne.

"Whatever," said Dodd. "They're good. How can I help you?"

"I was wondering if I could ask you about last Friday's fire."

"What do you want to know?" asked Dodd.

"Anything you've got."

"We don't exactly have picture windows facing the street," said Dodd. "So I wasn't really aware of the whole mess until the building blew up and the fire trucks came screaming in."

"You catch anything on your cameras?"

"Sheriff Doogie already asked me about that. Took a look at the tape, too." Dodd shook his head. "Nothing caught his attention."

"Did you see anybody hanging out around the County Services Building? Jack Venable, Ricky Wilcox, a guy named Marty Wolfson, or . . ."

Dodd cocked a finger at her. "That kid that was arrested. Wilcox."

"He was hanging around?"

"Not hanging around. He came in here a week ago and bought two gold wedding bands."

"What?" said Suzanne. She wasn't sure if she was more

surprised at Ricky coming in here or Dodd selling wedding bands. Finally she said, "You actually sell wedding bands?"

Dodd pretended to be offended. "Rings happen to be my stock-in-trade. I weigh the gold and charge according to the current market rate, so my prices are more than fair. Yup, we're always on the lookout for used rings to polish up and resell. You have no idea how many people come in and want to sell their wedding rings. Divorced guys, angry women, you name it." He chuckled. "I've seen it all. Had a ring thrown at me, too."

Suzanne thought for a minute. "Have you bought any rings recently?"

"Sure," Dodd replied with a crocodile smile that made Suzanne's skin crawl.

"From who?"

"I couldn't tell you offhand. All sorts of people come through these doors. The economy being what it is, business is booming."

"Do you think you could check?" Suzanne knew she might be grasping at straws, but she'd learned that sometimes the smallest detail could yield a bit of information.

"I suppose," said Dodd. "The state attorney general requires us to keep records on that sort of transaction— they're always worried about stolen goods."

"I can't imagine why," said Suzanne.

Dodd disappeared into a back room for a few minutes, and Suzanne had the uncomfortable feeling she was being watched on closed-circuit TV. When he returned he was clutching a black ledger and had a pair of reading glasses perched on the tip of his nose. He laid the book on the counter and said, "Let's take a look-see." He flipped through a few pages and said, "How far back do you want to go?"

"Maybe . . . three weeks?" said Suzanne.

"Three weeks," muttered Dodd, flipping more pages.

While Dodd was sorting through his ledger, the front door beeped and a customer shuffled into the store. Suzanne didn't turn around to look, but instead stayed focused on Dodd.

Finally, when he'd perused his notations, Dodd straightened up and said, "Well, isn't this interesting."

"What?" said Suzanne.

His dark eyes bored into her. "Jack Venable sold me a gold wedding band some twelve days ago."

"Really?"

"Sounds kind of hinky, doesn't it?" said Dodd. "Guess I better tell the sheriff." He let loose another chuckle that turned into a smoker's hack.

Suzanne thought this sale not only *sounded* hinky, but was downright incriminating. Had Hannah's husband actually stolen her wedding ring and sold it? If the lowdown, dirty coward had done something like that, would he also have had the guts to kill her?

"Is the ring still here?" Suzanne asked. "Do you have it?"

"Sure," said Dodd. "Why? You want to buy it?"

"No thanks. But call the sheriff, will you? Tell him about this?"

"Sure," said Dodd. "You got it. Anything to help."

Suzanne was practically shaking with anger as she made her way out of the shop. Now that there was actual documented evidence that Jack Venable had sold Hannah's ring, Suzanne decided she was going to make it her mission in life to find out why. And put him behind bars if he deserved it!

As she brushed past a stack of truck tires, Suzanne glanced sideways at the customer who'd just come in. And her heart caught in her throat.

Marty Wolfson was standing silently in front of a locked glass cabinet that was packed with a huge assortment of handguns. His eyes seemed to scuttle across the snub-nosed pistols and guns that carried scary names like Glock and

SIG Sauer. He looked just as angry as he had when he'd confronted Doogie at the Cackleberry Club last Saturday morning!

Dear Lord, this can't be good, Suzanne told herself. And on the heels of that, *I have to tell Doogie about this, too!*

SUZANNE was grateful for the fresh air and sunshine as she hurried out to her car. Hopefully, a protracted background check would delay, if not prevent, Wolfson from getting his hands on a gun. The man seemed like a ticking time bomb and surely had no business donning a holstered weapon.

Grabbing her phone, Suzanne quickly dialed Doogie's office number. He answered on the second ring.

"Doogie," Suzanne said, a little breathless.

"This ain't a good time," Doogie told her. "I'm up to my ears in alligators."

"I have to talk to you—now. It's really important."

"Life-and-death important?"

"Well . . . not quite *that* hot. But I just picked up some new information that could be critical to your arson case."

She heard him sigh and then mutter something that sounded like, "Driscoll, did you ever find that blah-blah-blah?" Then he was back on the line. "Where?"

"Where what?"

"Where do you want to meet?"

"Well, I'm downtown right now. Parked outside the bakery."

"Five minutes," said Doogie. "I'll be there in five minutes."

Doogie was there in eight minutes, which was about as on time as he ever got. And Suzanne was jumping out of her skin to talk to him. Of course, Doogie took his own sweet time, parking his car, hoisting himself out of his cruiser, walking slowly over to her car as if he was doing a perimeter check.

She rolled down the window so he could lean in.

"What was so danged important that you had to pull me away from my work?" Doogie asked.

She flipped a finger toward Dodd's Pawn Shop. "I was just in there, talking to Joe Dodd. Did you know that he buys and sells wedding rings?"

"Yup," said Doogie. "Fact is, I was in there checking his surveillance tapes. And a couple months ago, when Mrs. Davenport's sapphire ring went missing, we had to go through his inventory and sales records."

"Take a wild guess who was in his store recently and sold a wedding ring."

"Just tell me straight out," said Doogie. "I got no time for games."

"Jack Venable sold Hannah's wedding ring," said Suzanne.

That clearly got a rise out of Doogie. He gave a low whistle. "Seriously? He told you that?"

"It was in his records," said Suzanne. She waited a couple of beats and then said, "Don't you wonder why? Don't you think this shows Jack must have been up to no good?" Suzanne could see the wheels turning in Doogie's head. The man was no fool. In fact, he was a chess player who was generally three moves ahead of his opponent. Of course he recognized the implication.

Doogie played it cool, though. He stroked his chin and said, "Gotta think about this."

"There's something else," said Suzanne. "When I was leaving Dodd's I saw Marty Wolfson shopping for guns."

"Long guns or handguns?"

"Handguns," said Suzanne.

"That's not good."

"No kidding," said Suzanne. "And he still had that hostility thing going, too."

"I guess that means I should . . ."

Click click . . . ha-hoooo!

Doogie reacted as if he'd been punched in the gut. He hopped backward, his hand groping for his revolver as he nearly tripped over his own size-twelve cop shoes. Then he recovered, shook it off, and returned to Suzanne's car. He peered carefully at the box on the backseat. "What the heck you got in there anyway? A wild bobcat?"

"It's a baby owl," said Suzanne. "Technically an owlet."

Doogie seemed relieved that he wasn't going to be attacked. "Something you found?"

"That's right."

"Fell out of its nest, huh?"

"I suppose," said Suzanne. She was disappointed that Doogie hadn't reacted more strongly to her news about Marty Wolfson and his predilection for guns.

"Or maybe the owl was pushed out," said Doogie. "You know, natural selection and all that. Survival of the fittest."

"Hah," said Suzanne. "You're a fine one to talk."

SUZANNE sat in her car, watching as Marty Wolfson exited Dodd's Pawn Shop. Once he'd climbed into his jacked-up Ford F-150 and driven away, she dialed the number at the Cackleberry Club.

"Hello?" said Petra.

"You okay?" Suzanne asked.

"Of course I'm okay. Why wouldn't I be?" Petra was sounding a lot more upbeat, like she was back to her old spunky self.

"I need to tell you something," said Suzanne.

"Well, make it snappy," said Petra. "I've got a pan of blond brownies in the oven and I don't want them to turn into brunettes."

"You're not going to like this, but I stopped at Dodd's Pawn Shop . . ."

"You're right, I don't like it. Any more than if you'd

stopped at a tattoo parlor, strip club, dirty movie, or . . . well, I don't know." She chuckled. "I think I just ran out of sins."

"Petra," said Suzanne. "That funny feeling you had about Hannah's wedding ring? You were right. Turns out Jack Venable sold it to the pawn shop."

There was a long-drawn-out silence and then Petra said, "What?" And then, "That just breaks my heart. If Jack would do something that nasty and underhanded, could he . . . um . . . ?"

"Could he have started the fire that killed Hannah?" said Suzanne. "I don't know."

"Have you talked to Doogie about this yet? About the ring?"

"I just got done talking to him."

"What did he say?" asked Petra.

"Doogie's still playing it close to the vest," said Suzanne. "Jack Venable may be his prime suspect now, but Ricky Wilcox is still on the hook, too. Oh, and I ran into Marty Wolfson. He was looking at guns."

Petra sighed deep and long. "Well, when do you think Doogie is gonna make up his mind about who the killer is? When is there going to be an arrest?"

"I have no idea," said Suzanne. "I think he needs more concrete evidence."

"I wish we could get *some* sort of resolution," said Petra.

"I know. But take it easy, okay? We can talk more at the memorial tonight."

"Okay," said Petra. "Bring a candle."

"I'll do better than that," said Suzanne. "I'll bring Sam."

CHAPTER 13

SOME stereotypes are true—men really do like steak. Sam, of course, was no exception, and Suzanne was more than happy to oblige his inner caveman. Tonight it would be with a nice lean filet mignon sauced with a mixture of Dijon mustard and Madeira wine. At Petra's suggestion, she'd elected to balance out the savory flavor of the meat with lemon and garlic green beans, rosemary cheddar biscuits, and chocolate cake.

As Suzanne chopped, whirled, and shuffled pans on the stove, the heavenly aroma of sautéing shallots permeated her kitchen. In the dining room, soft candlelight danced a medley of shadows on the walls as a Joshua Redman song played on iPod speakers set next to a recently uncorked bottle of Cabernet.

Suzanne decided that a quiet dinner with Sam was a fine way to end a long, difficult day. She didn't have any definitive answers about Hannah's killer yet, but she did feel like she'd helped nudge Doogie another step forward. At least she hoped so.

A shuffle outside the front door, punctuated by the ring of her doorbell, told her that Sam had arrived. The usual barking and mad scramble of dogs followed.

"Come in," Suzanne called out. "Door's open."

She turned off the heat and scraped her shallots into a bowl. Then, toenails clicking briskly against tile, throaty woofs, and Sam's friendly voice caused her to turn around and smile.

"Hey there," he said. He was standing in her doorway, wearing faded jeans, a gray Rolling Stones T-shirt, and white sneakers. One hand rested gently on Baxter's head, the other on top of Scruff's head. "I hope I'm not totally underdressed." He smiled. "I was late getting out of the clinic and didn't have time to stop by my apartment. This was all I had stashed in my locker."

"Not a problem," said Suzanne. "The *Vogue* shoot called and cancelled at the last minute, so I sent the wardrobe people home. Looks like it'll just be the two of us tonight. Oh, and the dogs." She wiped her hands on her apron, skipped across the floor, and gave him a quick kiss.

"I hope there's more where that came from," he said.

"Probably is," she said.

"I found this in my car, too," Sam said, holding out a bottle of tawny port.

"Just sitting there in your car? How convenient."

"You said you were making chocolate cake, so my wine guy said this would be the perfect complement."

"I'm suitably impressed," said Suzanne. "You have a wine guy? Your own personal sommelier?"

"Well, maybe not a *real* guy, per se." Sam grinned. "It's actually an app on my phone called *My Wine Guy.*"

"And this guy just happened to recommend tawny port? Knowing it's one of my all-time faves?"

"Guess so," said Sam as he followed her into the kitchen. Followed, of course, by the dogs. "Man, it smells good in here."

"It's amazing what food companies can stuff into a can these days."

"Hah," said Sam. "A confirmed foodie like you? I don't think you even own a can opener."

"C'mere," said Suzanne, crooking her finger. "I want to show you something."

He headed for her stove, like it was a homing beacon.

"No, over here."

Sam came closer and Suzanne grabbed his hand and pulled him over to the small box that was perched at the far end of the counter. Baxter and Scruff sat down quietly on the floor beneath the box, their eyes imploring Sam to look inside the box. Or at least show them what was in there. Since whatever it was *smelled* pretty dang interesting.

"What have you got there?" Sam tiptoed closer.

Suzanne pulled a cardboard flap aside. "Take a look."

Sam peered down into the box at the fuzzy little ball that stared wide-eyed back at him. "It's a real live dust bunny," he said. "I've always heard rumors . . ."

"It's a baby owl," said Suzanne. "Isn't it cute?"

"Uh . . . yeah," he said. "How'd you get this little guy? Is it a guy?"

"I have no idea. I found him on the ground behind the Cackleberry Club. I think he tumbled out of his nest."

"Poor thing," said Sam. "He looks hungry. Will he be dining with us this evening?"

"That's kind of a problem. I've been fixing him a puree of hamburger and rice, but it's not easy getting him to eat it. I was going to use one of Petra's old turkey basters, but it's too big."

Sam thought for a minute. "I might have an idea."

"What's that?"

But he was already out the door. "Gotta grab something from my car," he called back.

When Sam returned he was carrying two plastic-wrapped packages.

"Eyedroppers," he told her, opening one of the packages and showing her a row of small blue bottles. "Let's see if this works. Put some of your owl food in one, then add a little warm water and shake it up."

"Like an owl smoothie," she said.

Suzanne used a funnel to transfer some of her puree into one of the glass bottles. Then she added some water, shook it vigorously, and handed it to Sam. Reaching carefully into the box, he moved the eyedropper toward the little owl, but the owl cowered and crept quickly to the rear of its box.

"Poor little thing is scared," said Suzanne. "Let me try."

"Couldn't hurt," said Sam.

Suzanne took the dropper and reached into the box. "It's okay, little one," she cooed. The owl stared at her, its tiny chest heaving with panic. Suzanne didn't push it, but neither did she pull away. Finally, gradually, the little owl quieted down. She moved the dropper closer until its mouth opened. She pinched the bulb to release some food and the owl's mouth clamped around the eyedropper with an audible *click*. Slowly, Suzanne squeezed the dropper some more. Food leaked out of the owl's tiny beak, but it was eating.

"It's working," she whispered. "He's eating."

Sam placed his hand on her shoulder and said, "You're magic, Suzanne."

DINNER was fantastic. At least Sam said it was. He chatted about his day, listened while Suzanne told him all about her discoveries at Dodd's Pawn Shop, and then got even more attentive when she started floating theories past him.

"You're really into this, aren't you?" he said.

"Oh yeah, we're going to figure this out. Hannah's killer is not going to go unpunished."

"But there are so many suspects," said Sam. "It's really baffling."

"Ricky Wilcox is out of the picture," said Suzanne. "I can pretty much guarantee he didn't do it."

"What about that fireman? Dale something."

"Darrel Fuhrman? I still want to talk to Fire Chief Finley about him. I mean, you saw him at the bar Saturday night, he's one angry guy."

"Maybe he's just unhappy," said Sam. "Lot of that going around these days. Tough economic times can take their toll. We see more and more people coming into the clinic just to get antidepressants."

"Is Darrel Fuhrman on antidepressants?" Suzanne asked.

"You know I can't give out personal medical information like that."

"Sure, you can."

"He's not my patient, so I really don't know," said Sam, finally.

"And then there's the gun-loving husband of that rescued woman," said Suzanne. "Marty Wolfson."

"Don't know anything about him, either," said Sam.

"I think he's pretty much of a scuzzball. But the guy who's really caught my attention is Jack Venable. That business about selling Hannah's ring . . . it's just awful. Traitorous."

"So you think Venable set the fire in order to kill Hannah," said Sam.

"I'm leaning that way, yes."

Sam put his hands flat on the table and said, "Doogie and his inspectors are fairly certain it was arson?"

"That's right."

"But what if Hannah wasn't really the intended victim?"

"What do you mean?" said Suzanne.

"What if Bruce Winthrop was really the target?"

Startled, Suzanne opened her mouth, started to say something, and then hesitated. Finally, she said, "I never looked at it from *that* angle before."

"Think about it," said Sam.

"I will," said Suzanne. "Because you make . . . an interesting point."

As wonderful as their evening had been, as creepy as their dinner-table conversation had been, Suzanne still wanted to attend the candlelight vigil tonight for Hannah Venable.

Sam drove her, one hand curled possessively around her hand, to downtown Kindred, where they parked in front of Kuyper's Hardware and then hiked over to a small plot of land that the downtown council had spiffed up with grass and flower beds. It sat kitty-corner from the burned-out County Services Building.

There were about forty or fifty people gathered there already, talking in low voices and just beginning to light their candles.

"There's Petra," said Suzanne. "And Toni." She tugged on Sam's hand as they threaded their way through the subdued crowd.

Petra waved when she saw them. "Glad you could make it," she said. "You, too, Dr. Hazelet."

"Sam," he said. "Please, just Sam."

"I was supposed to help Bruce Winthrop kick things off," said Petra, "but you-know-who was late." She fixed Toni with an accusing look. "Honey, I specifically asked you to pick me up at seven-forty-five. If I'd known you were on Pacific time I'd have said five-forty-five."

"I wasn't *that* late," said Toni, tugging at her jacket. She was dressed to impress in a pair of tight jeans, a black T-shirt, and a bedazzled jean jacket. She looked, Suzanne decided, like she was on her way to a snazzy hoedown.

"We're all here now," said Suzanne, ever the peacemaker. "That's what counts."

"And there's Kit," said Toni. She lifted a hand. "Over here, Kit."

Kit Kaslik eased her way through the crowd, looking youthful and pretty as ever in jeans and a camel turtleneck. But she also seemed subdued.

"Hi," Kit said, ducking her head as she approached.

"Where's Ricky?" asked Toni. "Isn't he here?" She stood on tiptoes and looked around.

Kit's face suddenly looked tight and drawn and she edged closer to Suzanne as if for protection. "Ricky was afraid to come," she whispered. "He was afraid to show his face."

"You mean he thought the villagers might come after him with torches and pitchforks?" said Suzanne.

"Jeez, Suzanne," said Sam. "You certainly have a knack for vivid description. What are you doing, writing a screenplay or something?"

But Kit just nodded sadly. "Ricky is basically terrified. He feels like he's persona non grata all over town."

"But he's innocent," said Toni.

"Try telling that to Sheriff Doogie," said Kit. "Especially when he's still on the list."

WITH everyone's candle lit and flickering softly in the night, Petra and a few friends from her church choir kicked off the singing. They started with "Yesterday," by the Beatles, and then segued into "You've Got a Friend," by James Taylor. Halfway through the second song, Suzanne spotted Jack Venable in the crowd. He was thin and wiry, with a head that seemed to perpetually poke forward as if he were walking into a heavy wind. He had watery blue eyes, a fluff of reddish brown hair, and prominent cheekbones. His lips, drawn into a tight line, were what Toni always referred to as turtle lips. That is, a thin, almost nonexistent top lip.

Of course, he'd be here, Suzanne told herself. Not everyone in town knew he was a suspect. Not yet, anyway.

Suzanne continued to watch Jack Venable as a few people came up to him and hugged him or patted him on the back. The entire time, Venable's expression never changed and she wondered if Jack Venable was trying to bravely hold his emotions together or if he was hiding a terrible secret.

As one of Hannah's friends spoke briefly about how kind she was and how much she'd be missed, Suzanne noticed a young woman moving around on the fringe of the group. Dark haired with lovely, almost slanted eyes, she wore a low-cut pink sweater and tight white pants tucked into brown suede boots. She also made sure Jack Venable was never out of her sight.

Suzanne nudged Toni. "Do you know who that is?" she whispered as she nodded discreetly toward the girl.

Toni's eyes searched the crowd then fell upon the dark-haired girl. She seemed to study her for a few moments, and then whispered back. "Yeah, I think I've seen her before." Then Toni gave Kit a nudge and they had a whispered exchange.

"What?" said Suzanne.

"Marlys Shelton," said Toni. "That's her name."

Suzanne reached a hand behind Toni and tapped Kit on the shoulder. "Do you think she's the young woman Jack Venable is having an affair with?" she asked in a low voice.

Kit grimaced and whispered back, "I think . . . definitely."

Then Petra and her chorus broke into Eric Clapton's "Tears in Heaven," their third and final song. At the last bar, as their sweet tones faded and died on the night wind, there wasn't a dry eye in the house.

"Wonderful," Toni and Kit breathed together.

"Very moving," Sam agreed.

But Suzanne had spotted Bruce Winthrop shuttling through the crowd, and quickly hastened over to have a word with him.

"Bruce," she said, "this must be awfully hard on you."

Winthrop blinked back tears. "Suzanne, you have no idea. Hannah and I worked together for six years, so I feel . . ." He wiped at his eyes, clearly embarrassed by his emotions. "But this . . . this amazing gathering tonight . . . well, I'm stunned and thankful that so many people turned out." He gazed about at the crowd that lingered. "What a blessing," he whispered. Then he leaned forward, so no one else could hear, and said, "Have you come up with anything yet that I should know about? I know I probably came on a little strong to you before, asking for your help and all, but I trust you, Suzanne. And with so many suspects . . ." His voice suddenly choked with emotion. "I just wish this case could be solved and done with."

"Bruce," said Suzanne. "I want to ask you something but I don't want to upset you."

"What, Suzanne?"

"Is there any chance that *you* could have been the intended target?"

"Wha . . . what?" Winthrop looked shocked beyond belief. "Me?"

"The thought just occurred to me," said Suzanne. *Thanks to Sam.*

"It never occurred to me. Never."

"Sheriff Doogie and his investigators are fairly certain it was arson," said Suzanne. "So either some*thing* in the building was the target, or possibly you or Hannah."

"That's a very disorienting thought," said Winthrop.

"I know it is and I apologize for even bringing it up. The thing is, it's looking more and more like Ricky Wilcox is out of the picture, suspectwise."

"Really?" said Winthrop. "Because . . ." He stopped abruptly and shook his head, as if he felt discombobulated.

"Because what?" said Suzanne.

"Oh, it's probably nothing."

"Tell me anyway," Suzanne prompted.

"I was just thinking about a little run-in I had with Ricky a couple of weeks ago."

"Concerning what?"

Winthrop waved his hand. "It was a silly thing, really. A misunderstanding over a pesticide permit."

"A what?" said Suzanne. She'd never heard of such a thing.

Winthrop explained. It seems that Ricky had been spraying some land for his brother and had been required by city ordinance to obtain a permit. But he hadn't done so. When Winthrop found out about the spraying, he confronted Ricky and told him there'd probably be a fine. And that's when Ricky got in his face.

"The kid has a nasty temper," said Winthrop. "He threatened me with . . . oh, I don't remember what. Anyway, I figured that was the end of it." He looked suddenly thoughtful. "But maybe not."

"Did you tell Doogie about this?" Suzanne asked.

"No," said Winthrop, "because it really just occurred to me."

"You've got to tell him," Suzanne urged. She hated getting Ricky in trouble all over again, but this was important. It was evidence that shouldn't be withheld.

Doggone it, now Doogie's going to have even more heaped on his plate. Winthrop's going to tell him about the pesticide incident and I have to tell him about Jack Venable's girlfriend. Oh joy.

Suzanne worried about these things as Sam drove her home, kissed her at the front door, and asked if he could see

her again tomorrow. "Of course," she told him, but everything was still rattling around in her brain as she fixed a cup
of chamomile tea, let the dogs out, and got ready for bed.

In fact, Suzanne was so caught up in these newly learned
snippets of information that it was only when she was drifting off to sleep that she remembered the token she'd found.
She got up, dug in the pocket of her hoodie, and set the
token on the nightstand next to her cell phone. Tomorrow,
she told herself, she'd take it to work tomorrow and give it
to Doogie. When she spilled the beans on everything else.

CHAPTER 14

ON Tuesday mornings Petra always made her cheesy omelet rolls, which usually brought an influx of customers to the Cackleberry Club. Her recipe started out the same as if she was whipping up a typical omelet—combining eggs, milk, flour, and seasonings in a blender. But instead of cooking it in a sauté pan, she poured her egg mixture into a cake pan and baked it for about twenty minutes. When the eggs were golden and bubbly, she pulled it from the oven, sprinkled on shredded cheddar cheese, and loosened the edges. Then she simply rolled up the omelet and cut it into pieces.

"How are we garnishing these omelet rolls?" Suzanne asked. She'd dealt out half a dozen white plates like playing cards and was watching Petra place an omelet roll in the center of each plate.

"Just drop on a dollop of sour cream and sprinkle on some of your homegrown chives," said Petra. "Oh, and don't forget, two slices of whole wheat toast with little pots of apple jelly."

"Got it," said Suzanne.

Petra turned back to her stove, where she quickly plopped eight slices of French toast onto her grill.

Suzanne carried the omelet rolls to the pass-through and caught Toni's eye. Toni nodded and hustled over. "We got more requests for sticky rolls and old man Wyckle says there isn't enough pepper on his eggs. You want me to get out my pepper spray and give him a shot?"

"No," said Suzanne, handing her a pepper mill. "I think just regular pepper will do the trick."

"Okeydoke," said Toni, grabbing two more orders and balancing them down the length of her arm.

Suzanne turned back to Petra, who'd just flipped her French toast over. It was looking golden and smelling heavenly. "We're getting more requests for sticky rolls," she told her.

"Of course we are," said Petra. Her baking skills were both terrific and prolific, and she reveled in the fact that her rolls and breads were requested as well as much enjoyed. Her donuts, cookies, and cakes were also in high demand when her beloved church held a bake sale or sponsored a church supper.

"Did you ever think of entering one of your pies in the county fair?" Suzanne asked.

"Thought about it," Petra replied.

She said it casually enough so that Suzanne knew she'd definitely been considering it.

"Yet you never do," said Suzanne. "Though you'd win hands down."

"Maybe."

"Oh, you would," said Suzanne. "Trust me."

"Is that tea group still coming in this afternoon?" Petra asked. "The one who requested a sunflower tea?"

"They're still coming as far as I know," said Suzanne. "Are you still planning to make sunflower seed muffins?"

"Yup," said Petra. "And I hope Toni remembered to bring in those bunches of sunflowers so we can fix up table bouquets."

"They're bobbing their shaggy heads in a big white bucket on the back steps even as we speak."

Petra glanced toward the back door, where a familiar cardboard box was sitting. "I see you brought your little owl back with you."

"He's commuting," said Suzanne. "Wherever I go, he goes. The thing is, I have to feed him, like, five or six times a day. But after this morning's feeding I'm going to put him outside and see if the momma owl comes looking for him."

"What will that accomplish?" asked Petra. "The little guy can't fly yet. He's too young."

"No, but if she's been looking for her baby, it will put her heart at rest. And then I can get a ladder and try to put the little owl back up in his tree."

"I guess it's worth a shot," said Petra.

The swinging door flew open as Toni burst into the kitchen. "I got two more orders," she told Petra. Both . . . um . . ." She squinted at her own crooked handwriting. "French toast and bacon."

Petra immediately dropped a few more slices of bread into her batter.

"Hey, do you guys know what's going on tonight?" Toni asked.

"As far as I'm concerned, absolutely nothing," said Petra. "I'm going to flake out in front of the TV in my fleece jammies and munch chocolate chip cookies to my heart's content."

Toni seemed so whipped up Suzanne just had to ask, "What's going on, Toni?"

"It's cherry bomb night at Schmitt's Bar!" said Toni.

"What on earth is that?" asked Petra.

"Maraschino cherries that have been soaked in Ever-clear," said Toni. "And they're just twenty-five cents apiece."

"Everclear?" said Petra. "Isn't that ninety-proof grain alcohol? Toni, shame on you. Don't you know that stuff can rot your brain?"

"It's not like I'm chugging it by the glass," said Toni. "The cherries are just soaked in it. Marinated, really."

"Sounds awful," said Petra.

Toni turned a hopeful gaze on Suzanne. "Suzanne, you're up for this, aren't you?"

"I don't know," Suzanne hedged. "We were just at Schmitt's Bar the other night. A little of their gung ho, guzzle-it-up atmosphere goes a long way."

"But this is a whole 'nother thing," said Toni. "And it's a good deal, too. I mean, twenty-five cents . . . two bits. How can you possibly say no?"

"Easy," said Petra.

"Let me think about it," said Suzanne. She grabbed her purse from under the counter, pulled out her cell phone, and saw the little red token sitting on top of a pack of Kleenex. She grabbed it and set it on the counter as a reminder to hand it over to Doogie when he came in.

"What the heck, Suzanne," said Toni, zeroing in on the token. "When were you hanging out at a casino?"

Suzanne glanced at her sharply. "What? What did you just say?"

"That chip," said Toni. "It's from Prairie Star Casino over near Cornucopia. What were you doing there? Playing the slots?" Then she looked thoughtful. "No, a chip like that would be from one of the table games, wouldn't it? Like poker or roulette."

"Toni," Suzanne said, feeling a little breathless. "Are you *sure* about that?"

"Sure, I'm sure," said Toni. She picked up two plates of

French toast that Petra had just set out, and then stopped. "Sure about what?"

"That this is some kind of casino chip?" said Suzanne. She picked it up and studied it a little more carefully, as if it were something she'd unearthed in an archaeological dig. Which she kind of had.

Toni peered at the chip again. "Yeah, it's from the casino. I know that for a fact 'cause Junior took me over to Prairie Star a couple of months ago. They were having an all-you-can-eat crab leg buffet." She jerked her chin at the chip that rested in Suzanne's outstretched hand. "Where'd you get that thing anyway?"

"I found it in the ruins of the fire," said Suzanne.

Toni's double take was so abrupt she almost dropped the plates she was balancing. "What? Are you serious?"

"The fire?" said Petra. "Hannah's fire?"

"Yes," said Suzanne. Her mind had suddenly leapt into overdrive, bombarded with questions and strange possibilities.

"Wait a minute," said Petra. She tapped her wooden spoon against a pot of vegetable soup and set it down. "Let me see that thing." She walked a few steps and peered at it.

"It's definitely from the casino," said Toni.

"But I found it in the ruins of the fire," said Suzanne. She knew she was repeating herself, she just couldn't help it.

"Creepers!" said Petra. "Do you think that chip could be some sort of clue?"

"I don't know," said Suzanne. "Maybe." Her throat felt suddenly dry.

"Has to be," said Toni.

"Are you going to give the chip to Doogie?" Petra asked. "You really should, you know."

"I guess I pretty much have to," said Suzanne.

"What about the information Kit confirmed last night?" said Toni. "About Marlys Shelton being Jack Venable's possible lover. Are you going to tell him about that, too?"

"He's not going to like any of this," said Suzanne. "But maybe I can trade her name for some of his inside information."

BUT Doogie didn't come in for breakfast. And when lunchtime rolled around he was still a no-show. But another familiar face came creeping in, looking tentative and more than a little unsettled.

Jack Venable. Hannah's husband. The newly minted town widower.

Suzanne was standing behind the counter, filling her coffeepot with Blue Mountain coffee when he came in. "Oh no," she said to Toni, who was humming away as she assembled a ham and cheese sandwich for a take-out order.

"What?" Toni stopped her humming and glanced up. Then her eyes landed on Venable and she said, "Good grief. Him." Her tone dropped to a bone-chilling thirty-two degrees. "Well, *I'm* not going to wait on him. He can just sit and spin for all I care."

But Jack Venable, murder suspect or not, was a customer. And Suzanne figured that he deserved to be waited on just like anyone else.

"What?" she said, coming up to Venable's table. Waited on, yes. Friendly banter, no.

Jack Venable looked up at her with sorrowful eyes. "Suzanne," he said, "thank you for coming to the vigil last night. I'm sorry we didn't get a chance to talk."

"The way I see it, there's not much to talk about," said Suzanne.

Venable sighed and said, "You, too?"

Suzanne's right eyebrow raised up a notch and quivered.

"You know me," said Venable. "I've lived in Kindred all my life. You have to believe that I wouldn't kill Hannah." His voice cracked. "I . . . I couldn't do that. I *didn't* do that."

"Actually, Jack, I don't know anything of the sort. But I'm starting to put a few pieces together and, frankly, I don't like what I see."

Venable looked shocked. "What on earth are you talking about?"

"First I hear you want to leave your marriage," said Suzanne. "And then, when your wife of twenty-eight years protests, lo and behold, she dies in a mysterious fire. And to top it all off, you stole Hannah's wedding ring and sold it at a pawn shop!"

"I never . . ." Venable began.

But Suzanne held up a hand. "I happen to know that you did. I visited Dodd's Pawn Shop and heard all about it. Sheriff Doogie also knows that you disposed of her ring there. So I have to ask myself . . . why would someone do all this? What exactly was their motivation?"

Venable stood up so suddenly his chair almost flew over backward. "I can't believe you . . ." He bellowed so loudly every head in the place turned to look at him.

"Follow me," Suzanne ordered. She turned and walked stiffly into the Book Nook, which she decided was becoming a regular routine.

Jack Venable stalked after her, looking unhappy. Finally, when they were away from prying eyes and ears, Suzanne whirled on him like a vengeful wraith and said, "Why did you steal Hannah's ring and sell it?"

"I didn't steal it."

"Have it your way. Why did you take it?"

Venable just stood there for a few moments looking angry and forlorn. Finally, his eyes misted up and his nose began to twitch.

Suzanne decided she could wait him out. Heck, she could stand here all day if she had to.

Finally, Venable said, "I don't know why I did any of that. I suppose because I was angry. Things hadn't been going well for us for a long time. I wanted to leave . . . I wanted *her* to leave . . . I wanted to . . ."

"Kill her?" said Suzanne.

"No!" said Venable. "Of course not. I would *never* do that."

"But you were cheating on Hannah."

"Absolutely not," said Venable. But one corner of his mouth twitched as his eyes slid sideways, and Suzanne could tell that he was lying.

"Look," said Suzanne, "I don't know who your new paramour is or what she does . . . in fact, I don't *want* to know. But you are in a deep pile of doo-doo right now—and more of it is about to come tumbling down on your head. So my advice to you is to think long and hard about hiring a really good criminal defense attorney."

"Suzanne," said Venable, suddenly looking contrite, "I've really come here with my hat in my hand."

She looked at him sharply. "What are you talking about?"

"I was hoping you'd help me."

"What?" Suzanne whooped. "Are you *serious*?"

"I don't know what else to do," said Venable. "Turns out a lot of folks in town think *I* set that fire . . . and now word is spreading! So what am I supposed to do? Move out of town and start my life over again? I'm too old for that." He shrugged. "And I'm too tired."

Suzanne held up a hand. "Whoa, whoa, wait a minute, Jack. You're starting to sound a little crazy."

"Suzanne?" said Toni. She was suddenly hovering at the door. "Is everything okay? Are *you* okay?"

"We're just . . . conversing," said Suzanne. But Toni didn't budge an inch from the doorway.

"The thing is, I'm *not* talking crazy," Venable said in a rush. "In fact, the logical thing is for you to help me. You and Petra and Toni were good friends with Hannah . . . you were there when the fire started. And . . ."

"And what?" said Suzanne.

"The simple fact of the matter is, you're also a friend of Sheriff Doogie's so you can bend his ear a little. And I hear you're smart, real smart. You were the one who figured out that awful business with the prison warden."

"That was pure luck," said Suzanne.

"That was pure brilliance," said Toni, sidling over to interject herself into the conversation.

"Jack," said Suzanne. "I can't help you."

"Then who can?" said Venable.

"A lawyer," said Suzanne.

"Private investigator?" said Toni.

"But whatever you do," said Suzanne, "be honest with the sheriff."

"Petra needs you in the kitchen, Suzanne," said Toni. "Like . . . right now."

"Good luck, Jack," said Suzanne.

"Hit the road, Jack," said Toni.

"YOU really didn't need me to help out, did you?" Suzanne asked Petra. The mingled aroma of homemade soup and fresh-baked bread was comforting after her strange confrontation with Jack Venable.

Petra turned from her stove, where she was overseeing a pan of grilled chicken sausages. "Hmm?"

Toni spoke up quickly. "I was staging an intervention," she said. "You looked like you needed rescuing."

"I didn't really," said Suzanne.

"Oh?" said Toni. "I think you should tell Petra exactly why Jack Venable came skulking in here today."

"Did the jerk come here to confess?" said Petra. Her words tumbled out uncharacteristically harsh for her.

"Noooo," said Suzanne. "He actually asked for my help. Apparently people are beginning to talk."

Petra sniffed. "I'd say Jack's got some nerve." Then, "You wouldn't do that, would you? Help him?"

Toni held up a finger. "I actually have a theory concerning that."

"What are you talking about?" said Petra.

Toni looked thoughtful for a few moments, as if she was pulling her words together. Then she said, "Don't you think any effort that goes into solving Hannah's death is a good thing?"

"You mean solving her *murder,*" said Petra.

"Right," said Toni.

"No," said Petra. "I don't want Suzanne to help Jack Venable in any way, shape, or form. In fact, I think we should let him stew in his own juices until he gets arrested."

"Okay," said Toni, "I guess we know how you feel about *that.*"

WHEN Doogie finally came in for lunch, Suzanne was feeling decidedly nervous about the poker chip. She knew she should have turned it over to him sooner, but the truth of the matter was, it had simply slipped her mind.

Of course it had. With owl issues, candlelight memorials, and a half dozen suspects popping their heads up like errant gophers, it had been a busy couple of days. Still, the chip could be important. Which is why she positioned it on the butcher-block table, then snapped a quick photo of it with her cell phone. Because . . . well, you just never know.

"Sheriff," Suzanne said, placing a gingham napkin in front of him and laying down a knife, fork, and spoon. "I have something to show you."

"Now what?" Doogie whipped off his Smokey Bear hat and stuck it on the stool next to him. His customary hint that he didn't want to be bothered during lunch. Actually, he didn't want to be bothered *any*time.

"I have something I need to show you, but I don't want you to be upset." She poured a cup of coffee for him into a large ceramic mug.

"No problem," said Doogie. "Because I'm already upset. Mayor Mobley and the city fathers are breathing fire down my neck. And that dang Mrs. Duesterman called my office three times this morning, yapping at me because the neighbor's dog keeps digging up her garden." He gritted his teeth. "You see what a poor county sheriff has to contend with? Scratched-up pumpkins and ruined rutabagas, on top of an arson and murder investigation."

"My news might pertain to two out of three of your issues," said Suzanne.

Doogie reached for his coffee and cocked an eye at her. "Oh yeah?"

"It kind of slipped my mind, but this past Sunday morning, when I was walking Baxter and Scruff down the alley behind that burned-out County Services Building, I found this."

Suzanne placed the chip on the counter.

Doogie stared at it. "You found this in the wreckage of the fire?"

"Well, more like on the edge."

Doogie poked at the chip with an index finger. "It's a casino chip, right?"

"Toni thinks it's from the Prairie Star Casino."

"And you waited until *now* to tell me?" Doogie sounded steamed.

"Like I said, I kind of forgot. There's been so much going on . . ." Now Suzanne just felt stupid. If it was a clue, Doogie should have had this right away. The arson investigators should have had it.

"Doggone it, Suzanne, you were withholding evidence."

"I wasn't, really. I wouldn't do that."

"Who else has handled this besides you?" asked Doogie.

"Nobody," said Suzanne. "Well, not that I know of."

"Scoot in the kitchen and get me a plastic Baggie, okay? A fresh one untouched by human hands."

"Sure," said Suzanne, still feeling unsettled.

"And while you're at it, you can have Petra rustle me up a nice meat loaf sandwich while I sit here feeling aggravated."

"DOOGIE's ticked off, right?" said Toni. She peered out through the pass-through at Doogie, who had tucked into his meat loaf sandwich with the gusto of Henry VIII.

Suzanne seesawed a hand back and forth. "Sort of."

"Does he know he's eating chicken meat loaf instead of beef?" asked Petra.

"No," said Suzanne. "And don't you dare tell him."

"He's almost done," said Toni, still keeping an eye on him. "He's gonna want dessert."

"That's what I'm counting on," said Suzanne. She was already slicing an enormous piece of carrot cake for him.

"Compliments of the house," said Suzanne as she set the cake in front of Doogie.

Doogie blinked, smiled at the cake, and stifled a belch. "You're trying to butter me up, Suzanne. I can tell. Whenever you want something you ply me with sugar."

"Look," said Suzanne. "All I want is a little quid pro quo. I gave you the chip—which may or may not help advance your investigation. Now I'd like a little information from you."

Doogie sat poised with his fork. "What kind of information?"

"A couple of things. First, did Bruce Winthrop call you about the dustup he had with Ricky Wilcox over the pesticide permit?"

"He did," said Doogie. He aimed a finger at Suzanne. "Said it slipped his brain just like finding that doggone chip slipped your brain. Duh."

Suzanne let his insult go by. "The other thing I was wondering about concerns the woman who got saved in the fire. The woman who lived in that second-floor apartment."

Doogie's nod was imperceptible. "Marty Wolfson's wife."

"Yes," said Suzanne. "Is she still in town?"

"As far as I know, she is," Doogie said cautiously.

"And Wolfson's still a suspect, right?"

"You certainly are fishing for inside information," said Doogie.

"That's because I've got something to trade," said Suzanne.

Doogie patted his shirt pocket and smiled. "No, you don't. I've already got the chip."

"I've got something else," said Suzanne. "A key piece of information."

Doogie's gray eyes studied her for a moment, then he leaned back and said, "Wolfson's still a suspect, yes. He's not exactly on my A-roster, but he's certainly sitting squarely on my B-list. Especially since you saw him perusing handguns yesterday afternoon." He gestured with his fork. "Now what have you got for me?"

"Marlys Shelton? One of the dancers at Hoobly's?"

Doogie nodded.

"That's who Jack Venable is having an affair with."

CHAPTER 15

SUZANNE wasn't a huge fan of Facebook, but a lot of her customers had urged her to start a Cackleberry Club page. And then Petra warmed up to the idea because she figured they could update folks on their breakfast and lunch specials as well as her various knitting classes.

So that's what Suzanne was working on this early afternoon. Sitting in her office, trying to figure out which photos to add, what captions to write.

Toni rapped her knuckles on the door frame. "Knock, knock, can I interrupt you for a second?"

Suzanne spun around in her office chair. "Please do."

Toni scrunched up her face and peered over Suzanne's shoulder at the computer screen. "How's it going?"

"Okay."

"Do you understand the allure of Facebook? Of getting all those photos and random musings from your so-called friends? To me it always feels like my aunt Ethel's Christmas letter coming at me every couple of days."

"I hear you," said Suzanne. She wasn't that big a fan of social media, either.

"So here's the deal, the luncheon crowd has pretty much cleared out and I'm working on those sunflower arrangements for the tea tables."

"Okay."

"So do we want to set up two tables or three tables?"

"Let's see," said Suzanne, opening her reservation book and quickly paging through it. "We've got twelve people coming in . . . so let's seat six guests at each of the large round tables."

"Got it," said Toni. "Oh, and Petra wants you to come and taste her sunflower cheese spread."

"Perfect," said Suzanne. "I wasn't getting very far with this anyway."

"I think it's wonderful," said Petra. "Then again, I'm the one who whipped it up." She dropped a generous scoop of sunflower cheese spread atop a triangle of whole wheat bread and handed it to Suzanne. "But I want to know what *you* think."

Suzanne took a bite, smiled, and took another bite. "Very tasty."

"Good," said Petra. She was standing in the middle of the kitchen, hands on hips, surveying her realm. "I've also got sunflower pumpkin muffins baking in the oven and I already made two batches of sunflower raisin cookies."

"This really is a sunflower tea," said Suzanne. "Somehow I figured that particular theme only applied to the décor."

"Oh no," said Petra. "We aim to please, no matter how outlandish the request."

"So I'll have Toni put out the yellow plates and the gold silverware."

"Maybe you could even tie some of that yellow netting

around the chair backs," Petra suggested. "We've got about a zillion yards left over from that baby shower we hosted for Trina Sjoblad a couple weeks back."

"I think that netting would look nice and festive. Really brighten the room."

"Oh, and Suzanne . . . I think I might have heard your momma owl hooting and flapping around out back."

"Really?" Suzanne crossed the kitchen and peered expectantly out the window. She didn't see the owl, but she had a feeling it was up there, watching and waiting for just the right time.

"The only problem is," said Petra, "I'm pretty sure she thinks you're doing a wonderful job in caring for her baby."

"Oh dear," said Suzanne, glancing at the cardboard box where the little owl was nestled. "I wish you wouldn't say that."

Toni hustled in with a tub of dirty dishes. "This is the last of 'em," she said, setting them next to the sink. "Now I'm gonna set up the tea tables." She stuck a clean spoon into a bowl of cookie dough and grabbed a taste. "Yum. So our group is coming at what time?"

"Three," Suzanne told her.

"Kind of late," said Toni.

"Kind of good to have so much business," said Suzanne. She glanced at Petra. "You want me to help make tea sandwiches?"

But Petra waved her off. "Naw, I've got this."

"Petra?" Suzanne hesitated. "Do you know Marty Wolfson's wife? The lady who was rescued from the second-floor apartment?"

"I do know her," said Petra. "At least I've met her. Sometimes she brings her little boy to the children's Bible study classes at our church."

"What's her first name again?"

"Annie," said Petra.

"Do you know where she lives?"

"Why? Are you going to talk to her?" said Petra. She seemed surprised.

"I thought I might," said Suzanne. "Her husband's still on Doogie's short list and . . . well, do you want me to keep investigating or not?"

"Absolutely, I do," said Petra. "Especially since you told me that Wolfson was looking at guns! You know, the one thing that's constantly been in my prayers is that Hannah's murder—and I'm convinced that's what it was—gets solved."

"Okay then," said Suzanne.

"I happen to know that Annie is staying with her sister right now," said Petra. She snatched up a pen and piece of paper. "I don't know the exact address, but I can draw a little map that will show you exactly how to get there."

TURNS out the tea group was really a garden club. A group of women who called themselves the Sunnyside Garden Club and got together for coffee, tea, garden parties, and whatever a few times a year.

This year's president, Molly Owens, was the first one to arrive. She bounded through the door, glanced around with a smile, then let out an excited little "Ooh!" as her eyes focused on the two tables.

Suzanne rushed over to greet her. "Mrs. Owens, I hope everything is to your liking."

"Molly, call me Molly," said the woman.

"And I'm Suzanne."

"You've done a marvelous job," said Molly. "Everything's so pretty and bright and yellow . . . and, well, the sunflower arrangements look like something Van Gogh might have painted. The ladies are going to be thrilled."

Toni came skittering out. "Hey there, Molly," she said. "Great to see you. Welcome."

"Hi, Toni," said Molly.

"You two know each other?" said Suzanne.

"Oh sure," said Toni. "Molly's husband races monster trucks. Me and Junior have run into them a bunch of times over at the Golden Springs Speedway."

Molly rolled her eyes. "I keep telling Matt to sell that awful thing."

"Aw, it's not so bad," said Toni.

"Yes, it is," said Molly.

THE sunflower tea was a huge success. Once the rest of the guests arrived and were seated, they oohed and aahed over Petra's tea sandwiches with their tasty fillings of sunflower cheese spread, chicken salad, and egg salad. Then, as the tea continued, they begged for recipes for the muffins and cookies. And as Suzanne and Toni refilled steaming cups of Assam tea, several of the women asked to buy tins of that particular tea as well.

"We're killing them out there," Toni told Petra when she and Suzanne popped in to grab small squares of white picnic cake, the final tea course.

Petra yawned. "That's the general idea, isn't it?"

"Are you okay?" Suzanne asked her.

"I'm okay," said Petra, wiggling her shoulders. "I just feel a little crumped."

"You're stressed because Hannah's funeral is tomorrow," said Toni.

Petra gazed at her. "I'm stressed because Hannah's killer still isn't in jail."

BY five o'clock, Suzanne was driving along Nicholson Street with Petra's map clutched in her hand, searching the house where Annie Wolfson lived with her sister. She was in the older part of town, where a lot of the homes were really more like small cottages. Suzanne guessed that eighty or ninety years ago, there had been a kind of lake over here. Of course, that was before city planners had tampered with nature, draining swamps and rerouting streams. Or putting in pipes that took the water underground. When would we learn, she wondered, not to keep tampering with nature?

Probably when all the lakes are dry and the trees are gone, she thought grimly. *Then somebody's going to look around and say,* Oops.

Suzanne was generally a pragmatist, but she never stood idly by when the natural order of mother earth was threatened. She signed petitions to save the wolves, protested when Mayor Mobley suggested cutting down a sliver of the original Big Woods to accommodate a go-nowhere road, and tried to grow as many of her own herbs and vegetables as humanly possible.

Petra had once suggested putting a chicken coop behind the Cackleberry Club, since so many people were into raising urban chickens, but Suzanne didn't want to drive her current egg suppliers out of business. It just wouldn't be right. They'd been with her from the beginning, so she was going to stick with them to the very end.

Suzanne consulted her map again and determined that the last house on this block had to be the one she was looking for. She pulled over to the curb and sat there for a few moments, gathering her thoughts and making her plans. First she'd talk to Annie Wolfson, then she'd zip over to the hospital and share a few leftover tea sandwiches with Sam, and then she was going to meet up with Toni for cherry bomb night. And somewhere in between, she had to find time to run home, change clothes, and feed Baxter and Scruff.

When Suzanne knocked on the door of the little white house, she wasn't quite sure what she was going to say. She was just winging it, trying to figure things out as she went along. But when the door creaked open and a familiar face appeared, Suzanne knew exactly what to do.

"Mrs. Wolfson?" she said. "I'm Suzanne Dietz. I don't know if you remember me or not, I'm one of the owners of the Cackleberry Club?"

"Petra's partner," said Annie Wolfson. She brushed her blond hair back from her face, pulled the door open wider, and said, "Sure, I remember you." Then she hesitated. "What's up?"

"I just wanted to ask you a couple of questions," said Suzanne.

"Come in," Annie invited. "I'm sorry this place is such a mess. My sister's a little laissez-faire when it comes to house-keeping, and Joshua's been running around like a maniac."

"Joshua," said Suzanne. "That's your son?"

"Five years old and quite the terror." She paused. "What kind of questions?" She led Suzanne into the small living room and indicated for her to sit down on the couch, which was the only piece of furniture not covered with a fleet of toy trucks. She picked up a small yellow truck from a worn armchair and sat across from Suzanne, fiddling nervously with the toy.

"I was there last Friday," said Suzanne. "At the fire. I saw you and Joshua being rescued."

Annie touched a hand to her heart and said, "An ordeal that was truly terrifying. But I am so indebted to that fire-fighter. Jason, I think his name was. Scrambling up the lad-der like that, reassuring me the entire time, telling me we weren't in any danger, when I'm sure we really were."

"The firefighters did a great job," Suzanne acknowledged.

Annie furrowed her brow. "But you're not here to talk about firefighters."

"I wanted to ask you about your husband."

"Marty," said Annie. She blew out a glut of air and her blond bangs ruffled outward. "Marty," she said again.

"I'm fairly close with Sheriff Doogie," said Suzanne. "So I know that he's a suspect."

"Yes." Now Annie sounded bitter. "I've already been questioned several times by Sheriff Doogie." She shook her head. "Marty and I did have our differences."

"The two of you are separated, correct?"

"Yes," said Annie. "We have been for the past four months. Which is why I was living . . . well, you know."

"I ask about this," said Suzanne, "because . . . um . . . I understand there's the matter of an insurance policy."

"That's exactly why Sheriff Doogie is on Marty's case! But there's just no way he would have intentionally set that fire. He would never hurt Joshua. He loves him."

"But Joshua wasn't supposed to be home that day," Suzanne said softly. For some reason, she figured that speaking softly might cushion the blow.

Annie dropped her head into her hands and her shoulders started to shake.

Suzanne felt awful. She jumped up, scurried across the room, and put an arm around Annie's shoulders. "I'm so sorry. I didn't mean to upset you like this. The woman who died in the fire . . . Hannah Venable . . . she was a friend of mine. That's why I'm kind of digging into this."

"You didn't upset me," said Annie, wiping at her tears. "I've been upset for days. Ever since the fire."

"I'm so sorry," Suzanne said again.

Annie waved a hand. "Don't be. The crazy thing is, Marty and I were separated and probably headed for divorce. Now . . . the fire, this terrible thing . . . may have actually brought us back together."

"Seriously?" said Suzanne. Petra had heard rumors that Annie Wolfson had sustained a few injuries at the hands of her husband.

Annie nodded. "It's made us . . . reconsider our priorities. Made us take a good hard look at our relationship."

This was the absolute last thing Suzanne had expected to hear. She thought there might be an angry tirade laced with some regret, but certainly not news of a possible reconciliation. This was a shocker.

"So there's no doubt in your mind that your husband had anything to do with that fire?" said Suzanne.

Annie gazed at her, her face a picture of sadness. "I guess . . . not," she said.

But to Suzanne, her answer didn't sound convincing. Not convincing in the least. And all she could hope was that Annie Wolfson didn't end up in the battered woman's shelter over in Jessup. Or shot dead with a newly purchased handgun.

CHAPTER 16

"WHAT is this cheese again?" asked Sam. They were sitting in the hospital cafeteria, nibbling leftover tea
sandwiches that Suzanne had brought along. The room was
sterile white and clattery, lit with too many fluorescents.
Not very conducive to romance. Or even pleasant conversation.

"Cream cheese and sunflower seeds," said Suzanne. "You
like it?"

"Man cannot live by bread alone, he needs a little cheese,
too," Sam said as he gulped another sandwich. "Besides, fat
combined with salt, what's not to like?"

"You can't eat healthy all the time," Suzanne said with a
rueful smile.

"I generally try."

"What about those pancakes you scarfed last Sunday?
Drenched in syrup? And the steak last night?"

"Those are very specific instances of being a guest in your
home," said Sam. "I can hardly climb up on my high horse and

lodge a protest. When you're a guest in someone's home you eat what they serve. It's the polite Emily Post thing to do."

"And if I serve bacon, hash browns, gravy, and buttermilk biscuits?"

"Be still my heart," said Sam, rolling his eyes. "Or maybe I'll need a stent. Either way, I'd hate to pass that up."

"You're incorrigible," said Suzanne.

Sam held up a finger. "And easily corruptible. Your cooking could so lead me down another path. And it's obviously not the straight and narrow."

"I thought all doctors ate crap," laughed Suzanne. "Cheese bits from vending machines, French fries from the hospital cafeteria . . ."

"That was only in med school," said Sam. "And under the most dire circumstances. I've since reformed."

"Yeah, right," Suzanne said. She snapped the lid off a plastic container and offered him a cookie.

His eyes shone. "Ooh, there are *cookies?*"

While Sam munched away, Suzanne told him about her meeting with Annie Wolfson. Sam listened carefully, asked a couple of questions, and then said, "The whole thing sounds problematic. Their relationship, the fact that she doesn't seem to trust him . . ."

"That's my read, too," said Suzanne. "I mean, what if Marty Wolfson is playing the role of a lifetime? What if he's just pretending to turn over a new leaf and reconnect with Annie?"

"And he'd do that for what reason?"

"To throw Doogie off his trail," said Suzanne. "Eliminate suspicion."

"I suppose that's plausible," said Sam. "If he's roughed up his wife in the past, like you think he has, that's an indication of an almost sociopathic personality. A person who tends to be quite adept at smoke screens and deception."

"There you go," said Suzanne. She decided she wasn't one

bit fooled by Marty Wolfson's attempt to reconcile with his wife. And she was determined to make sure that Doogie wasn't taken in, either. The investigation was still alive and well and she wasn't going to rest until Hannah's killer—whoever he might be—was brought to justice.

"So you've already talked to Doogie about Wolfson?" Sam asked.

"No, but I'm going to," said Suzanne. "And earlier today I did hand over what I think might be a kind of clue to him."

"You found a clue? Where?"

"Okay, I didn't tell you about it because it slipped my mind. But when I was walking Baxter and Scruff last Sunday morning, before you came back for breakfast, I found something."

"Found what?"

"What Toni and I think is some kind of casino chip from Prairie Star Casino. I was walking the dogs down the alley behind the burned-out County Services Building and there it was."

Sam looked suddenly concerned. "You had no business going back there, Suzanne. It's still a dangerous area and you could have been injured."

"I was careful."

"Then one of the dogs could have been hurt."

"Now you're trying to guilt me."

"Well, sure. If that's what it takes to keep you safe."

Suzanne snuggled closer to him. "I'm safe. When I'm with you I feel safe."

"It's the times you're *not* with me that make me worry. You do tend to roam a bit."

Suzanne shoved the cookie container toward him and smiled brightly. "Have another cookie."

"You scare the crap out of me, you know?"

"You're such a sweet talker."

Sam sighed. He knew when he was defeated. "So . . . you still have your owl?"

"Oh yes. In fact, he's out in my car waiting patiently. With a cozy down quilt tucked around him."

"I can't remember," said Sam. "Did you ever do that to me?"

"I think so," said Suzanne. She pretended to look puzzled. "Hmm, maybe not. Perhaps you'll have to come by again and let me take care of that. The cuddly thing with the quilt, I mean."

"You're on."

"Just not tonight," said Suzanne. "I promised Toni I'd meet her for cherry bomb night."

"What's that? Something to do with fireworks? For the county fair?"

"I wish," said Suzanne. "No, it's a kind of drink promotion over at Schmitt's Bar. Apparently, they marinate maraschino cherries in grain alcohol and then sell them for a quarter."

"That sounds like something we used to do in med school."

"With cherries?" said Suzanne.

Sam looked amused. "Well, no. With . . . um, maybe we shouldn't go into detail while we're still eating."

"Maybe we shouldn't," Suzanne agreed.

TONI was already sitting in a booth at Schmitt's Bar when Suzanne arrived. Looking very curvy in a tight white tank top and blue jeans, Toni grinned and waved a hand, happy to see her.

"I was afraid you wouldn't come," said Toni when Suzanne settled into the seat across from her.

"I had to take the owl home. But I promised I'd come and I did. I try never to break my promises."

"Like how you promised Petra you'd help figure out who killed Hannah?"

Suzanne nodded.

"And then you promised Kit that you'd try to get Ricky off the hook."

Suzanne could see where this was leading.

"And when you promised . . ."

"Okay," said Suzanne. "I catch your drift."

Toni offered a mousy little smile. "You're a genuinely good person, Suzanne. But sometimes you get in over your head."

"And you don't?" said Suzanne. "How about that thing with Lester Drummond? And that awful . . ."

"Okay, okay," said Toni. "What you're saying is we're a couple of busybodies."

"I think 'concerned citizens' might be a nicer term."

"How about observant and mindful?"

"I'll buy that."

"Better yet, I'll buy you a couple of cherry bombs," said Toni. She held up a hand. "Garçon?"

"Aren't we fancy tonight," said Suzanne.

"Two years at the Sorbonne," Toni joked. "You can really pick up the language skills."

But Freddy was more than happy to go along with Toni's good cheer. "How many cherry bombs do you gals want?" he asked. "Better order up now 'cause they're going fast and we'll probably run out."

"Maybe a half dozen?" said Toni.

"And they're really soaked in grain alcohol?" said Suzanne.

"Darn right." Freddy rapped his knuckles against the table. "This ain't Applebee's, Suzanne."

SUZANNE glanced around the bar. The place seemed crowded for a Tuesday night. Then again, she didn't make a habit of hitting Schmitt's Bar on a school night, so she wasn't sure if they were operating at full capacity or not.

"How'd your meeting with Annie Wolfson go?" Toni asked.

"Okay. I think she feels bad that her husband is on Doogie's suspect list, so she's talking about getting back together with him."

"Is that so? Because something tells me that Marty Wolfson isn't all that hot to put his little family back together again."

"Why do you say that?" said Suzanne.

Toni gave a harsh chuckle. "Because he's sitting right there at the bar."

Suzanne's head spun around like it was on ball bearings. Then she spotted him. Marty Wolfson was sprawled at the bar and leaning heavily toward a woman in a purple sweater who was seated next to him. A pitcher of beer and a basket of pull tabs sat in front of him. Suzanne half expected Darrel Fuhrman, the ex-fireman, to be sitting at the bar, too. Just as he had last Saturday night.

"Wolfson looks like he's drunk," observed Suzanne.

"Well . . . yeah," said Toni. "That's like his third pitcher of beer." She paused. "He's a real picture of a family man, huh?" She smirked, then ducked her head and locked eyes with Suzanne. "Oh crap."

"What?" said Suzanne.

"I think he's looking at us. I think he knows we were talking about him."

"No, he doesn't," said Suzanne. "He's all wrapped up in that woman with the ghastly purple spangles on her sweater."

Turns out, he wasn't.

"Hey," yelled Wolfson. "Hey, you."

"I'm pretty sure he's talking to you," said Toni.

"I don't think so," Suzanne muttered.

"You, Cackleberry lady," said Wolfson, louder this time.

"That would definitely be you," Toni said in a singsong voice.

Suzanne stole a quick glance toward Wolfson. He was glaring at her.

"I hear you're a regular little Miss Marple," Wolfson said to her. "Playing the role of Sheriff Doogie's sidekick, investigating the fire, asking questions all over town."

"I think you heard wrong," Suzanne said in an even tone. There was something about Marty Wolfson that frightened her. He was one of those men who looked like he was perpetually angry at the world. Even now, she was picking up a weird vibe from him, as if he might be the kind of man who wouldn't mind slapping a lady around. And enjoying it immensely.

"You mind your own business!" Wolfson barked. "And if you dare point a finger at me, I'll come after you with everything I've got!"

Hot anger flared inside Suzanne. "Is that a threat?" she asked, mindful that the man might be armed.

"It's a warning!" said Wolfson.

"Ladies," said Freddy, suddenly interjecting himself between them and Wolfson. "Your cherry bombs."

Suzanne crossed her arms. "I don't think I'm all that interested anymore."

"Aw, don't let that dude get to you," said Freddy. "He's just whacked out of shape over all the questions Sheriff Doogie's been putting to him. And he's been drinking like a fish."

"Are you gonna throw him out?" asked Toni. She loved nothing better than to witness a good saloon dustup.

"Pretty soon," said Freddy. "So try to ignore him for now, okay?"

"Sure," said Suzanne. "Whatever." She poked a finger at a cherry bomb, then said, "Really?"

"Just pop it in your mouth and chew it," Toni urged.

Suzanne popped it in her mouth and chewed.

"So whadya think?"

"Bracing," said Suzanne. "And it tastes a little medici-nal." She smiled to herself, thinking about Sam's remarks concerning grain alcohol, and suddenly wished he were with her tonight.

"So," said Toni, grabbing another cherry bomb, "Doogie was pretty shocked by that poker chip today."

"He was pretty annoyed," said Suzanne, popping another cherry bomb into her mouth. "On the other hand, the chip might mean nothing at all."

Toni inclined her head toward the bar. "What if Wolfson was the jackhole who dropped it there?"

"That would make it a serious clue," Suzanne agreed.

"Or maybe Jack Venable dropped it?" said Toni.

Suzanne stared at Toni as a little lightbulb clicked on inside her brain. "Toni, do me a favor, will you?"

"Sure. Hey, are you gonna eat that last cherry bomb?"

"No, help yourself."

Toni did. "So what's your favor?"

Suzanne pulled out her iPhone and slid it across the table to Toni. "Take a picture of Marty Wolfson, will you?"

Toni stared at her. "You want me to waltz right up to Mr. Hothead over there and say, 'Watch the birdie'?"

"No, I want you to do it surreptitiously. Go to the ladies' room and then come back. But, for gosh sakes, be careful."

"I'm always careful," said Toni.

"This time you have to make like a cat burglar," said Suzanne. "Wolfson might be armed, he might have a gun."

"Pish," said Toni, "I'm not afraid of that." She slid out of the booth and walked past Wolfson. He didn't take any notice of Toni, but his eyes seemed to constantly dart back to Suzanne.

Good, she thought. *Now if Toni can just . . .*

Toni was strolling back along the bar now, with the cell

phone tucked discreetly in the palm of her hand. When she was a couple of feet away from Wolfson she aimed it at him and took a photo!

Gotcha! Suzanne thought to herself.

"WHAT was that all about?" Toni asked once they were standing outside on the sidewalk.

"I had a kind of brainstorm," said Suzanne. "What if we took photos of Marty Wolfson and Jack Venable over to that casino and asked around? See if they're regulars there?"

"That's a stupendous idea!" said Toni. "We'd be following the trail of the chip." She hesitated. "Except that . . ."

"Except what?"

"We don't have a shot of Jack Venable."

"Not yet we don't," said Suzanne.

Toni narrowed her eyes. "What are you thinking, girlfriend?"

"Hop in the car and I'll show you."

CHAPTER 17

TONI aimed her car toward the curb and slid behind an enormous acacia bush that sprouted on the boulevard. She'd insisted on driving and Suzanne was terrified. Every time she heard a rattle, bing, or boing, she figured Toni's car was about to give up the ghost. Engineered by Junior, of course, the car was a complete rattletrap. Or was it more of a death trap?

"Now that we're here," said Toni, "how are you going to get Venable's picture? I mean, you can't just run up to the front door, yell 'Trick or treat,' and snap his photo."

"We've got to lure him outside somehow."

"How we gonna do that?" said Toni. Then her face took on a snarky look and she said, "I've got an idea."

"Ring the doorbell?" said Suzanne.

"Rock," said Toni.

"You're gonna smack him with a rock? That really will ring his bell. And, besides, won't that count as a felony assault?"

"No, silly, I'm gonna toss a rock at his *window* and when Venable comes paddling out to see what the heck's going on, you're going to snap his photo. Easy peasy."

"That sounds crazy," said Suzanne. "Even to me."

Toni nodded sagely. "Which is why it'll probably work like a charm."

Jack Venable lived in a white clapboard house that looked sturdy and sedate, and had probably been built in the '30s. Lights blazed in the downstairs windows, there was a large front porch with a railing around it, and a door-bell with a little blue light, so they figured their whacked-out plan just might work.

"See," said Toni, whispering now. "You hide off to the side of his porch and I'll aim my rock at that big front window. All you have to worry about is taking his picture."

"Okay," Suzanne whispered back. "But where will you be when he comes rushing out?"

"Not here," said Toni. "I'm gonna make like an egg and beat it."

Together they crept toward the house. Halfway there, Toni detoured into a small garden that was built around a blue plastic birdbath, and picked up a small rock. She hefted it in her hand, nodded at Suzanne, and the two of them got into position.

"Here goes," said Toni. She slung the rock toward the window, where it hit with a loud smack followed by a crash of glass!

"Oops," said Toni as she dashed off into the darkness.

Suzanne crouched next to the porch, feeling terrified. The rock had hit way too hard, Venable was going to be angry, and . . .

Jack Venable came flying out the front door in his stocking feet, cracked his knee against a giant ceramic pot, and howled loudly. "Who did that!" he screamed as he hopped up and down. "I see you kids! Don't think I don't see you!"

If he'd been a cartoon character, hot steam would have poured out of his ears.

Suzanne chose that moment to poke her head up, aim the camera, and hope for the best. And so, that's how she got him. Venable in a fit of rage, shaking his fist, his mouth gaping wide open.

As far as Suzanne was concerned . . . mission accomplished.

"THAT'S some arm you have," said Suzanne as they drove through the night toward Cornucopia, where the casino was located.

"I guess I put a little too much elbow grease on it," Toni admitted.

"You're stronger than you look."

"Aw," said Toni, "it's 'cause of that slow-pitch softball team I played on for a while. It whittled my waist but built up the muscles in my arms."

"You must have been their star player," said Suzanne.

When they pulled up in front of Prairie Star Casino and shuddered to a halt, the valet was reluctant to park their car.

"What kind of car is that?" he asked Toni warily. He was a young kid—maybe sixteen, in a red jacket and baggy black slacks—working for tips.

"It's your basic Frankencar," Toni told him. "Some Chevy parts and the front end of a Buick. A Chevuick." They got out, prepared to let the car just sit there, a giant metallic heap, blocking the valet parking lane in front of the casino.

"Never heard of that model before," the kid said, ducking his head and climbing into the driver's seat.

"It's crafted by hand," Toni shot back. "Like those fancy British cars."

Then they were sailing through the front doors of the Prairie Star Casino, swallowed up in a whirling, swirling haze of flashing lights, tinkling slot machines, loud rock music, and raucous, frustrated gamblers.

"This is awful," said Suzanne as she looked around. The casino seemed to be arranged in concentric rings. Slot machines on the outer ring, electronic blackjack machines a few steps down in another ring, and then down another ring to the table games. It was, she decided, architecturally similar to Dante's rings of Hell.

"I think this place is a hoot," said Toni. She was already digging in her purse, looking for loose change to feed the hungry slot machines. "Let's see if I can win myself that cute little Mercedes-Benz."

Suzanne glanced up. Sure enough, positioned on a podium directly above a row of 25¢ slot machines was a copper-colored Mercedes. Its lights were on, there was a film of dust on the hood, and a sign on the grill proclaimed, Progressive Slots—Win Big!

"Shoot," said Toni. She pulled the handle on a one-armed bandit again. "Doggone it."

"Not having your usual run of luck?" asked Suzanne.

"Not having any luck at all," said Toni. "Ah well. The gambler's lament."

"So what do you think we should do? Maybe find the casino security office?"

But Toni had another idea.

"You see that girl over there?" she said. "The cocktail waitress with the tray of drinks?"

"You mean the girl in the absurdly minuscule gold hot pants and white leather halter top?"

Toni nodded. "Yeah. I know her. She used to work at Hoobly's."

"The poor dear," said Suzanne, and she wasn't kidding.

But Toni was already waving her arms like mad. "Hey, Candy, hey, over here. It's me! Toni!"

"Hey," said Candy, strolling over. "Toni. How you doin'?"

"Good," said Toni. "This is my friend Suzanne."

"Nice to meet you," said Candy. "Would you guys like a drink?" She tipped her tray toward them. "I've got rum and Cokes here, compliments of the house."

"Thanks," said Toni, taking two and handing one to Suzanne. "That's quite an outfit you're wearing."

Candy made a face. "Kind of skimpy. But the customers seem to like it."

Toni gave her a wink. "Not as skimpy as the lingerie you wore at Hoobly's."

"Tell me about it," said Candy. "Compared to Hoobly's this is like . . . I don't know . . . working at a swanky nightclub."

"So you work here full-time?" asked Suzanne.

Candy nodded. "Five, sometimes six nights a week. The tip situation is real good."

Toni sipped on her drink, and then said, "Listen, my friend Suzanne and I are looking for a couple of guys."

"Bernie usually takes care of that," said Candy. "But you're gonna have to slip him a couple of . . ."

"No, no, no," protested Suzanne. "We're not looking for a *hookup*. We just want to know if a couple of fellows we know have been hanging out here."

"Oh, okay," said Candy, looking relieved.

"Show her the photos," said Toni.

Suzanne dug out her phone and scrolled to the photo of Marty Wolfson.

"Recognize him?" asked Toni.

Candy studied the photo. "No, I can't say that I do."

"Okay, how about this guy?" said Toni as Suzanne scrolled to the shot of Jack Venable.

"Whoa," said Candy. "What happened to him? He looks kind of surprised, like he just swallowed a bug."

"Yeah," said Toni. "It was kind of an impromptu shot. *Candid Camera* and all that. Anyway, you recognize him?

He might be a regular customer here, at blackjack or one of the other table games."

"I don't think I've seen him here," said Candy. "Or if I have, I don't remember."

"We're striking out," said Suzanne.

"Maybe you could try the casino security office," Candy suggested.

"You think they'd talk to us?" asked Suzanne.

"Ask for a guy named Rufus," said Candy. She smiled sweetly. "He owes me."

"Will do," said Toni. "And thanks."

Suzanne and Toni pushed their way through a crowd, past the buffet line, and into a red-carpeted corridor that was lined with posters of comedy and musical acts.

"Look at that," said Toni. "Bogus Bob and the Ridge Riders are coming here next month. We should get tickets."

"Absolutely," said Suzanne, who was focused only on locating the security office.

RUFUS Boeckman turned out to be one of those big, teddy bear–type guys. Broad shoulders, baby face, and friendly smile. He was wearing khakis and a burgundy golf shirt that said Security, and probably tipped the scales at two-eighty.

"Rufus," said Toni. "Candy said you'd be a sweetie pie and help us." They'd squeezed into a small office that smelled of burned coffee and was packed floor to ceiling with closed-circuit monitors. Three other security guards were smooshed in there, too, studying the screens, looking professionally bored.

"Oh yeah?" said Rufus. He had kind of a high, squeaky voice.

"We're looking for a couple of guys," said Suzanne. She scrolled quickly through her phone to the picture of Wolfson. "Do you recognize him? Is he a regular here?"

"Why are you asking about him?" said Rufus.

"Because he could be in trouble," said Suzanne.

"And you're trying to help him in some way?" said Rufus.

"Uh . . . something like that," said Suzanne.

"Candy said you owed her one," said Toni.

Rufus bent his head and studied the photo. "No."

"No, you won't help us or no, you don't know him?" said Suzanne.

"Don't know him," said Rufus.

"How about this guy?" said Suzanne, offering up the photo of Venable.

Rufus shook his head. "I don't think so. Weird-lookin' guy, though. So I'd probably remember him."

"Well, shoot," said Toni.

"It seemed like a good plan," said Suzanne.

"It sure did," Toni agreed.

"You'll have to leave now," said Rufus, attempting to close the door.

"Thanks anyway," said Suzanne.

"Do you think that rules them out?" Toni asked as they headed back through the casino.

"Maybe," said Suzanne. "I don't know."

"Look at this place," said Toni. She seemed jacked up by the bright lights, free flow of money, and crush of anxious gamblers.

"It's awful. Why do I see people losing their hard-earned money and then not being able to pay their mortgage?"

"There have to be *some* winners," said Toni. She plucked at Suzanne's sleeve. "Come on, let's walk by the table games, see what's shakin'."

"Do we have to?"

"Yeah, it'll be fun."

It wasn't fun, not for Suzanne anyway. But it was eye-opening.

"Holy shih tzu!" said Toni. "Look over there, just past that pai gow poker table. Do you see . . . ?"

"Ohmigosh," said Suzanne. "It's Darrel Fuhrman!" She could hardly believe her eyes.

Darrel Fuhrman, the ex-firefighter, was sitting at a blackjack table, staring intently at his hand of cards, sipping away at a drink.

"I think he's winning," said Toni. "Look, he's got a decent-sized stack of chips in front of him."

"Chips," said Suzanne. Suddenly, all she could think of was the dirty red chip she'd picked out of the ruins of the fire. Had that chip come from this casino? Had it been in Darrel Fuhrman's pocket when he snuck down the alley and started the fire at the County Services Bureau? Or was this just a huge, crazy coincidence?

Suzanne knew one thing for sure—she needed to find out a lot more about Darrel Fuhrman.

SUZANNE and Toni were both quiet on the ride home. Both wondering if there was a connection between Fuhrman and the fire that had killed Hannah.

"See you tomorrow," Toni said when she let Suzanne out on Main Street.

"Okay, take care." Suzanne's car was still parked a few doors down from Schmitt's Bar. The lights were on in the bar, she could hear Hootie and the Blowfish blasting from the jukebox, and the Blatz Beer sign in the window was blinking blue and white.

Suzanne drove home, still pondering their discovery, wondering what kind of person Fuhrman was, and why he'd been fired.

I have to talk to Doogie about him. Or Chief Finley. Because maybe Fuhrman is the missing piece in the puzzle.

Suzanne waited while the dogs went out, and then turned

off all the lights downstairs. She trudged upstairs, remembering that Hannah's funeral was tomorrow morning.

Ugh. I have to pick out a funeral-appropriate suit. Or dress.

Suzanne pulled a black dress off the rack, held it up to herself, and stared in the mirror. She knew it was silly, but she still had a few residual issues about her body. Was she thin enough? Pretty enough? Was she young enough to keep up with a guy like Sam?

Narrowing her eyes, Suzanne scrutinized herself in the mirror. She'd always thought that maybe, just maybe, her shoulders were a little too wide. Then, a couple of months ago, she'd read an article that said hers was the exact body type George Balanchine, the ballet impresario, had looked for in his premier dancers. Wide shoulders, slightly shorter torso, somewhat longer legs. She'd actually felt heartened after reading that. Vindicated in some way for the DNA that had been responsible for her growth.

She hung the dress on the back of the closet door, shucked out of her clothes, and brushed her teeth. Not five minutes later, Suzanne drifted off to sleep, dreaming of ballerinas. Ballerinas in pink toe shoes who danced across a bed of hot coals while flames roared in the background.

CHAPTER 18

ELEVEN o'clock at night, across town. The arsonist looked out his window at the lopsided yellow moon hanging low in the sky and the darkened houses surrounding him. And smiled a drunken smile. He'd fixed himself another drink and flipped on CNN, where a couple of talking heads argued back and forth about instability in the Middle East.

He was vaguely interested. On the other hand, he was a little bit drunk and it was hard not to feel gleeful and self-satisfied. Okay, let's be totally honest here, he was feeling more than a little smug.

I'm too smart for them, he told himself as he dropped heavily into his leather Barcalounger. *Too smart for all of them. They'll never catch me in a million years, because small-town people have small-town minds.*

He nuzzled his scotch and closed his eyes momentarily, convinced a thousand times over that he was forever safe.

On the other side of town, Suzanne stirred in her sleep and, unconsciously, ground her teeth as she dreamt of sweet revenge.

CHAPTER 19

SUZANNE, Toni, and Petra, each turned out in black, sat like a trio of somber crows at Hannah's funeral.

It was Wednesday morning at Hope Church and there was standing room only. It seemed like the whole of Kindred had turned out to pay their respects and bid Hannah a final farewell. The choir was warbling sadly in the choir loft overhead, while tiny little Agnes Bennet pumped away at the enormous pipe organ, just as she had at weddings, funerals, and Sunday meetings for the last forty-five years.

Suzanne recognized the song; it was Paul Simon's "Homeward Bound." The sentiment always made her feel sad and she could see that Petra was sad, too. The poor dear was oozing tears and dabbing at her nose with a lace hankie. Toni, on the other hand, was craning her neck around, inquisitive as always, eyes roving about, studying the crowd.

Suzanne decided to follow her lead. Leaning sideways, almost out into the center aisle, she tried to see what was happening at the front of the church. Ah, there he was. Jack

Venable. Sitting in the very first pew, looking sober and sub-dued, surrounded by a sprinkling of people that all had his same sharp nose. Relatives, probably.

"Look," Petra whispered. She'd been watching carefully even as she mumbled her quiet prayers. "Hannah's sister, Joyce, is sitting on the *other* side of the church."

Then Toni had to slip in her two cents and nail it. "I wonder if Jack Venable's little chickie-poo is here?"

Petra sniffled. "I don't know. Maybe he wasn't having an affair after all. Maybe the man is just . . . lost."

Suzanne and Toni glanced quickly at each other, a move that wasn't lost on Petra.

"What?" she said.

"He was," said Suzanne.

"Is," said Toni.

"Really?" said Petra.

Suzanne and Toni both nodded.

"Then what I'd really like to do," whispered Petra, "is sit down and *talk* to him. Shake the cold, hard truth out of him."

Wouldn't we all? Suzanne thought.

The church's double doors swung open with a loud *clunk* as George Draper, the town's leading (and only) funeral director, entered and then marched slowly down the center aisle. He was tall and storklike with a sad countenance, as though *he* was one of the bereaved parties. Draper was wearing one of his typical sedate black funeral suits, though Suzanne had once seen him at a Jaycees' event, wearing the same suit and dancing a wild merengue.

Draper stopped, turned, and made a subtle hand ges-ture. Then the men carrying the casket entered the church and followed slowly down the aisle behind him. Topped with a spray of white roses and gladiolas, the casket was a creamy off-white that reminded Suzanne of the ivory keys on an old piano.

Sheriff Doogie was one of the pallbearers; so was Mayor

Mobley. They struggled their way down the aisle, eyes bulging, suits almost bursting at the seams from their effort. Suzanne wondered if the current generation might be getting a little old for this sort of thing. Maybe let some younger fellows do the heavy lifting, so to speak.

Then Reverend Strait came out to stand at the altar, looking dapper and handsome with his slicked-back white hair, regal bearing, and dark suit.

There were prayers, testimonials, more prayers, and songs. Everyone who spoke referred to the funeral as a celebration of Hannah's life. But Suzanne knew it was really all about mourning her death. Having buried Walter not that long ago, she understood the harsh truth. That death is an inevitable part of life. You can celebrate death, rail against it, or fear it. But sooner or later, death was going to come calling for everyone.

Petra sobbed openly as the final hymn, Sarah McLachlan's "I Will Remember You," rang through the church. Toni put an arm around her, while Suzanne took her hand and squeezed it.

And then the service was over. Everyone hurried out of the church, looking sad-eyed but a little anxious to resume their everyday lives. Because that's what you did. You simply got on with things.

"We're heading right back to the Cackleberry Club," Toni told Suzanne out on the front steps. "Petra's positive we've got a line waiting at the door."

Suzanne glanced around. "Some of these folks will turn up there, I suspect."

"I think so, too," said Petra, sniffling. "You coming with us?"

Suzanne thought for a moment. "In a little while. I've got a couple of things I need to take care of first." She'd just noticed Gene Gandle standing across the street, snapping pictures like crazy. The nerve of him.

As Suzanne pushed her way through the crowd, she was suddenly buttonholed by Bruce Winthrop.

"Suzanne," Winthrop said. He looked sorrowful but well turned out in a charcoal gray suit. "You were right. I met with Sheriff Doogie and told him about the encounter I had with Ricky Wilcox."

"I think that's smart," said Suzanne. "Doogie needs all the information he can get. Then he can analyze it, ask the tough questions, and hopefully move forward."

"We can only hope," said Winthrop. He ducked his head and added, "And thank you for all your help."

"Thanks for your faith in me, Bruce, but I haven't really done that much."

Winthrop gazed at her, his eyes filled with kindness and concern. "Ah, whether you know it or not, Suzanne, you serve as a kind of sounding board for Sheriff Doogie. You're his moral compass. He trusts you and I know he always appreciates your input."

"Really? You think so?" Suzanne knew that Doogie would sooner spit a rat than acknowledge her help.

Winthrop looked sideways and said, "Speak of the devil . . ."

They both glanced across the street where Doogie was striding briskly toward his cruiser. He was parked directly across one of the neighbor's driveways, blocking it completely. But nobody had come out to yell at him or tell him to move his car. Or even leave a nasty note.

Suzanne put a hand on Winthrop's forearm. "Excuse me. I want to have a word with Doogie."

Winthrop nodded as Suzanne dashed across the street.

"Doogie," she called, holding up a hand.

Doogie saw her but chose to ignore her. He unlocked the door to his cruiser and yanked it open.

Suzanne caught up to him just as he'd settled his bulk into the driver's seat and turned over his engine.

Doogie looked up at her and said, "Ah jeez, and I was this close to a clean getaway."

"I'm sorry," said Suzanne. "I know this has been a rough day for you. For all of us, really."

Doogie's radio suddenly burped. He grabbed the handset and said, "What?" There was a burst of static and a few garbled words. "Write him a ticket, for cripes' sake," he snarled. "You know what to do." He hung up his radio and turned back to Suzanne. "Now what?"

"I just happened to be at the Prairie Star Casino last night."

Doogie's wooden stare morphed into one of suspicion. "Wait a minute, run that by me again. You just *happened* to be at the casino last night?" He clenched his jaw as if fighting for control. "Please don't tell me this sudden gambling foray of yours had something to do with the casino chip you turned over to me yesterday afternoon."

"It was related to the casino chip, yes," Suzanne admitted.

Doogie exploded. "Gosh dang it, Suzanne! Didn't I tell you to leave the investigating to me?"

"Believe me," said Suzanne. "You're going to want to hear this." She saw the fury in his eyes, found it unnerving, and stumbled with her words. "The thing is, I . . . well, we . . . Toni was with me . . . we saw Darrel Fuhrman playing blackjack there."

"Playing blackjack," Doogie repeated.

"That's right."

"You've got to learn to mind your own business, Suzanne. Leave the investigating to the professionals."

Now it was Suzanne's turn to push back. "Wait a minute, bucko. You're the one who *told* me about Fuhrman. You're the one who let the cat out of the bag!"

Doogie's face turned pink, then seemed to bloom bright red. "Well, let's just stuff that pussycat back in the sack for now, okay?" And with that he hit the accelerator, and rocketed away.

"You're welcome," Suzanne called after him. "Glad you can use the new information."

SUZANNE was headed for the Cackleberry Club when she suddenly hooked a right, sped down Catawba Parkway, and caught up with the tail end of the slow-moving funeral cortege. She put her lights on and followed the last car in the procession up the bumpy, twisted road to Memorial Cemetery.

It wasn't Suzanne's idea of a bucolic resting place. For one thing, the cemetery always looked old and decrepit. There were dozens of ancient, half-felled trees hanging over rows of rounded stone tablets that had been so battered and bruised by the elements that they reminded her of rotted teeth. A kneeling stone angel, its right wing broken off and its sorrowful face pitted with age, added to the overall spookiness of the place.

Pulling her car off the road and onto the grass, Suzanne climbed out and watched the graveside services from a safe distance. Then, when the final prayers had been uttered, when all the Venable relatives had scattered, she ambled over to Jack, who was left standing there alone.

He was staring fixedly at Hannah's coffin, jaw tensed, as if he was grinding his teeth. He didn't seem to be aware of Suzanne's presence next to him until she said, "Jack."

Venable jumped as if a banshee had just materialized from the nearby woods and dropped a cold hand on his shoulder.

"What? Jeez!" he cried, startled as he clapped a hand to his heart. "I didn't see you there, Suzanne. Wow, you scared the crap out of me." He shook his head, still looking nervous and unsettled. Then he remembered his manners. "Thank you for coming to Hannah's funeral . . . and to the graveside service."

"I came out of respect to Hannah," said Suzanne. "And because I was curious as to how you're holding up."

"How do you *think* I'm holding up?" he rasped.

"Why don't you tell me?" said Suzanne.

"You still believe that I killed her, don't you? Set fire to that building so she'd be out of my life."

"You not only sound angry, you make it sound as if you had it all neatly planned out."

Venable hunched his shoulders as if to ward off a blow. "No. Of course I didn't! Because I didn't *do* anything." His almost nonexistent upper lip made an appearance and curled outward. "You've been putting a nasty bug in Sheriff Doogie's ear, haven't you? Or maybe he put a bug in your ear. I understand the two of you are thick as thieves."

"And yet you sold Hannah's ring," Suzanne said softly.

"I told you I made a mistake," said Venable. "A terrible mistake." He looked like he wanted to say more; instead he staggered across the grass, placed both hands on Hannah's coffin, and sank to his knees.

"I'm sorry," he sobbed. "I'm so sorry."

Suzanne watched Jack Venable express his sorrow without a single touch of emotion on her part. She decided that Venable was either extremely grief-stricken or a very accomplished actor.

In any case, she left him there, his knees pressed into the freshly turned earth, weeping uncontrollably, possibly trying to reconcile his own past actions.

"WHERE did you run off to?" Petra asked as Suzanne slid in the back door, her trusty cardboard box in hand. "Oh, and I see you brought your little owl along."

"Wherever I go, he goes," said Suzanne. "We're a team."

"And where did you go?" asked Toni. She was standing

at the butcher-block table, deftly slicing a stick of butter into individual little pats.

"Cemetery," said Suzanne. She set her box down, grabbed a clean apron off a peg, and draped it around her neck. There were a dozen cars parked out front and she was anxious to pitch in and help.

"I expect you were taking one more run at Jack Venable?" said Petra. She was standing at the stove, stirring a pan of golden, caramelized sauce. When it was to her liking, she dumped in a dozen precooked breakfast sausages and stirred it all up together.

"Yes, I tried to get in one last wheedle," said Suzanne. "And, pray tell, what is it you're making there?"

"Sweet and spicy glazed sausages," said Petra. "It's just a quick trick to get things moving."

"You should have seen her make that sauce," said Toni. "Like alchemy. She mixed hot and sweet mustard with a jar of orange marmalade."

"Sounds wonderful," said Suzanne. "So that's our today's special?"

"That and baked apple pancakes," said Petra. "Along with scrambled eggs, corn muffins, tomato basil soup, and crab salad, which you can either have as a sandwich or tucked inside a tulip tomato. We're serving a single menu today, a sort of brunch menu, seeing as how we got such a late start."

"Works for me," said Suzanne.

The door between the kitchen and café opened quietly and Kit slid in. "I delivered that order to table six like you asked," she told Petra.

"Thank you, dear," said Petra. "Now if you could run into the cooler and grab me another dozen eggs?"

"Sure thing," said Kit, but she sounded tired and listless. Not her usual perky self.

Suzanne caught Kit's arm as she went by. "How are you doing?" she asked. "How's Ricky doing?"

"I'm okay, I guess," said Kit. "Ricky's shaking in his boots."

Petra turned and frowned. "Now what?"

"Doogie wants to question him again," said Kit. "Something about an argument over pesticide?"

"Pesticide?" said Toni. "What's that about?"

"Kit," said Suzanne, "you don't look so good."

"I don't feel very good," said Kit. She really did look pale and shaky.

"Is it the baby?" Toni asked, suddenly concerned.

If Kit's pregnancy was bothering her, Suzanne didn't want to take any chances. "Maybe you should go home," she suggested.

"I hate to do that," said Kit. "I don't want to leave you guys in the lurch."

"We're always in the lurch," Petra muttered.

"Go home and rest," said Suzanne. "Really."

"Put your feet up," said Toni.

"Only if you're sure it's okay," said Kit.

"We're sure," said Suzanne.

"Thank you," said Kit. "But I promise you ladies that I'll be back here Friday night for the dinner theater. I know you're going to be incredibly busy and I know you're counting on me to help serve."

"Bless you, sweetheart," said Petra. "We'd appreciate that."

"The dinner theater," said Suzanne, looking a little startled. "I almost forgot. We're having a run-through tonight—a rehearsal."

"That's right," said Toni. "So nobody break a leg!"

CHAPTER 20

PETRA leaned backward, grabbed a tin of muffins from the oven as her right hand stirred a kettle of tomato basil soup. Then she set down her spoon, whirled again, and seemed to lose her balance for a split second. That's all it took for the hot tin of muffins to crash to the floor.

"Oh shizzle!" she cried.

"What?" said Suzanne, leaning through the pass-through from the café side. "Oh." She rushed into the kitchen to see if she could be of assistance.

"Five-second rule?" she asked Petra. Everyone knew the five-second rule: if you could snatch dropped food off the kitchen floor within five seconds' time, it was okay to eat or serve.

But Petra was shaking her head. "Afraid not. I worry that the state health board would swoop in and take our restaurant license away."

"Crumbs for the birds then," said Suzanne. "Or maybe my momma owl."

"If she's still out there."

"She's out there, all right," said Suzanne. "I heard her hooting away when I drove in this morning. I think she's just waiting for the right time to put in an appearance."

"Or for you to adopt her baby so she can be carefree and single again," said Toni, popping into the kitchen to see what all the fuss was about. Then, when she saw the ruined muffins scattered on the floor, she grabbed a broom and dustpan and set to work.

"Clumsy of me," Petra fretted. "I guess I'm still rattled from the funeral."

"You know what's really wrong with you?" said Toni.

"No," said Petra. "But I'm sure you're going to tell me."

"You're suffering from apocalyptaphobia," said Toni.

"That's an awfully big word to come from such a little woman," said Suzanne. "What does it mean exactly?"

"It's like end-of-the-world syndrome," said Toni. "Fear of zombies and nuclear war and the apocalypse."

"Nuts," said Petra. "I don't give a second thought to any of that doom and gloom nonsense. I'm more concerned with practical issues. Like will my cheese soufflé fall and go splat, or will we receive our shipment of Jade Sapphire cashmere yarn. Or, how about this . . . do I dare wear a bathing suit to Flo Miller's end-of-summer party that I've just been invited to?"

"A pool party?" said Suzanne.

"Yes," said Petra. "And of course I forgot my workout at the gym. I mean, that's four years in a row now."

"Are you gonna wear a bikini or a tankini?" asked Toni.

Petra stared at Toni as if she were spouting a foreign language.

"Ho!" said Toni. "I bet you don't even know what a tankini is."

"Okay, so I'm not up on your hot fashion lingo," said Petra. "But a tankini doesn't sound good. It sounds like it'd be clingy and nasty and reveal way too much of my love handles."

"If the shoe fits," said Toni.

"It's not my feet I'm worried about."

THE big luncheon rush never did materialize. There was just a gentle trickle of customers from around eleven in the morning until two in the afternoon. So by early afternoon, with customers finishing their dessert or lingering over coffee, Suzanne, Toni, and Petra were starting to relax. And talk about the upcoming Logan County Fair, which kicked off tomorrow night with a big parade through downtown Kindred.

"What I really love," said Toni, "are all the rides on the midway. The Tilt-a-Whirl and the Mad Mouse coaster. Even the Tunnel of Love." She winked at Suzanne.

"Speaking of rides," said Petra, focusing on Suzanne, "did you ever decide if you're going to enter your horse in the barrel racing competition?"

Suzanne was hesitant. "I *think* I am, but I'm going to work Mocha one last time as soon as I can get out of here. I'll see how it goes and make my final decision then."

"I've still got to decide about that pie baking contest," said Petra. "The fair officials are requesting that all food entries—jams and jellies, cakes, pies, cookies, and bars—be brought in tomorrow afternoon." She drummed her fingers on the counter. "So what do you guys think?"

"Nobody can hold a candle to your rhubarb pie," said Suzanne.

"Or your lemon meringue," said Toni. "So I think you should go for it. I love the idea of a big purple ribbon hanging on the wall of the Cackleberry Club."

"I think maybe I will enter a pie," Petra said slowly. "Or maybe my banana bread. But I'll come in real early tomorrow morning and do my baking, so everything's just fresh from the oven."

Suzanne nodded. "Atta girl."

Toni picked up a frosted chocolate brownie and took a big bite. "Jeez, you guys, if Suzanne rides in the rodeo and Petra enters the baking competition, I'm gonna be the odd gal out." She sniffed. "Kind of makes me feel like a big fat zero."

"Wait a minute," said Suzanne. "Didn't you tell me that Junior was entering his beer in the craft beer competition?"

Toni shrugged. "Yeah, I guess. So what?"

"Maybe you could be Miss Hubba Bubba Beer," said Petra.

Toni looked askance at that suggestion. "I'm not sure that counts as actually participating."

"What if you were the brand ambassador?" said Suzanne.

Toni smiled. "Brand ambassador. I like the sound of that. Kind of like the Kardashians for that weight-loss crap or Diddy for his vodka?"

"Uh . . . yeah," said Suzanne. "Something along that line."

Toni was clearly warming up to the idea. "That could be a lot of fun. I'm gonna give Junior a call right now."

MID-AFTERNOON, Suzanne slipped out of the Cackleberry Club and drove on the narrow, packed dirt road to the farm across the way. The sun glowed bright and warm in the western sky, and the cornstalks that rustled softly in the breeze were a good six feet high. In another few weeks they would be golden and ripe for harvesting.

Suzanne wasted little time in saddling Mocha, and then rode him out across the farmyard to a newly mown alfalfa field. Though there weren't any barrels set up, she imagined invisible barrels. She practiced hurry-up starts; quick, intricate turns; and lead changes as they spun in tight circles. After half an hour's work she felt good. Felt a renewed confidence in her riding ability and the adeptness of her horse.

So yes, Suzanne told herself. *I'm pretty sure the answer is yes. I'm going to burn some sage, cross my fingers, figure out the feng shui, and enter him on Friday.*

Back at the barn, Suzanne gave Mocha a quick rubdown and served up an extra ration of oats for both him and Grommet. Then she was off for home to grab Baxter and take him to his appointment at the vet. He'd been shaking his head the last two days and she suspected there might be an ear infection brewing. Baxter, who was growing gray in the muzzle, was her sweetheart, her one, final connection to Walter. So she wasn't about to take any chances.

BAXTER laid his furry head in Suzanne's lap and rolled soft, expressive brown eyes at her. He let out a low *woof* that started in the back of his throat and vibrated all the way down to the tip of his tail. Then he threw a commiserating glance at the fluffy white poodle that occupied the chair next to them. Baxter was not one bit happy about being at the Paws and Claws Veterinary Clinic and he didn't care who knew it.

Suzanne stroked Baxter's graying muzzle, then leaned forward and gave him a kiss. "Five minutes," she promised. "Let the doctor take one quick peek inside your ears, prescribe a tube of medicine, and then we're outta here."

Baxter, still hoping to elude the veterinarian's evil clutches, scrambled to his feet, tugged at his leash, and gazed anxiously toward the door.

"No," Suzanne told him. "Nice try, but not yet."

Helene, the receptionist, glanced over the top of her desk and said, "It'll just be a couple of minutes. Dr. Sievers is finishing up with a minor surgery."

"You see?" Suzanne told Baxter. "Nothing to worry about."

But Baxter was worried. His tail was down and his eyes

darted back and forth. He tilted his muzzle upward, gave a sniff, and then tugged even harder on the leash.

"C'mon, Bax," said Suzanne. "Take it easy." Truth be known, she was anxious to get going, too. She was due back at the Cackleberry Club at seven for the rehearsal. And she'd promised to honcho things as well as help Petra with the refreshments.

Now the poodle sitting next to them was tugging at his leash, too.

Suzanne stood up, just as Helene said, "Why don't you go into exam room two. Your dog might be more comfortable waiting in there."

"Thank you," said Suzanne.

She walked Baxter over to the door that had the number two on it, pushed it open, and then had to physically pull Baxter in.

"What's with you?" she asked. "You're not usually like this." She sat down on a chair that was positioned right next to a long metal exam table. She figured if she relaxed, Baxter might follow suit.

He did not.

Instead, he walked to the opposite door, which led into the back room of the veterinary clinic, and pawed at it. Then he lay down, sniffed, and came back to her.

Suzanne knew he was trying to tell her something, she just wasn't sure what it was. She spoke limited canine and Baxter's lexicon of English ran more to phrases such as Food, Walk, Out, and Treat. Although Ride and Bed were in there, too.

"What is it, big guy?" Suzanne put her hands on either side of Baxter's head and gazed at him. And that's when she smelled something funny.

Chemicals from the back room?

Suzanne sniffed expectantly. No, that wasn't quite it.

Baxter let out a low, anxious whine.

Probably just burning coffee. Sure, that has to be it.

Baxter's soulful eyes locked on to hers.

Wait a minute, Suzanne thought, startled. *Burning coffee? That's what I thought I smelled when I was at Root 66. That was right before . . .*

Her eyes traveled around the room.

A tiny, diaphanous tendril of smoke seemed to waft from beneath the door.

No, it couldn't be. I must be imagining things.

But when another puff of smoke seemed to seep under the door, Suzanne sprang to attention.

But what if . . . ?

She flew across the exam room and yanked open the door that led to the back office. Smoke billowed up, causing her to choke abruptly and her eyes to burn fiercely.

"Fire!" Suzanne yelled, even as her brain coughed up the thought, *Another fire?* She felt awkward, self-conscious, and terrified all at the same time. Like she'd been caught inside some weird kind of time loop. A déjà vu of sorts.

She stared into the smoke again and suddenly saw Dr. Sievers rush toward her. Cradled in his arms was a basset hound with one bandaged foot.

"Out the front door!" Dr. Sievers ordered. "Everybody out."

As Suzanne, Baxter, Helene, and the lady with the white poodle scrambled out into the street, Dr. Sievers stopped at the front desk, shifted the dog in his arms, and hastily dialed 911. Once he'd tersely informed the dispatcher about the fire, he ran out the door, too.

Two minutes later the fire department showed up with a roar of engines and clatter of equipment. Half of the firemen rushed into the building, while the other half of the team remained outside, connecting hoses, quickly laying out equipment.

Suzanne glanced about as people ran out of adjacent buildings to see what was going on. The little white poodle was shaking like crazy. Interestingly, Suzanne was not. She just felt a cold, white-hot rage for whoever had caused this mess.

"Did everyone get out okay?" she asked Dr. Sievers. "No pets left behind?"

"Everyone's fine," he said, still holding the dog.

Then Doogie's cruiser came careening down the street, siren blaring and light bar flashing.

Just as he sprang rather inelegantly from his car, Fire Chief Finley appeared in the door of the clinic and announced that the excitement was over.

"What the heck?" cried Doogie. He charged past Suzanne and Baxter, bumping her hard with his shoulder as he rushed up to talk with Fire Chief Finley. Finley, a short, stocky man in his early fifties, wearing an asbestos coat and a fire hat with an emblem on the front of it, was holding a hand up, trying to calm the gathering crowd.

"Go back to work," Finley told the inquisitive group. "It's over, just a scare, that's all. Nothing to worry about."

To Suzanne it felt like more than just a scare. It seemed like an ominous coincidence.

"What happened?" asked Doogie, hastening up the two front steps to confront Chief Finley. Suzanne also wanted to know what had happened, so she and Baxter pressed forward, too.

"Aw, somebody set a heap of rags on fire and then stuck them inside the back door of the vet's office," said Finley. His eyes were like hard blue marbles and had little puffy bags beneath them. Like little pink pillows.

"You think it was a prank?" said Doogie.

"Possibly," said Finley. "Probably."

"It didn't feel like a prank," said Suzanne.

Both men turned to look at her, startled to find her standing right there, boldly listening in on their conversation.

"You were in there?" Doogie asked.

Suzanne nodded. "Yes, with Baxter here." At hearing his name, Baxter gave an acknowledging tail wag.

"Hmm," said Doogie. He was looking at Baxter, but Suzanne could see the wheels turning in his brain.

"Doesn't this seem like a strange coincidence?" she asked. "In light of the fire at the County Services Bureau?"

"If I thought every fire we dealt with was connected to the one before it," Chief Finley said in a slightly condescending tone, "we'd constantly be chasing our tails."

"Still," said Doogie, "Suzanne might have a point."

"Are those arson investigators still in town?" she asked.

Doogie and Finley both shook their heads. "No," they said in unison.

"Too bad," said Suzanne. "So . . . you really do know how the fire started?"

"Like I just said," said Finley, "as *you* were listening in . . . somebody doused a ball of rags with gasoline and jammed it in the back door. Set it on fire."

"That sounds like more than just mischief," said Suzanne. "It sounds like arson."

Finley gave her a wide, mirthless smile. "Why don't you let me worry about that, okay?"

"Sure," said Suzanne, stepping back and pulling Baxter with her. "No problem." Out of the corner of her eye, she'd just seen a familiar car pull up. A blue BMW. It was Sam. How he'd heard about the fire, she had no clue.

Sam spotted her and pushed his way through a crowd that never really had dispersed. "What are you doing here?" he demanded. "Are you all right?"

"I'm fine," said Suzanne. "How did you find out about this fire so fast?"

"I was standing outside in the ambulance bay at the hospital," said Sam. "Shooting the breeze with Dick Sparrow, one of the paramedics, when the call came over the radio. But I didn't know *you* were here."

"In other words," said Suzanne, "you came by to gawk." It was getting more and more difficult to remain anonymous, she decided. To do her own brand of investigating. Of course, there was a flip side to that, too. It was sublimely comforting to have people you love worried and concerned about you.

"Yeah, something like that," muttered Sam. "But you haven't answered my question. What were you doing here?"

"Baxter," she said. "I think he might have an ear infection."

"I can take care of that," said Sam. He took her by the hand and led her away from the crowd. "Especially if it's a simple case of otitis media. I can stop by the clinic and grab a sample tube of antibiotics."

"Great," said Suzanne as Baxter gave Sam a dubious look.

"So what started the fire anyway?" Sam asked. "Was it wiring or something electrical?"

"Chief Finley found a ball of rags stuffed inside the back door," said Suzanne.

Sam's expression turned even more serious. "That sounds worrisome."

"My thoughts exactly," said Suzanne. "In fact, it feels a little like arson."

Sam gazed at her. He knew she'd been investigating, he knew she was right there in the middle of things.

"What I can't figure out," said Suzanne, "is why someone would try to set a fire here. I mean, the Paws and Claws Veterinary Clinic? Come on."

"Think about it, Suzanne," said Sam. "What is it you've been doing lately?"

"Um . . . attending a funeral, training my horse, and having dinner with you?"

"Noooo," said Sam. "You've been investigating. And everybody in town knows it."

Suzanne blinked, and then gave a nervous hiccup. "You

think somebody's trying to stop *me*?" The notion that she might suddenly be a target was so foreign to her that it made her stomach churn and her head throb.

"I wouldn't rule it out," said Sam.

"You're saying somebody was following me? Tailing me? And then tried to, um, scare me?"

"Scare you?" said Sam. "That's not exactly the word that comes to mind."

"But I don't *know* anything," Suzanne cried. "Really, I don't."

"Doesn't matter," said Sam. "If some crazy person, some whacked-out arsonist *thinks* you do, then you're clearly in his sights."

"Oh dear," said Suzanne.

"Hey," Sam said as he circled his arms around her and pulled her close. "Be careful, but don't let it prey on your mind, okay? Because I intend to take very good care of you."

CHAPTER 21

PETRA stood in the middle of the kitchen, a pan of lemon bars in her hand. "What?" she said, gaping at Suzanne, her eyes growing bigger by the moment. "The *vet* clinic?"

It was seven o'clock in the evening at the Cackleberry Club, and the actors were due to show up any minute for their big rehearsal. Suzanne had just stammered her way through her story, telling Toni and Petra about the nasty fire at the Paws and Claws clinic. And, just as she had feared, they were clearly knocked for a loop.

"Jeez," said Toni. "Another fire? That's kind of an odd coincidence, wouldn't you say?"

"More than a coincidence," said Petra. "It's a warning."

"That's what Sam thought, too," said Suzanne. "That somebody was worried about me investigating. Sam didn't even want me to come here tonight, except for the fact that he's in the play so he'll be here to keep an eye on me."

"Now why would poor Sam be worried at all?" said

Petra. "Since you've only been dashing all over town, keeping company with Kindred's most unsavory characters."

"Really?" said Toni. "Unsavory?" Now she was even more interested.

"First Suzanne paid a visit to that awful pawn shop," Petra said accusingly. "And then the two of you went carousing off to that casino." She dropped the word "casino" like she was referring to a pile of manure.

"But not the tattoo shop," Suzanne said, trying to inject a spot of humor and diffuse the tension.

"I'm sure you'll get there eventually," said Petra.

Toni nudged Suzanne with an elbow. "If you go, let me know, okay? I'm thinking of getting a yellow rose on my . . ."

"But we're *not* going to go there, are we?" said Petra. "In fact, we're not going to talk about this anymore."

"Sure," said Toni. She winked at Suzanne, then grabbed a stack of plates, ready to carry them out into the café. When she got halfway through the door, she called back, "Hang on to your hats, ladies, here comes our illustrious troupe of actors."

IT was a group of ten actors that came tumbling through the door, ready to recite their lines, figure out their marks, and do a final rehearsal of *Blithe Spirit.*

Connie Halpern, the executive director of the Kindred Community Players, greeted Suzanne and Toni with over-the-top enthusiasm.

"You're not going to believe this," said Connie, "but we're completely sold out! All fifty tickets for the dinner theater."

"We thought that might happen," said Suzanne. Actually she'd known about it for a week.

"Which is why we're gearing up for an onslaught," laughed Toni.

"This is going to be a grand experiment," Connie continued. "And we're just so delighted that you agreed to host us. We were going to present our play in a church basement, but that's really not a dinner theater atmosphere."

"Too reminiscent of pancake breakfasts and booyah suppers," said Toni.

Connie clapped her hands at her group. "Okay now, cast, we've got to decide the placement for our main set. And figure out entrances and exits."

All the actors gathered around. Sam was there, of course, since he was playing the role of a doctor. And Carmen Copeland, their prickly local author, was playing the role of Madame Arcati, the medium.

Suzanne gestured toward the far end of the café. "We figured you should probably do all your staging down at that end. We can hang a curtain there and you can use the Book Nook and Knitting Nest for dressing rooms and makeup. You can pop in and out as your script demands, which means you won't have to contend with us running in and out of the kitchen while we serve a three-course dinner."

"Perfect," said Connie.

Sam sidled up to Suzanne and gave her a quick kiss. "You doing okay?" he asked.

"Never better," she said.

"You're being awfully flippant," said Sam. "In light of today's events." He gave her a slightly stern, listen-to-your-doctor type of gaze. "I want you to be extra careful."

She smiled back at him, feeling an intense flutter in her heart for her handsome boyfriend. And his willingness to look out for her. "I promise I will."

The actors broke up into tight little groups then, discussing their roles, running their lines, gesturing to one another, and discussing how each actor or set of actors would negotiate their entrances and exits.

Carmen, never a wallflower, always pushing her fashion

quota to the max, was poised near the Book Nook, reciting her lines loudly to anyone who would listen. Dressed in skintight leggings and a leopard-print tunic top, she also wore a matching turban that was held in place with an enormous, glittery rhinestone pin.

"Holy baloney," Toni muttered to Suzanne. "Did Carmen come for the rehearsal or is she here to tell our fortune?"

Carmen overheard Toni's remark and took umbrage. "I heard that. And, for your information, my head wrap happens to be a very expensive Saint Laurent scarf. One you might *never* be able to afford."

Toni snorted. "For your information," she replied, pivoting fast and wiggling her shapely backside, "I happen to be wearing a very expensive pair of Levi jeans. Ones you'll probably never *fit* into!"

"Uh-oh," said Suzanne, sensing a disaster in the making. She grabbed Toni by the arm and yanked her away. "You need to come in the kitchen and help Petra with the refreshments. I'm *positive* she needs you."

Toni was still grumping and sputtering as Suzanne spun her through the swinging door.

"Carmen better watch out," Toni threatened. "Somebody might just drop a *house* on top of her."

"Funny," said Petra, as she mixed diced apples into a bowl of chicken salad. "You mean like the Wicked . . ."

"Witch," said Toni. "Yeah, yeah, yeah."

As far as Suzanne could tell, the rehearsal went very well. The actors spoke their lines with a commanding presence, and the exits and entrances appeared flawless. So much so that she was starting to really look forward to Friday night's dinner theater. The Cackleberry Club had never undertaken anything this heroic, but if the dinner theater proved to be a success (and wasn't it already a hit with all the tickets sold?) this might pave the way for more dinner theaters to come.

At the end of an hour, Connie called a halt to the rehearsal. She praised her actors for their skill and commitment, and urged them to let her know if they needed any help with their costumes. Then she looked toward Suzanne, who was waiting expectantly, and said, "Suzanne? I understand you and your partners have been kind enough to prepare a delicious surprise for us?"

"Just a few goodies," said Suzanne, stepping aside to reveal the treat table they'd set up while the actors were busy rehearsing. "Some tea sandwiches, cookies, and brownies, as well as coffee and tea."

"Actors?" said Connie, holding up her hands to indicate applause.

There was a moment of enthusiastic applause for the food, and then everyone rushed for the table to help themselves.

"You were great," Suzanne told Sam. They were sitting at a table with two other actors. Sam was nibbling a chicken salad sandwich, while Suzanne sipped a cup of oolong tea.

Sam held up a tiny bit of sandwich. "This is so great. Acting always makes me hungry."

"How much acting have you really done?" Suzanne asked in a teasing voice.

"Enough."

"Oh really."

"Okay," said Sam. "Confession time. This is the first acting I've done since I played a mushroom in fourth grade."

"In a play about healthy food groups?" said Suzanne.

"Nah," said Sam, reaching for another sandwich. "*Alice in Wonderland.*"

Sam hung around, joking, kibitzing, keeping a watchful eye on Suzanne, until all the actors had departed and the place was once again spiffed up, ready for breakfast tomorrow.

"I thought I'd follow you home in my car," he told her. "Just to make sure you get there safely."

"Not to worry," said Toni, cutting in. "I'll take good care of our girl. I'll follow her home and all that."

"You're sure?" said Sam. He didn't look all that confident in Toni's protective skills.

"Sure. It's called the BFF Club," Toni explained. "We always look out for each other."

"Okay," Sam said, yawning. "But I want you guys to drive straight home. No stops for cherry drops or whatever they're called."

"Will do," said Suzanne.

But out in the parking lot, Suzanne had other ideas. "I'm dying to do a look-see on Jack Venable," she confessed to Toni.

"You think he's the one who set the fire today at the vet's office, don't you?"

"I don't know. But something about his involvement feels right."

Toni considered this. "Let's see . . . Jack Venable sets a fire at the County Services Bureau and kills Hannah so he can cavort around with a sleazy piece of fluff. Then he finds out you're hot on his trail, so he sets another fire to try to scare the poop out of you." She squeezed her eyes shut, thinking. Then they popped open and she said, "I don't know, it's so perverted and offbeat that it sounds kind of right to me."

"The thing is," said Suzanne, "what exactly can we do? Just drive over to Jack Venable's house for a reconnaissance mission?"

"We pretty much did that last night," said Toni.

Suzanne thought for a few moments. An idea was forming in her head and it was a doozy. "What if we actually went *inside* his house?"

Toni gazed at Suzanne as if she'd just suggested they smuggle their way into North Korea. "How on earth are we going to do that? Break a basement window and creepy-crawl our way in?"

"No," said Suzanne. "We can't do that because I'm fairly sure Jack Venable's at home tonight. In fact, I think his relatives are probably still hanging around. So . . . what if we used the old casserole ploy?"

Toni snapped her fingers. "Ha! You mean take one to his house."

"You got it," said Suzanne. Delivering a casserole after a death, dismemberment, graduation, or football victory was standard operating procedure in the Midwest. As long as said casserole contained oodles of noodles, bits of meat and cheese, and was bound together by a can of cream-of-something soup.

"You've got a casserole handy?" Toni asked.

"I just happen to have one at home in my freezer."

Toni grinned wickedly. "What are we waiting for?"

THEY drove to Suzanne's house, grabbed the casserole, then climbed into Suzanne's car. As they drove across town to Jack Venable's house, they were nervous but giddy. This was going to be a classic frontal assault, after all. Kind of like a two-man team storming Mount Everest without the use of supplemental oxygen.

"If you could have seen Venable this morning at the cemetery," said Suzanne, "you'd truly believe he'd just lost the love of his life."

"But you think he's a phony?" asked Toni. "That he's crying crocodile tears and making a bigger deal out of his grief than it really is?"

"The thought has crossed my mind," said Suzanne. "Several times."

When they pulled up in front of Venable's house, half a

dozen cars were parked in front and lights blazed brightly from every available window.

"Lit up like a Christmas tree," breathed Toni. "Excellent. We're not the only ones here."

"See, I told you," said Suzanne. "The relatives are still hanging around."

"Schmoozing and boozing," said Toni. "Probably a few neighbors here, too."

"Sure," said Suzanne. "At least the ones who still think he's innocent."

Solemnly carrying the casserole, as if it were a gift from the Magi, Suzanne and Toni waltzed up the front walk.

"Looks like Jack got his front window fixed," Toni muttered.

"I'm just glad he didn't call the police and have them check for fingerprints," said Suzanne. "Or footprints."

"Ditto," said Toni.

Getting inside Jack Venable's house was a snap. Suzanne and Toni didn't have to knock on the door or ring the bell or bluff their way past a bouncer and a velvet rope. Since the front door was standing wide open, they just sauntered in, cool as you please.

"Piece of cake," Suzanne whispered. They walked into a living room that was furnished with mission-style furniture and a large blue and gold Oriental rug. They smiled pleasantly as they blended in with the two dozen or so people who milled about. Because they were acquainted with a few of the neighbors, they were able to ingratiate themselves even more by saying hello and exchanging pleasantries.

A woman in a plum-colored suit noticed them and came over to greet them. "Aren't you ladies kind. Is that a casserole I see?"

"Yes, it is," said Suzanne, trying to look appropriately sad.

"Chicken with baby peas," said Toni. "Are you, uh, by any chance related to Jack?"

"I'm his sister Bernice," said the woman, with a slightly officious nod.

"We'll just take this into the kitchen and stash it in the refrigerator," said Suzanne. "So it stays nice and fresh."

"Be sure to help yourself in the dining room," said Bernice. "There's quite a lovely buffet."

"Will do," said Toni.

They ducked around a potted plant and eased their way through the dining room and into the kitchen, managing to avoid Jack Venable at all costs. The dining room table had been laid out with the good china and a generous buffet, but the kitchen was a complete jumble. The table was heaped with plastic storage containers containing bits of cakes, cookies, and bars. When they opened the refrigerator, it was jammed with bowls filled with fruit salad, platters of cold cuts, and at least five casseroles.

"Curses," chuckled Toni. "Somebody beat us to it."

"What we need to do," said Suzanne, wedging her casserole dish in among the others, "is get serious. Take a look around this place and see what we can see."

"What is it we're looking for again?" asked Toni.

"I'm not sure, but maybe we'll know it when we see it."

They stood quietly for a moment, surveying the kitchen. It was an old-fashioned place, homey and lovingly assembled. The appliances were very '70s-looking, but Hannah's décor of rosebud wallpaper, white lace curtains, stenciled cabinets, and hand-embroidered tea towels more than made up for it.

"This kitchen looks like Hannah," Toni said, with a kind of reverence in her voice. "With the hanging copper pots and plants and things. Oh, and look at that collection of ceramic angels on the windowsill." She walked over and touched one of the angels gently, as if she could divine some crucial information from it.

"This is heartbreaking," Suzanne whispered. "I feel like Hannah's essence is still here, though her physical self is gone forever."

"She's in a better place," Toni whispered back.

They opened drawers, peered in cupboards, and peeked behind a row of cookbooks.

"Anything?" said Toni.

"Nada," said Suzanne. "Zip, zero, zilch."

Then Toni pulled open a door, peered down into the darkness, and sniffed. "Basement. Think we should see what's down there? A dungeon perhaps?"

"Let's check it out," said Suzanne as they flipped on a light and descended the stairs.

Suzanne wasn't sure what they would find down there, but the furniture, wood-paneled walls, and distinctly masculine vibe weren't what she'd expected.

"Gack," said Toni, expressing her distaste as she looked around. "It's a man cave. Look at this place, all tricked out with a leather sofa, big-screen TV, and foosball table."

"And a bar," said Suzanne. "With lighted beer signs and beer steins, and bottles of scotch and tequila up the wazoo. Why do some guys feel the compulsion to create their own saloon?"

"My guess is they're trying to reclaim their lost youth," said Toni. "Get back into the mind-set of the good old frat-rat, kegger days." She curled a lip. "Junior would probably go ape over this place." The disgust was all too evident in her voice. "Only he'd probably have installed a stripper pole."

"Not for you, I hope!" said Suzanne, horrified.

"Good heavens, no," said Toni. "I'm not that kind of girl." She lifted a shoulder. "Although, back in the day . . ."

"C'mon, let's go back upstairs. There's nothing here."

Back in the kitchen, they looked around again. Baskets hung on the walls along with muffin tins and a couple of framed needlepoints.

"I'm afraid we might have struck out," said Suzanne. She was looking for something—anything—that would point to Jack Venable as either an angry husband or a killer with a motive.

Toni touched her hand to the knob of another door and tentatively pushed it open. She gave a low whistle. "Hey, take a look at this."

"What?" said Suzanne.

Toni eased the door open a little more. "Look at this little room. I think it must have been Hannah's home office. It's way too cute for Jack's taste."

Suzanne studied the room. It was windowless, cozy, and small, about ten feet by twelve feet. The wallpaper was a pale pink morning glory pattern, there was a small desk, a narrow bookcase, and next to it an old-fashioned wooden stand with a '70s-era Singer sewing machine on top.

"This must have functioned as her sewing room, too," said Suzanne.

"Hannah liked to sew?" said Toni.

"She was a quilter. That's how she and Petra first met."

They eased their way in and poked around.

"Look at this," said Toni, pointing to several little jars of colored paint. "She was a crafter, too. I bet she hand-painted some of those angels in the kitchen." She sniffled. "Kind of breaks my heart thinking about it."

But Suzanne had wasted no time in pulling open Hannah's desk drawers and riffling through them.

"Suzanne!" said Toni, a little taken aback. "Do you think we should really be rummaging through her desk? There might be personal papers in there."

"That's exactly what I'm hoping for," said Suzanne. She dug past bank statements, a savings and loan passbook, and a few letters, until her fingers touched a brown leather-bound book. She pulled the book out and looked at it.

"Whatcha got?" asked Toni.

"I think Hannah kept a diary," said Suzanne.

"Holy smokes, are we gonna read it?"

"We came this far, didn't we?"

Toni glanced around, a little wild-eyed. "We can't do it here. Somebody might come in and catch us. So . . . we have to smuggle it out."

"I'll stick it in my purse," said Suzanne. But when she opened her hobo bag the diary wouldn't quite fit.

"I know," said Toni, "I'll stick it down the front of my pants. It'll just look like I ate too much. I'm kind of like that anyway. If I gobble a couple of burgers my stomach pops out. Like a snake that swallowed a gopher."

Suzanne shoved the diary into Toni's hands. "Do it," she said. Then, "Let's get out of here!"

They made it through the dining room without being accosted or stopped by anyone, then through the living room. When they hit the front porch Toni was looking decidedly gleeful.

"What are you smiling about?" Suzanne asked. "We didn't exactly stage a heist at the National Archives."

"It's not that. I think one of the women sitting in the living room was that waitress from Hoobly's," Toni tittered. "You know . . . Marlys whatever."

Suzanne glanced back over her shoulder. "The one Jack's having an affair with? Are you sure about that?"

Toni nodded so rapidly she looked like a bobblehead doll. "Oh yeah. I'd recognize those blue hair extensions anywhere!"

IN the darkness and relative safety of her car, Suzanne paged through the diary.

"Is it Hannah's?" Toni asked.

"It most certainly is."

"Try to find the most recent entry," Toni urged. "Maybe that'll give us something to go on, some kind of clue."

Suzanne continued to page through the diary. Then she stopped, scanned a couple of pages, and said, "Oh dear Lord."

"What?" said Toni. "*What?*"

"Listen to this," said Suzanne. "And this is in Hannah's own handwriting. 'I don't know how long we can keep up this charade, Jack and I. He is so unhappy and uncaring, and nothing I say to him seems to get through.'"

"Whoa," said Toni. "What else?"

"She writes a lot more about being unhappy. About feeling unable to connect with Jack." Her eyes met Toni's. "This makes me so sad. That Hannah was this unhappy. She . . . she should have just left the bum. I would have."

"Like I left Junior," said Toni. She looked thoughtful. "Still . . . this diary's not exactly incriminating evidence. A lot of couples live their lives that way, just going through the motions. Look at me and Junior with our love-hate relationship."

Suzanne continued to page through the diary. She studied her most recent entry, blinked, and looked at it again as something seemed to click inside her brain.

Toni, sensing Suzanne had discovered something, said, "Now what?"

Suzanne cleared her throat and said, "There's an entry here that says, and I quote, 'Things have now gotten to the point where I definitely must talk to Chuck Hofferman.'"

"Huh?" said Toni, looking puzzled. "Who's he?"

"The county attorney."

"You think she was going to ask for his advice about a divorce?" said Toni.

"I don't know. Maybe."

"That's it?" said Toni. "That's all Hannah wrote? There's

nothing else, nothing that expounds upon what she was thinking?"

Suzanne closed the book with a snap. "That's where it ends."

"What do you think was nagging at Hannah?" said Toni. "Why did she want to talk to this guy Hofferman? Do you think it was about Jack?"

Suzanne could only shake her head.

CHAPTER 22

"YOU two girls are plumb crazy, you know that?" said Petra.

It was Thursday morning, Egg in a Biscuit Day at the Cackleberry Club. And Petra wore a look of supreme disapproval on her broad and usually kindhearted face.

"What are you talking about?" said Suzanne, feeling a little blip of uncertainty bubble up within her. Petra hardly ever got mad, but when she did—*kaboom!* It was like World War III had launched.

"Aw," said Toni, looking sheepish. "I told her about our little escapade last night. I fessed up about finding Hannah's diary."

"Now why would you go and do something like that?" Suzanne demanded. "When we do something really stupid and a little outside the law, why can't you keep your mouth shut like any normal criminal would?"

"Because I pried it out of her," said Petra. "Toni came skulking in this morning with such a guilty look on her face, I just knew she'd been up to no good. And that you were probably involved, too."

"Thanks so much for your vote of confidence," said Suzanne.

Petra shook her head, still muttering to herself. "And I suppose you forgot to bring along my sprigs of fresh rosemary, too. So I can bake a couple pans of rosemary cheese rolls."

"I brought the herbs," said Suzanne, setting a small basket on the counter. "I had to get up at the crack of dawn and fight off marauding insects, but I brought them."

"Good for you," said Petra, finally cracking a semblance of a smile. "At least *something's* going as planned."

"You're just cranky because you've committed to baking your pies today," said Toni.

"You're baking pies?" said Suzanne. "So you're for sure going to enter the fair?"

"Yes," said Petra. "And the entry forms are about driving me crazy. The pies I can manage, but the forms . . ." She grabbed a spatula and flipped over a dozen strips of turkey bacon that were sizzling in her frying pan.

"Let me handle the forms for you," Suzanne volunteered. "I don't mind being a paper geek. Besides, I have my own rodeo entry to do."

Petra looked up from the stove. "Really?"

"Sure, no problem," said Suzanne.

"You see?" said Toni. "No problem. Everything's simpatico."

Petra grabbed the basket of herbs. "You're not getting off that easy," she said. But a smile played at her lips.

Suzanne and Toni got busy in the café, delivering breakfasts, pouring refills on coffee, brewing a pot of Darjeeling tea.

"Do you think Doogie's gonna drop by today?" Toni

asked as she twirled past Suzanne, on her way to grabbing a sticky roll.

"Probably."

"Are you going to tell him about the diary?"

"I haven't decided yet."

"I heard that," Petra called from the other side of the pass-through.

"Okay," Suzanne called back. "I probably am."

TWENTY minutes later, with all of their customers munching away, Suzanne and Toni took their own quick coffee break.

Toni bit into a chocolate donut and, with a mischievous look on her face, said, "Do you think we should tell Petra about the woman we saw at Jack Venable's house last night?"

Petra, who'd been carefully rolling out her piecrust dough, glanced up, a look of intense curiosity on her face.

"Ah, now she's interested," observed Toni. "As opposed to ticked off."

Petra waggled her fingers. "Who was Jack Venable snuggled up with?"

"Not exactly snuggling," said Suzanne.

"Not yet," said Toni. "Since there were relatives hanging around. And a few neighbors."

"Okay, now you *have* to tell me," said Petra. "Was it that Marlys person?"

Toni nodded. "Yup."

"Why am I not surprised?" said Petra.

A few minutes later, Suzanne went to work on the chalkboard. Today's luncheon specials were a roast chicken

Reuben, citrus salad, pita pizza, and a chicken meatball sub sandwich. And since Petra was busy baking pies to enter in the fair, she was offering just one dessert today, something called Cake in a Mug.

When Toni had quizzed her about this, Petra just smiled and said, "Wait and see." So Suzanne guessed they'd all have to wait and see, even though Petra had told her the single-serving cake was available in chocolate, red velvet, and lemon.

Toni stood behind the counter, slicing a hunk of white cheddar cheese, assembling a cheese and bologna sandwich for a take-out order. When she had it wrapped, bagged, and tagged, she sauntered over to Suzanne and said, "There's a kind of parade down Main Street tonight in honor of the opening of the Logan County Fair. Are you going?"

"Sam mentioned something about it," said Suzanne. "So, yes. Probably." She glanced out the window toward the front parking lot and said, "Doogie just pulled in. He's early."

"Depends if he's here for breakfast or lunch," said Toni.

Turns out Doogie had really just popped in for coffee and a donut. And to grumble about Gene Gandle's article in today's *Bugle*.

"Did you see Gandle's story?" Doogie asked, shifting his bulk on the stool at the counter.

Suzanne shook her head. "Haven't read it yet. Is there a problem?" She figured there had to be since he was favoring her with a grumpy face.

Doogie did a quick glance over his shoulder. "It sure ain't complimentary to law enforcement, I can tell you that."

"Gene Gandle's a putz," said Suzanne. "And everybody in town knows it. I think the only reason Laura Benchley keeps him on at the paper is because he handles ad sales, too. I know he keeps pestering me with his deals, offering a quarter page for the price of an eighth page." She poured Doogie a steaming mug of coffee and placed two donuts on his plate, the kind he liked best, chocolate donuts with multicolored jimmies all over them.

Doogie snatched one up and took a bite, causing a mini flotilla of jimmies to course down the front of his shirt. "All those questions you asked Chief Finley yesterday, you almost gave the old fart a brain aneurysm."

"That's too bad," said Suzanne. "All I wanted were a couple of simple, straight-ahead answers. Which he could have easily provided, without acting like he was divulging classified CIA information."

"Sometimes pulling an answer out of Finley is like pulling taffy," Doogie chuckled.

"What's your take on the fire at the vet's office? Do you think it was just kids up to no good?"

Doogie took a long sip of coffee as he formulated his answer. Then he said, "I do think it might be connected to the fire last Friday. I think a lot of things are connected. But I'm still a little stumped as to how to pull all the pieces together." He took another sip of coffee and looked up at Suzanne. He seemed a little anxious, as if he was ready to divulge a nugget of important information.

"What?" she said.

"I discovered something a little strange," said Doogie. He reached into a glass bowl of toothpicks, grabbed one, and stuck it in the corner of his mouth.

Suzanne put her elbows on the counter and leaned forward, the better to be complicit.

"Chuck Hofferman," said Doogie. "You know him, the county attorney?"

"Yes," Suzanne said with a start. "He's a real fan of Petra's chicken chili." *And Hannah mentioned him in her diary!*

"Well Chuck was telling me that Hannah had scheduled a meeting with him for Monday morning."

"This being the Monday after the fire." Suzanne's heart was beating faster now.

"Correct."

Suzanne held up a hand. Now she knew she had to reveal her information. "Stop right there," she said.

"What?" said Doogie, looking puzzled.

"I also found out that Hannah was going to talk to him."

Doogie narrowed his eyes. "How would you know something like that? Did Hannah Venable mention something about a meeting to you or one of your cohorts?"

"She did in a manner of speaking." Suzanne gulped a deep breath and said, "Give me a minute." She ducked into the kitchen, grabbed the diary, and carried it out to Doogie.

When she set it on the counter in front of him, he said, "What the Sam Hill is this? Are you trying to nag me into joining your book of the month club again? I told you I don't read thrillers, only westerns. I'm a cowboy hat and sagebrush kind of guy."

"It's Hannah's diary," Suzanne told him. "That's how I knew she was planning to meet with Hofferman."

Doogie set a new land speed record for going from cranky to utterly astonished. "Where'd you get this?" he demanded as his hands closed around it.

"From her house last night."

"You *stole* it?"

"Nothing quite that dramatic," said Suzanne, flinching inwardly at her little white lie. "Toni and I took a casserole over and . . . uh . . . we kind of stumbled upon it. Appropriated it you might say. The critical thing is, Hannah actually wrote in her diary about needing to meet with Hofferman. It's one of the last entries. In fact, it's *the* last entry."

Doogie tapped the book with a stubby index finger. "Does she say what the meeting was supposed to be about?"

Suzanne shook her head. "No. Did Hofferman know what the meeting was all about?"

"He had no idea," said Doogie. "Hofferman just told me that Hannah called him a few days before the fire and said she had something important to discuss."

"I wonder what it was?" said Suzanne. And then, "Do you think that's the reason someone set her building on fire? That Hannah was privy to some sort of secret? She had some damaging information on someone?"

Doogie switched his toothpick from one side of his mouth to the other. "That's *exactly* what I think."

JUST as Suzanne was setting plates of meatball subs in front of two farmers dressed in bib overalls, Sam walked in. He stood in the doorway for a moment, looked around, and caught her eye. When she held up a finger, indicating she'd be with him in one second, Sam seated himself at the small table by the window and spread open his newspaper.

A few minutes later, as quick as was humanly possible, Suzanne hastened over to greet him.

"You should have told me you were coming in for lunch today," she said, sounding both flustered and excited. "I would have had something special waiting for you."

Sam winked at her. "I do have something special waiting for me. You."

"Dr. Hazelet, your table manners are awfully flirtatious," she scolded. But inwardly she was pleased. Thrilled, really.

"You ought to see my bedside manner," he said. "Oh, excuse me, you have."

Suzanne blushed fiercely and gave him a playful shoulder punch. *Please don't let anyone overhear this conversation*, she thought to herself. *Especially those two farmers over there, because then I will never, ever hear the end of it.*

"So what's good?" Sam asked. "I've got, like, thirty minutes, then I'm off to the hospital to attend a very boring committee meeting."

"I'll ask Petra to whip something up. Make it a surprise."

"That'd be great," said Sam.

"PETRA!" Suzanne cried once she was safely in the kitchen. "Sam's here!"

"That's nice," said Petra. She was busy cutting thin strips of pastry to top her rhubarb pie.

"What can we serve him that's really special?"

Petra straightened up and gazed at her. "Seems to me you're always fixing something special for that guy. A few nights ago it was filet mignon, last week it was veal Prince Orloff. I even gave you my aunt Edith's secret recipe for wine and morel sauce."

"Your point being?" said Suzanne.

"If you keep feeding him like he's dining out at the Four Seasons every night, then that's what he'll come to expect."

"You're training him," said Toni. "Like Pavlov's dog."

"Exactly," Petra laughed. "He'll come to expect a nifty combination of Martha Stewart and Boom Boom LaRue."

Suzanne could see some logic in this. She *had* been indulging Sam of late, with food, wine, appetizers, pancakes, and homemade fudge. "So you're saying I should tone it down a little. Hot dogs and beans one night, grilled cheese sandwiches another time. Make my meals a little more . . . casual."

"More Midwestern," said Toni. "Throw in a casserole or two. Wink wink."

"Toni's right," laughed Petra. She wiped her hands on her apron and glanced around the kitchen. "Tell you what, how about I fix the love of your life a nice bacon and egg panini? You think that would slide down okay?"

"That would be superlative!" said Suzanne.

"I guess I'm just a pushover for romance and love," said

Petra. Her eyes crinkled merrily. "Speaking of which, is there anything I should know about? Any foreseeable change of marital status on the horizon?"

"You'll know when I know," said Suzanne.

"Not the answer I was hoping for," said Petra, plopping a fat pat of butter in her sauté pan.

Me neither, thought Suzanne.

WHEN Suzanne delivered Sam's panini to his table, he whistled and said, "Wow, you made this?"

"It's basically Petra's recipe," said Suzanne. "But I helped."

"You're going to spoil me. You *are* spoiling me."

Good. Well, maybe not so good. Because I probably am.

Sam's hand thumped against the newspaper. "Did you get a chance to read the article Gene Gandle wrote about the County Services fire and the sheriff's ongoing investigation?"

"Not yet, but Doogie was in before and seemed pretty cranked up about it."

"He should be. Gandle seems to have taken it upon himself to be Kindred's very own muckraking journalist."

"Not what we need," said Suzanne. She lingered at his table, loving that he was enjoying his lunch, but worried that she *was* indulging him. "So, do we still have plans to go to the parade tonight?" she asked. "Because Toni was wondering." *And so am I.*

"Sure," said Sam, in between bites. "I'll stop by and pick you up. What time's good?"

"Seven?" said Suzanne.

Sam suddenly scrunched up his face. "Ooh."

"What's wrong? Too much pepper sauce?"

"No, there's just something I have to do. Would it be okay if I met you there?"

"Sure," said Suzanne, wondering what was so important. "Maybe . . . in front of the bakery?"

"You got it," said Sam.

SUZANNE was nibbling at a meatball and Toni was loading dirty dishes into the dishwasher when there was a knock at the back door.

"Open," called Petra.

"Can I come in?" asked a girl's voice.

"It's Kit," said Toni. "Yeah, come on in, honey."

Kit's blond head appeared in the doorway, and then she popped into the kitchen, looking cool and breezy in a pale green sundress. "Am I too early?" she asked.

"For what?" Toni asked, looking befuddled. "Lunch is over. And you weren't supposed to work today anyway."

"You're right on time," Petra told Kit. Then to Toni she said, "Kit volunteered to deliver my pies to the judging committee."

"That's it?" said Kit. "Just pies?"

"A rhubarb pie and a cherry pie," said Petra. "As well as a loaf of banana bread." She glanced at Suzanne. "You already filled out the entry forms?"

"Got them right here," said Suzanne. "Forged with your very own signature." She grabbed the forms from one of the kitchen shelves and handed them to Kit.

"It's really kind of you to do this," said Petra. "I appreciate it."

"Not a problem," said Kit. "You've all been so nice and supportive of me . . ." Her smile faltered and she suddenly seemed ready to dissolve into tears.

"What?" Petra asked in a gentle voice.

Kit shook her head. "It's nothing."

"Why don't you let me be the judge of that," said Petra.

"Aw . . . it's Ricky. You know he's still on Sheriff Doogie's suspect list."

"Along with quite a few others," said Suzanne. "I really don't think you should take it all that personally. Doogie's just doing his job. Following leads, eliminating suspects and all."

"Then I wish he'd hurry up and eliminate Ricky," put in Toni. "Seeing that he's Kit's fiancé and almost husband. And by the way, what's the status on Ricky shipping out?"

"He's still in a holding pattern," said Kit. "He can't go with his National Guard unit because he's been forbidden to leave town."

"I'm sure this whole mystery will be solved in a matter of days," said Suzanne.

"Really?" said Kit.

"You think?" said Toni.

"I do," said Suzanne. At least she *hoped* it would be. She hoped that Doogie would finally pull the voting booth lever. That he'd figure it all out and make an arrest. So everyone could get on with their lives.

"Okay," said Petra. She nestled her rhubarb pie into a cardboard box alongside her cherry pie and loaf of banana bread, and then covered it all with an embroidered tea towel. "Off it goes. Fingers crossed."

Kit gently set the entry forms on top. "I'll take everything right over to the Home Arts Building," she said.

"Careful," said Petra, as Kit picked up the box. She was hovering like a mother hen.

"I'll get the door for you," said Toni, doing a stutter step and lurching for the back door. But before she could get a hand on the knob, the door swung open and Junior appeared.

"I got it, I got it," said Junior, pulling the door wide open and stepping aside for Kit to pass. "Headed for the fair, huh? Yeah, I just dropped my stuff off, too." He sounded chirpy and upbeat. As if he didn't have a care in the world—which he probably didn't.

"You entered your homemade beer?" Toni asked as Junior stepped inside the kitchen. He was dressed in his summer duds today. Lighter, baggier denim jeans and a scruffy orange T-shirt that said Hot Stuff on the front of it. A pack of Camel cigarettes was rolled up in his right sleeve. When he shrugged his dark forelock off his face, he looked like a frighteningly bad reincarnation of James Dean.

"I just took a dozen bottles of Hubba Bubba beer over to the fairgrounds," Junior proclaimed. "For their craft beer competition." He grinned like a crazed jack-o'-lantern. "The judging's first thing tomorrow morning and I figure I'm gonna blow everyone's socks off. The judges have never tasted the likes of my brew."

"Looks like we'll be rooting for both you and Petra," said Toni.

"Ha!" said Junior, grinning at Petra. "How much you bet we *both* walk away with blue ribbons!"

"We'll see," Petra murmured.

"I got another sideline going, too," said Junior. "In fact I got me part of a booth in that new Merchandise Mart."

"The Merchandise Mart," said Petra. "Didn't that used to be the old Swine Building?"

"Yeah, well, they cleaned it up," said Junior. "Aired it out."

"By 'sideline' you're talking one of your harebrained schemes," said Toni. "Which means I'm a little afraid to ask for any details."

"Ask," said Petra. "The suspense is killing me."

Junior dug into the pocket of his jeans and pulled out a piece of tinfoil. He proceeded to unfold it, puff it out, and place it directly on top of his head.

"Stupid," said Toni. She was referring either to Junior or the ridiculous silver thing covering his head. Or both.

"Are you planning to serve popcorn in that thing?" asked

Petra. Junior's headgear looked like a cross between a poufy silver shower cap and a pan of already-popped Jiffy Pop.

Toni tried to snatch the contraption off his head, but Junior backed away. "Where'd you get that dumb thing anyway?" she asked.

"George Duffert is selling them," said Junior, reaching up to straighten it out. "His wife makes them and he heads up the sales and marketing team. They got a regular cottage industry going."

"They sound like a couple of crackpots," said Toni.

"What are your tinfoil hats for anyway?" asked Suzanne. Didn't a new product have to address a particular need? Wasn't that Marketing 101?

"They're basically all-purpose," said Junior, comfortable now that he was launching into his sales patois. "Protection against UV rays, gamma rays, meteor showers, sunspots, you name it."

"Wait a minute," said Suzanne. "Isn't George Duffert the guy who claims to have seen a whole bunch of UFOs?"

"He *did* see them!" exclaimed Junior. "Said there was a whole flotilla hovering over a wheat field outside of town. Just glowing in the night sky and sort of scoping things out."

"And now he's pawned this crap off on you," said Toni. "Well, whoop-de-doodle-do."

"That's no way to talk to a regional sales manager," huffed Junior.

"Regional sales manager of what?" asked Suzanne.

"Doomsday Incorporated," Junior declared proudly.

"Jeez, Junior," said Toni. "How can you be so stupid?"

"I'll have you know," said Junior, "that when I attended that automotive trade school over in Jessup my GPA was 3.0."

"Hah," scoffed Toni. "That was probably your blood alcohol!"

CHAPTER 23

SUZANNE wandered through the Book Nook and into her office, a copy of the *Bugle* tucked under her arm. It was three in the afternoon and she was debating whether she should unpack and shelve a newly delivered case of books or just veg out at her desk and read the paper.

Vegging won out. Of course, the mug of fresh-brewed chamomile tea she had in her hand didn't hurt, either.

Slouched in her leather desk chair, Suzanne breathed in deeply and smiled. It took a lot of work to keep the Cackleberry Club alive and thriving, but she wouldn't have it any other way. Yes, she was a stickler for fresh, locally sourced ingredients. But fresh cheeses, eggs, vegetables, and hormone-free meat just tasted better. And, of course, it was better for you.

Suzanne liked to tell her customers that the Cackleberry Club served comfort food that had been kicked up a couple of notches. Not just a cheese omelet, but an omelet topped with melted baby Swiss cheese and fresh-picked butter-fried morels. Not just fried chicken, but oven-baked chicken that had been slathered with Petra's herb and homemade bread crumb mix. Both she and Petra worked hard to keep everything fresh and organic. No preservatives, antibiotics, added BHT, or factory processing. In other words, they were sneaky gourmets.

Taking a sip of tea, Suzanne spread the newspaper on her desk and shook her head at the sensational headline: *Blaze Blasts Downtown, 1 Dead!*

One dead. No, it wasn't just one dead, she told herself. It was one wife, one friend, one sister, one cousin that was dead. Hannah Venable had been dearly loved by many people. As such, she deserved a far better mention than *1 Dead.*

Suzanne skimmed the article, aware that Gandle had tried to punch it up as hard as he could. The only place his story wavered was when it came to actually naming suspects. Obviously, Doogie couldn't come right out and say that Jack Venable, Ricky Wilcox, Marty Wolfson, and Darrel Fuhrman were all viable suspects. But Gandle had talked to people and cadged rumors from all over town, so he made some fairly broad hints.

Gandle had taken pictures, too. On the front page was a fairly dramatic black-and-white photo of the burning building, right at the height of the blaze. Suzanne turned to page three where the story continued and found two smaller photos. One of them, strangely enough, was a photo taken at Hope Church. The hearse was featured prominently in the shot, and in the background were the mourners, filing out of church.

She leaned forward, studying the picture, wondering idly if she'd be able to recognize anyone.

Turns out she could.

Besides herself, Toni, Petra, and Jenny Probst, she recognized a sea of familiar faces. As well as one singular face in the lower-right corner of the photo. It was Darrel Fuhrman. She'd almost swear to it.

"Hello, Darrel," she murmured. "What are you doing here?"

Suzanne pondered this question for a few moments and decided there were several possibilities. Fuhrman could be somehow related to Hannah, though that seemed a little farfetched. He could be a friend of Jack Venable's, or he could be a weird looky-loo, a funeral freak.

The final possibility was that Fuhrman had attended the funeral because he wanted to somehow remain involved with Hannah Venable right to the bitter end.

Which would point to what? To Fuhrman having set the fire? To Fuhrman having a beef against Hannah? Had Fuhrman set the fire and then felt regret over Hannah's death?

None of those thoughts were particularly pleasant. Plus it felt like time was slipping away. Suzanne knew that if Hannah's murder wasn't solved fairly soon, it could get put on the back burner and never be solved.

Suzanne took a sip of tea. Suddenly, what had tasted bright and sweet now tasted bitter and flat. She knew it wasn't really the tea that had changed, it was her frame of mind.

What to do? Suzanne wondered, tapping her fingers against the desk. She leaned back in her chair and let her eyes be drawn to one of Petra's needlepoints that hung on the wall.

The colorful needlepoint was just a simple quote. It said, *Fill your heart with what's important and be done with all the rest.*

Suzanne ruminated on that. What *was* important to her? Sam, of course. Solving this arson case. Getting justice for Hannah. And the Cackleberry Club and her friends.

She and Sam would figure out where they were going as time went on. But Hannah . . . that problem needed to be kicked into high gear. So maybe she should investigate Darrel Fuhrman a little more thoroughly. Which meant she probably had to have a sit-down with Chief Finley.

If he'll even talk to me, that is.

Suzanne popped out of her chair and scurried through the kitchen, where Toni and Petra were finishing up for the day.

"Are you taking off?" called Petra.

"You're leaving us?" asked Toni.

Suzanne snatched up her box and grabbed her handbag off a peg. "See you guys tonight at the parade," she called back over her shoulder just as the door whapped shut behind her.

CHIEF Mulford Finley wasn't one bit pleased to see Suzanne. Yet, sitting behind his wide expanse of desk, staring across at her, he put on a fairly good show.

"You're here about the fire," he said. It was a statement, not a question.

"In a way, yes," said Suzanne. "But I'm more interested in learning a few more details about a particular, um . . . shall we say, suspect?"

Finley reached for a fat black pen and centered it carefully, buying time. Suzanne waited patiently.

"Who might that be?" said Finley. Of course, he knew the answer.

"Darrel Fuhrman," said Suzanne. "I know you're aware that he's on Sheriff Doogie's short list. As far as suspects go."

"Fuhrman is no longer employed by this department," said Finley.

"That's right," Suzanne said. "And I'd like to know why."

"His personnel records are sealed."

Suzanne decided the pleasantries were over. "Gimme a break," she said. "I'm not trying to con you out of his social security number or get details on his pension fund. I just need a few simple answers."

Finley shifted in his chair, clearly uncomfortable. "Fuhrman was problematic."

"In what way?"

"Oh . . . attitude, attendance, a lot of small things that added up to him being a constant pain in the butt."

"Okay," said Suzanne. Now they were getting somewhere. "So he was fired."

"Let's just say we came to a mutual agreement," said Finley.

"Severance pay was involved," said Suzanne. She knew how it worked.

"Generous severance pay," said Finley.

Suzanne figured Finley had bought Fuhrman off so the man wouldn't come back at the department and launch a wrongful termination lawsuit. In the long run, it probably made sense.

"Do you think Fuhrman had problems outside of work?" Suzanne asked.

Finley lifted a hand. "Possibly."

"Do you think Fuhrman might have had a hand in last Friday's fire?"

"You're asking me if I think he maliciously set that fire," said Finley. His nose twitched and he made a face. "I've given that quite a bit of thought, as you might imagine, and, in the end, I'd have to say no. We're talking a Class A-1 felony since there was a related death. I never saw that in Fuhrman. That sort of uncontrollable rage."

Related death, Suzanne thought. Now Hannah was being referred to as a related death. The phrase wasn't just cringe-worthy, it made her nauseous.

Suzanne pressed ahead anyway. "But do you think Fuhrman had an unhealthy attitude concerning fires?"

Finley stared at her with the unblinking façade of an old turtle. "Are you asking me if Fuhrman is a pyromaniac?"

"Okay, yes. Let's lay it on the table. Is he a pyromaniac?"

"Again, I'd have to say no," said Finley. "Sheriff Doogie asked me that very same question and I told him probably not. Fuhrman resents authority, appears to have societal problems, and didn't get along all that well with the other men, but I've never seen a single clue that would point to that type of truly antisocial behavior. You have to understand that true pyromania is a type of impulse disorder. On a par with kleptomania or compulsive gambling."

"Gambling," said Suzanne. Was it just two nights ago that she and Toni had seen Fuhrman at the Prairie Star Casino? Yes, it was. Sitting at the blackjack table, looking angry, drinking, and throwing down chips.

"Well," said Finley. "Did I answer your question?"

Not really, Suzanne thought to herself. *But you sure fanned the flames.*

"Yes," she said, standing up to leave. "Thank you for your time."

SUZANNE was deep in thought when she left Chief Finley's office.

How interesting that pyromania and compulsive gambling reside on the same impulse disorder spectrum.

As she drove across town, heading for home, she wondered what else might be on that spectrum.

Baby steps toward becoming a sociopath?

She also wondered about the mind-set of someone who would deliberately set a fire. Were they frenzied or coolly in control? Were they arrogant about their crime or a trembling neophyte turned on by the prospect of creating a raging inferno?

So many questions, but not many answers. Yet.

The dogs were crazed to see her. Baxter administered sloppy, wet kisses while Scruff spun in tight circles, like a circus performer. When they finally calmed down, Suzanne poured each of them a heaping bowl of kibbles and gave them bowls of fresh, cold water. And then, because she was going to go out again for the evening, she snapped leashes on their collars and took them for a meandering fifteen-minute walk.

When Suzanne returned home, she changed into her favorite pair of blue jeans—the ones that made her thighs look skinny and her legs longer than they really were—and shrugged into a pink cotton sweater. She splashed water on her face, ran a brush through her hair, and added a dab of Dior pink lipstick.

A few minutes later, she dashed out the door. The parade was scheduled to start at seven and she had barely fifteen minutes to spare. She drove along Magnolia Street, turned at Lawndale, and coasted into downtown Kindred.

Of course, the Public Works Department had put up signs prohibiting any parking on Main Street. It hadn't occurred to Suzanne that parked vehicles would obstruct the view of the parade, so driving slowly, because there were hundreds of people milling around now, she had to circle back behind the bakery and nose into a tight parking space a good three blocks away.

I should have walked. It would have been simpler.

Suzanne rounded the corner, the bakery almost in sight, when she ran smack-dab into Toni and Junior.

"Hey, girlfriend!" said Toni, greeting her.

"Huzzah," said Junior. "Whither thou goest?"

Suzanne stopped dead in her tracks. "What?"

Toni did a quick eye roll. "Junior got wind that the next play the Kindred Community Players might put on is Shakespearean, and he's got a mind to audition."

Junior nodded. "Thine shalt not tarry."

"I'll tarry you," said Toni.

"Cometh, mine wench," said Junior.

"Have you seen Sam around?" Suzanne asked. "He was supposed to meet me in front of the bakery."

"I don't know," said Toni, glancing around. "There are so many people downtown tonight . . . oh, hey!" She pointed. "There he is."

Suzanne turned and saw Sam threading his way through the crowd. He saw her, raised a hand in greeting, and then he was right there, wrapping his arms tightly around her. "Sorry I'm late," he said.

"You're right on time," said Suzanne, smiling as her heart pitter-pattered. Yes, she'd just seen him at lunch, but gosh, that was almost seven whole hours ago. She needed her love fix.

"Hey there," Sam said, nodding to Toni and Junior.

"Howdy," said Toni.

"Huzzah, good sir," said Junior.

"Excuse me?" said Sam.

"I think Richard III here just gave you a friendly greeting," said Toni. As Sam looked puzzled, they all four strolled toward the curb, the better to get a clear view of the parade.

"So what's this all about?" Sam asked Suzanne. "Will there be elephants and other exotic creatures prancing down the street?"

"You've never been to a county fair parade before, have you?" said Suzanne.

Sam shook his head no.

"It's more likely a couple of Percherons will be pulling a beer wagon," Suzanne laughed. "That's about as exotic as it gets."

"They're coming!" Toni suddenly squealed. "I can feel it. I can feel that big bass drum thumping inside my stomach."

"It's probably gas from the pepperoni pizza we nuked," said Junior.

But it really was the parade, rolling like a tidal wave of color and pageantry down Main Street.

The Kindred High School marching band had the honor of leading the parade. Two majorettes, wearing sparkly leotards and white boots, twirled their batons, tossed them high into the air, and then caught them between their fingers with graceful ease. The kids in their red and blue wool band uniforms, faces all red and sweaty, played their little hearts out as they managed a swing version of "When the Saints Go Marching In."

Next up were a few floats. Kuyper's Hardware was represented with a tractor pulling a flatbed trailer piled with stainless steel appliances. The Prairie Star Casino had a float with a giant roulette wheel, huge red dice, a few provocative-looking casino hostesses giving friendly waves, and a sign that said, Come and Play!

"Yeah!" yelled Junior.

"Eeyu," said Toni.

A tropical float carried six youthful queen candidates dolled up in prom dresses and corsages, their backdrop a mash-up of surfboards, fake palm trees, and a giant plastic parrot.

There were also marching contingents of Girl Scouts, Boy Scouts, and the local Jaycees. They were followed by the Circle K Riding Club, ten riders mounted on high-stepping matched palomino horses.

Suzanne wondered if any of these younger, lanky, determined-looking women would put up stiff competition for her tomorrow afternoon. She guessed they definitely would.

"This is great," said Sam, pulling her tight against him. "Very honest and small town. I love it."

"Do you really?" Suzanne asked. Sam was from the East Coast and had gone to school in Chicago. She sometimes wondered if this was all a little tame for his big-city sensibilities.

"I love everything about it," he said as he planted a kiss on her forehead.

A barnyard float came next, complete with live lambs and red hens against a backdrop of giant orange carrots.

"Look at that!" said Junior, snapping to attention. "World War II vets." A Jeep Wrangler, its ragtop pushed down, carried two white-haired fellows past the cheering crowd.

"Sad to say there's not many of them around anymore," Sam murmured.

Junior managed a combination salute and fist pump. "Good for you, boys!" he screamed. "You sure whipped them Nazis!"

"Sshh!" said Toni, tugging at his sleeve. "Pipe down, there are other vets here, too. From the Korean War and Vietnam and all the Middle East wars."

"God bless them all," Suzanne whispered.

"Holy crapola," said Toni, taking a step back. "Here come the Kindred Jesters."

"Who are they?" Sam asked. But a second later the clown club was virtually on top of them. A clown in a black-and-white jailbird costume drove a tiny race car with an *ah-oo-gah* horn directly at the crowd, swerving at the very last moment. A clown with a tattered red vest and purple pants juggled large white balls. There were almost a dozen more clowns, each with his own crazy costume and shtick.

As they buzzed about, one clown ran directly up to Suzanne, blew up a pink balloon, bent and twisted it into a so-so poodle dog, then handed it to her.

"Thank you," she said. "I think."

The Jessup High School band marched by, a few more floats glided past, and then there was the usual parade of bigwigs and politicos riding in convertibles: Mayor Mobley, a smiling congressman, and some other poor stiff that Suzanne didn't recognize because she probably hadn't voted for him.

There was a loud *whoop whoop* from Sheriff Doogie's siren

as he drove his cruiser past, looking both official and officious, and then the parade was over.

"You want to come home and have a bite with me?" Suzanne asked Sam. "I could fix us grilled cheese sandwiches." She was pleased she hadn't offered beef Wellington or something equally complicated.

"I'd love to, sweetheart," said Sam. "But I can't. I have to dash back to the hospital." He gave her a quick kiss goodbye and was off.

"Come with us," Toni invited. "We're gonna cruise down to Schmitt's Bar and see what's shakin'."

"No thanks," said Suzanne. "I think I'll just head home."

"Be careful!" called Toni as Junior grabbed her arm and pulled her away.

"Always," said Suzanne.

She figured Kindred would be buzzing with people tonight, but when she turned down Ivy Street, heading for her car, the street was practically deserted. No parade goers, no kids on skateboards, not even a stray dog. It was full-on dark now, with cars lining both sides of the narrow street, lights burning in a few of the homes. What had been a clear day had turned cloudy, so that added to the almost oppressive darkness.

I hope it's nice and sunny tomorrow for the barrel racing, Suzanne thought as she walked along. *Hope I'm ready to go for broke on my horse.*

When she saw her car up ahead, Suzanne hit her clicker and the taillights flashed red.

Good car, smart car, she thought. *Safe car.*

She climbed in, started the engine, and cruised to the end of the block. Now she had a choice. She could circle back the way she'd come and maybe run smack-dab into the tail end of the parade and all the buses for the marchers, or she could hang a right, cruise along Catawba Parkway, and then come out a few blocks from home. A little longer, but not so well traveled, and certainly very scenic.

Suzanne took the parkway. It ran parallel with Catawba Creek, a burbling little stream that tumbled down through a series of gorges and valleys, and boasted its fair share of rainbow and brook trout.

So pretty, she thought, as she skimmed past stands of birch trees and a few weeping willows. There were scenic turnoffs, too, that afforded postcard-perfect views of the creek. In high summer, kids rode the creek on inner tubes, boogie boards, and colorful rafts. A kayak club set up an obstacle course. Now, as the days grew cooler and a little shorter, no one ventured out.

It wasn't until Suzanne made a sweeping S-turn past a picnic area that she noticed the car behind her. She supposed it had been there all along, trailing along, just sort of dogging its way slowly like she was.

Only now it had crept up behind her.

Suzanne eased her foot off the gas and eased toward the shoulder. Maybe the driver was in a huff and wanted to pass.

But, no, instead of passing, the car slid right up behind her.

What? He doesn't want to pass me? Okay then . . .

Suzanne juiced the accelerator and sped up. In a move she didn't expect, the car behind her sped up, too. In fact, now the nose of his car was practically riding her bumper. If she decided to hit her brakes for any reason, he'd for sure rear-end her.

What's going on?

Suzanne felt the first tickle of apprehension work its way into the pit of her stomach. She was alone, driving a deserted stretch of road—what's not to worry about? She made up her mind that, first chance she got, at the very first road that intersected this one, she'd execute a speedy turn and leave this jerk in the dust.

She glanced into her rearview mirror. Yup, he was still

there. And, wouldn't you know it, the jerk had his brights on, so she couldn't see who was behind the wheel. Could she see his license plate? She squinted into the light. No. Couldn't make it out.

No matter, the turn onto Leandro Lane was just up ahead. She'd amble along, and then, without bothering to signal, hang a quick left.

Inhaling deeply, Suzanne glanced into her rearview mirror, then flicked her eyes on the road ahead. Twenty more feet. The sign for Leandro Lane loomed large.

She goosed the gas and sped into her left-hand turn.

And wouldn't you know it—her pursuer did the same thing!

Dang! This was getting serious. So what now? Grab her cell phone and call the Law Enforcement Center? Tell them some idiot was tailgating her and scaring her half to death? Or . . .

Suzanne slalomed right, then left, then right again. She saw the opening for the alley at the last minute. Could she make it without clipping that white garage? There was only one way to find out.

Zoom! Tires squealing, she cranked the wheel hard and headed down the alley.

Was he behind her? No. But what if he'd turned and was going to come down the alley from the other direction?

Suzanne saw an open garage and, without a moment's hesitation, pulled in. She killed the lights, then sat there, doors locked, engine ticking down slowly.

Am I okay? Did I lose him?

Thirty seconds later she saw a sweep of headlights. Someone was bumping down the alley. Was it the owner of this garage? Or her weird pursuer?

Suzanne waited, holding her breath, her hand on her cell phone, ready to press 911.

Gravel crunched as the car traveled slowly down the

alley. Something inside Suzanne, her female intuition, the innate sense all women have for knowing when they're in a dangerous situation, made her scrunch down.

The car rolled past her borrowed garage, slowly, stealthily, as if on the hunt.

At the last moment, Suzanne raised her head to grab a peek. And saw a man in a yellow-and-orange-striped costume with a red fright wig to match.

A clown! Probably one from tonight's parade. Why had he followed her? What did he want?

Was he one of Doogie's suspects come to call? Trying to scare her away from asking questions and investigating Hannah's murder? Or did he have something more sinister in mind?

Suzanne thought he might. Which is why she waited another twenty minutes before she backed her car out, gunned her motor, and drove home as if her life depended on it.

Which it probably did.

CHAPTER 24

"Do you guys know who's in the Kindred Jesters Club?" Suzanne asked. It was Fried Egg Friday at the Cackleberry Club and Petra was standing at the stove sizzling sausages with onions, yellow peppers, and plump mushrooms. Toni was busy dicing more vegetables. The kitchen smelled of baking bread, fresh oranges, and fennel sausage.

"Why do you ask?" said Petra. "Are you thinking about joining?"

"Ugh," said Toni, giving a little shiver as she set out a row of plates. "Clowns always creep me out. I particularly didn't like those guys last night. All frenetic and weird with their dinky little cars and silly antics. Reminds me of those killer clown movies."

"Clowns scare the bejeebers out of me, too," said Suzanne. And then she added, "I'm pretty sure one followed me last night."

"What are you talking about?" said Petra. "A killer clown?"

"No," said Suzanne. "A real clown. Some goofball in a yellow-and-orange-striped jumpsuit with a red fright wig and nose to match."

"Sounds like my boyfriend from high school," said Toni.

"Be serious," said Suzanne.

"I am!" said Toni.

"Wait a minute," said Petra. "What are you saying, Suzanne? That someone dressed as a clown followed you home?" She double-cracked two eggs into a bowl to punctuate her sentence.

"He didn't get the chance to follow me *home*," Suzanne explained, "because I drove my car down an alley and hid in an empty garage."

"Dear Lord," said Petra, putting a hand to her throat. "So you really were threatened."

"But you took evasive driving measures," said Toni. "Good girl."

"Not so good," said Suzanne. "Because I don't know who it was."

"Who do you *think* it was?" Petra asked. Suzanne had her full attention now.

Suzanne shook her head. "No idea."

"Take a wild guess," said Petra.

"Jack Venable, Marty Wolfson, Darrel Fuhrman?" said Suzanne. "Take your pick. They all know I've been asking questions about them. Investigating them."

"But not Ricky Wilcox?" said Petra.

"It wouldn't be Ricky," said Toni. "He's a pussycat. He didn't have anything to do with Hannah's murder."

"Still," said Petra, "he's on Doogie's list."

"Innocent until proven guilty," Toni reminded her.

"Are you going to tell Doogie about the clown?" Petra asked.

"I don't know," said Suzanne. "If I do, he'll make me back way off. When what I really want to do now is catch that horrible clown person and let my dogs rip him to shreds."

"Easy, girl," said Toni. "Save some of that wrath and rancor for later. We've got a mighty full day ahead of us."

"I know," said Suzanne. "I wish we didn't." She knew she had to get through breakfast and lunch, rush over to the farm and saddle up Mocha, try to work up her competitive spirit for the barrel racing competition, then run back here and be charming for their dinner theater.

After last night's close call, Suzanne felt nervous and on edge. Today would have been a dandy time to take a mental health day. On the other hand, if they lived in Europe, they could all go on holiday for months at a time.

"I feel responsible," Petra said. "After all, I'm the one who urged you to get involved in Hannah's murder investigation."

"You're not responsible," said Suzanne. "I went into this of my own free will."

"And now it's time to quit," said Petra. Tears glistened in her eyes as she twisted her hands and then wiped them flat against her apron. "We certainly don't want *you* in any jeopardy."

"Time to quit," Toni agreed.

But Suzanne, still angry from last night, determined not to be bullied or harassed, knew this was the time to get deadly serious.

WORKING on autopilot, her brain still mulling over possibilities, Suzanne took orders, poured coffee, worked the cash register, and honchoed the café in general. Because it was Friday, and because today was the start of the Logan County Fair, a big deal in these parts, the Cackleberry Club was extra busy. Breakfast became a blur of sausages, fried eggs, baking powder biscuits, pancakes, and coffee.

Lunch wasn't all that different. Chilled blueberry soup, caprese salad, tuna salad in a tomato cup, and egg salad sandwiches. Suzanne smiled and chirped friendly greetings, wrote down orders, readily agreed to substitutions, and delivered plates of food to their customers.

"Two more caprese salads," Suzanne told Petra. She waved her order sheet in front of Petra's nose, then stuck it on a spindle.

"We've been selling those like hotcakes," said Petra.

"Do we ever sell hotcakes like caprese salads?" asked Toni. She was poised by the stove, ready to grab an order.

"Let me think about that." Petra smiled. Then, "Suzanne, do you think you could make a trash run for me?"

"Sure," said Suzanne.

"As soon as we finish up with lunch," said Petra, "I'm going to roll up my sleeves and get everything prepped for tonight so we're good and ready. And I always like to start with a clean kitchen."

"I wish I was sticking around to help," said Suzanne, hesitating at the back door as she gathered up the trash. "Maybe I *should* stick around."

"No way," said Petra. "You're going to ride that horse of yours if I have to slap on a pair of chaps and do it for you."

"Whoa," said Toni. "That I'd like to see."

SUZANNE hefted the lid of the Dumpster, tossed in her bags of trash, and reached up to close the lid. That's when the sky went black and a rustle of beating wings filled her ears.

Raising a hand in surprise, Suzanne was stunned to see an owl swooping upward, like a glider pilot who'd dipped into an air pocket and then was rising straight up on a thermal.

It was the mother owl!

"Hey," Suzanne cried. "Come back here. I'm the one who's got your baby!"

The owl settled high up in the crook of the oak tree and gazed down at her.

"Yeah," said Suzanne. "I'm talkin' to you, Momma. He's a cute little critter and I have to admit that I've grown quite fond of him, but I think you're far better equipped to care for him than I am."

The owl pivoted her head sideways, then back again. She seemed to be contemplating Suzanne's words.

"So what do you think? If I climbed up there, I could hand him over to you. Plop him right there in your nest in the hollow tree. We'd call it even, no harm done."

The owl looked down at her, lifted a claw, and blinked.

"Was that a yes?" Suzanne said, just as a blue Ford pickup came rumbling into the back parking lot. She watched the truck roll to a stop and shudder once as it backfired loudly. When Suzanne looked up, the owl had disappeared.

Darn it.

Kit and Ricky climbed out of the truck. They were looking at her as if she was a little cuckoo.

"Is everything okay?" Kit asked.

"Fine," said Suzanne. She threw an arm up and made a vague gesture toward the tree. "Just trying to strike a deal with the momma owl up there. Trying to get her baby back to her."

Ricky pointed at the roof of his truck. "I brought along my extension ladder. I'm gonna use it to hang the metal rod and curtain for the play tonight. After I'm finished I could lean it up against your tree. Put your little owl back in his nest all safe and sound."

"That would be great," said Suzanne. "Except I'd like to be the one to do it, okay?"

Ricky nodded. "Sure. I'll leave the ladder out back once I'm finished with the curtain."

"We borrowed that velvet curtain from Petra's church," said Kit. "And is it ever gorgeous. The deep midnight blue is going to look elegant hanging in the Cackleberry Club." She grinned. "I think it's going to be a great night."

"Let's hope so," said Suzanne.

"I brought two shirts for you to try," said Toni. She and Suzanne were hunkered in the office just off the Book Nook. Toni, the queen of Western garb, had convinced Suzanne that it was crucial to dress the part and look like a real rodeo queen. So now she held up a red satin shirt with white pearl snaps and a black paisley shirt with gold insets and gold buttons.

"I don't know," said Suzanne. "Which do you think is best?" They were both a little gaudy for her taste. Still, it was a Western-style competition. Maybe if she looked the part she'd be able to live and breathe the part, too.

"You're wearing jeans and boots?"

"Sure. And my cowboy hat."

"What color's your hat?"

"Brown."

"Maybe the red shirt," said Toni.

"It looks a little tight."

"It's supposed to be tight. It's a *fitted* shirt."

Suzanne peeled off her T-shirt and struggled into Toni's red shirt.

"Is Sam coming to watch?" asked Toni.

"No. I told him not to, I'd be too nervous if he was there."

"Hey," said Toni, reaching out to brush away an invisible speck. "That shirt looks cool on you."

"It's *really* tight," said Suzanne, inhaling mightily as she tried to pull the shirt together in front. It was satin, so it didn't stretch. Instead, the shirt clung to her body as if it were spray-painted on. "I can barely snap it."

Toni smiled. "That's the whole idea, sweetie. You want to look just this side of hoochie momma so you'll get noticed favorably by the judges."

"And if my shirt pops open right in the middle of a cloverleaf turn?"

"Then you might even win."

"It's a timed trial," said Suzanne.

"So have a good time!"

SUZANNE drove across the field to the barn, her nerves tingling, her stomach churning but revved with excitement, too.

She'd polished her saddle two days earlier and now the rich leather fairly gleamed as it caught the rays of light that filtered into the barn.

"This is it," she whispered to Mocha as she slipped his bridle on, then tossed the saddle on his back. "There's no turning back now."

In his stall next to Mocha, Grommet raised his head and nickered softly. Good luck wishes from one four-legged friend to another.

And then Suzanne was cantering slowly down the driveway, warming Mocha up, warming herself up for what was to come. She could have borrowed a horse trailer and driven over in style, but she liked the idea of riding the two miles to the fairgrounds. It gave her and Mocha time to get in synch with each other, for him to feel her gentle hands jiggling the bit in his mouth and her knees pressing expertly against his sides.

And slowly, inexorably, the excitement built within both of them as they pranced their way down the lane to the fairgrounds. In the distance, Suzanne could see an enormous Ferris wheel, all yellow metal with pink neon lights glowing on the sides. She remembered how her stomach got that sinking feeling every time she rode a Ferris wheel and the car came over the top and dropped down. That's how she felt now.

But as she drew closer, where crowds hurried along and the flags atop the grandstand snapped hard in the wind, the roar from the midway suddenly sounded like a roar of victory.

THE entire area surrounding the show ring and barrel racing course was parked up with horse trailers and pickup trucks. Would-be cowboys and cowgirls were everywhere, doing last-minute grooming, adjusting equipment, spit polishing boots. Suzanne had her entry number, number twenty-three, pinned to the back of her shirt, and was walking Mocha in a lazy circle where the prevalent aromas consisted of horses, hay, and saddle soap.

She watched out of the corner of her eye as rider after rider entered the ring, kicked their horse into a galloping start, and swiftly flew around the barrels.

Then Suzanne's number was announced over the fuzzy loudspeaker and it was her turn. Heart pounding, she hopped onto Mocha's back and trotted smartly over to the starting line. Saying a little prayer, she kicked Mocha sharply and cried out, "Hyah!" Suddenly she was flying through the entry gate, where she broke the invisible beam and set the timer in relentless motion.

There was no time to think! The crowd cheered loudly, clouds of brown dust blew into her eyes, her legs flailed and mashed up against the barrels. She felt like she was traveling ninety miles an hour as she navigated the cloverleaf pattern, almost unaware of making the turns, relying strictly on instinct. The glimpses she caught of the crowd, the barrels, and Mocha's bobbing head felt like miniature snapshots in time. Just *click, click, click.*

And then, after what felt like about eight seconds but surely had to have been more, Suzanne was flying for home. Mocha charged across the finish line, her time was officially clocked, and the race was over. She reined him in hard, causing him to rear up slightly, and an appreciative "Oooh" rippled through the crowd.

I'm a cowgirl now, Suzanne thought. *A real live cowgirl. Well, at least I was for a few fleeting seconds.*

She leaned forward, patted Mocha on his lathered-up shoulders, and tried to relax. Now what? Oh, she had to wait for the final results. Of course, she did. That was the whole point of her jouncing wild ride. See what kind of time she was able to stack up against a bunch of riders who were almost twenty years her junior. She slipped off her horse and stood stock-still, trying to catch her breath, listening to the miniature thunder of pounding hooves as other riders navigated the course.

Ten minutes later, the women's barrel racing event was complete and her wait was finally over. The announcer, a white-haired man in a powder blue Western-style leisure suit and enormous white hat, mounted the viewing stand and started calling out numbers. His assistant, a girl in a brown vest and fringed suede skirt, held a handful of ribbons.

As the first- and second-place winners were called, they galloped jubilantly past Suzanne. She clapped good-naturedly. This had been an exercise in fun, she told herself. A personal challenge to see if she and her horse really could compete. But when number twenty-three, her number, crackled across the loudspeaker, she practically froze.

"That's you, ma'am," said a skinny cowboy standing next to her. "Looks like you won third place."

"I did?" Suzanne was stunned.

"Go get your ribbon," urged the cowboy. "Here, you need a leg up?"

She placed the toe of her boot in his interlaced fingers and sprang onto Mocha's back. "Thanks."

Suzanne rode into the ring feeling as if she were living a dream. Accepting a white ribbon from the judge, she smiled, shook hands, and posed with the first- and second-place winners for a quick promotional photograph.

Amazing.

As Suzanne rode out of the ring, head in the clouds, still not believing her good fortune, she heard a voice calling her name. It was Junior. She looked around and found him in the crowd. He was dressed in jeans, a black T-shirt, a Pennzoil trucker cap, and wore a silver belt buckle that was either an insect or a flower, depending on how you looked at it.

"Jeez Louise, Suzanne," cried Junior. He put both hands on top of his head as if his brains were about to bounce loose. "You won! You did it!"

"Third place," she said, secretly pleased that she'd done so well.

"Lemme see your ribbon."

Suzanne dismounted and held up her white ribbon, letting it flutter in the breeze.

"You're a genuine rodeo queen, you know that?" said Junior. "You oughta take your horse to the State Fair."

"I wouldn't go that far," said Suzanne.

"Oh, it ain't far," said Junior. "Maybe sixty miles, tops."

"No, I meant . . ." Suzanne chuckled. "What brings you to the fair, Junior?"

"I been in the Merchandise Mart, helping sell those gamma ray hats."

"Before you go back to that, Junior, would you do me a favor?"

"Sure, Suzy-Q. Anything you want."

"Hang on to Mocha for about ten minutes?"

"You mean I should just stand here and talk to him or can I walk him around?"

"Walk him around. In fact, that's a great idea, he'll stay nice and calm that way."

"Yeah, give him something to do," said Junior. "Where you off to?"

"I want to check the Home Arts Building and see how Petra did. See if she won any ribbons for her pies or banana bread."

"Bet she did," said Junior. "That lady can bake up a storm."

"I just remembered," said Suzanne, handing over the reins to Junior. "You entered your craft beer. How did the judging go on that?"

Junior grimaced. "Aw, there were a few minor problems. Seems the judges didn't take a liking to my beer."

"I'm sorry to hear that," said Suzanne. "I know you had high hopes."

"There's always next year," said Junior. "I'm a natural-born optometrist."

"Optimist," said Suzanne.

Junior nodded sagely. "That, too."

Suzanne held up her hand as she stepped away. "I'll be back in ten minutes, fifteen at the most."

TURNS out Petra had won a ribbon. In fact she won three ribbons. A purple grand prize ribbon for her rhubarb pie, a blue ribbon for her cherry pie, and a red ribbon for her banana bread. So a full sweep for the Cackleberry Club!

Suzanne wanted to grab the ribbons and take them home to Petra, but she knew they had to remain in place until late Sunday. That way everyone could admire her baked goods and know that she had won.

"Suzanne," said a friendly voice.

Suzanne turned to find Mark Binger, the local game warden, smiling at her. He was tall and thin with salt-and-pepper hair and a handlebar mustache drooped over a friendly smile.

"Mark," she said. "You're the perfect person to run into."

"I'm happy to hear that," Binger said. He was wearing olive drab slacks and a light green shirt with a game warden patch on it. He gestured at his outfit and said, "I'm going to give a talk in a few minutes. About pheasants and other game birds."

"About hunting them?" she asked.

"No, no, about preserving habitat," said Binger. "Trying to get folks to stop mowing their fields or ditches too clean. Leave some tall marsh grasses for the birds to nest in."

"I wonder," said Suzanne, "do you know anything about owls?"

Binger nodded. "Some."

"I found a baby owlet. Poor thing tumbled out of his nest, from a tree right behind the Cackleberry Club."

"And you've been caring for it," said Binger.

"Yes. But I don't want to," said Suzanne.

"Best thing to do, is put it back in the nest. Nine times out of ten that'll do the trick."

"If the mother owl rejects it, what then?"

"Worst-case scenario," said Binger, "is you'll have to hand-feed it before it can be released into the wild." He smiled. "Just mash up some crickets or mice."

"Crickets I can manage."

"Say," said Binger, shuffling a little closer. "Would you like to have dinner with me sometime?"

"You know, Mark," said Suzanne. "I'm seeing someone right now." Then she hastily wondered, was that what it was? *Seeing* someone? Is that what she had going with Sam? Because that handy-dandy little catchphrase sounded about as exciting as a mashed potato sandwich.

"Well, if circumstances should ever change," said Binger, looking a little disappointed, "you know where to find me. Out in the marsh grass."

Suzanne was on her way back to the horse paddock when

she heard a loud honking noise and a bunch of high-pitched laughter. She glanced around and saw a contingent of clowns running through the crowd. She ducked behind a hot dog stand and peered out at them, trying to see if her aggressor clown from last night was among them. But she didn't see him. No yellow-and-orange-striped costume and red fright wig.

Fright wig. She'd always wondered why they called it that. Now she knew.

CHAPTER 25

PETRA was thrilled beyond belief. At Suzanne's third-place ribbon and especially by the news that she'd won a rainbow of ribbons.

"And here I thought Edna Stang would win grand prize in baking," she crowed. "She's always so snooty about her pecan pie. Always going on about how you have to use special Georgia pecans and cane sugar."

"You use cane sugar," Suzanne pointed out.

"Well, sure," said Petra. "I use it because it's the best, but I don't get all snooty about it."

Suzanne had rushed home to shower and change, and now she (and her baby owl) were back at the Cackleberry Club. It was late afternoon and their dinner theater guests would probably start arriving in an hour or so.

"What's going on?" Suzanne asked. "What can I do?"

"For one thing, you could go eyeball things in the café," said Petra. "Toni, Kit, and Ricky have been busy setting tables and arranging things, but who knows how it'll all turn out?"

"How do you want it to turn out?"

"Somewhere between a state dinner at the White House and Chicken Pickin' Tuesday at a local barbecue joint."

"We should be able to manage that," said Suzanne.

But when she poked her head into the café, Suzanne was pleasantly surprised. White linen tablecloths camouflaged wooden tables, glassware sparkled, polished silverware gleamed. And when she quizzed Toni and company about the gorgeous floral bouquets, it turned out that Ricky had driven over to Jessup to buy bunches of roses, carnations, and baby's breath at a super discount price from a floral wholesaler that he was friendly with.

"This all looks gorgeous," Suzanne told them. "In fact, the whole room is practically glowing."

"Thank you," said Toni. "And I understand big-time congratulations are in order."

Suzanne grinned. "Who told you?"

"Junior," said Toni. "He was all whooped up over your third-place ribbon." She glanced over her shoulder and gave a slightly downturned expression. "In fact, he's here right now. Sitting in the office, playing games on the computer. Kind of hiding out."

"Hiding out from what?" asked Suzanne.

Toni, Kit, and Ricky all exchanged glances. Smirks, really.

"Uh-oh, tell me what happened," said Suzanne.

"Junior's Hubba Bubba beer?" said Toni. "It was a total disaster."

"Apparently his beer made the judges sick," said Ricky. "I guess two of them even tossed their cookies."

"That's terrible," said Suzanne. She almost giggled, but didn't.

"So if Junior offers you a brewski," said Kit, "run the other way."

"Suzanne," said Ricky, "I put my ladder out back just like you asked. Leaned it right up against that big oak tree."

"Thanks," said Suzanne. Once the dinner theater was under way, she'd run out and try to put the owlet back in his nest. "Try" being the operative word. She glanced around at the rest of the room, which really looked as if it had been professionally pulled together. "By the way, that curtain turned out great."

Ricky had draped the blue velvet curtain so that it closed off the entire end of the room. Once the curtain was pulled open, the stage set—really a round table and a few chairs—would be revealed. And the actors could make their entrances and exits via the Book Nook or Knitting Nest.

"Thanks," said Ricky, shuffling his feet. "I'm happy to help. You've all been so nice to me. In spite of things."

"Is it okay if Ricky hangs around?" asked Kit.

"He's been a big help so far," said Toni.

"I guess so. Sure," said Suzanne. She smiled at Ricky. "That's if you don't mind pitching in to bus dishes or load them in the dishwasher. We're going to be awfully busy tonight."

"I'm not afraid of a little hard work," said Ricky.

SUZANNE was just starting to light the candles when she heard a couple of cars roll into the parking lot. "The actors are here," she called.

Within minutes, Sam, Carmen Copeland, Connie Halpern, Lolly Herron, and three other actors had piled into the Cackleberry Club. As they rushed into their dressing rooms du jour, Sam pulled Suzanne aside into a cozy embrace.

"You won!" he exclaimed, giving her a quick kiss.

"Just third place," she told him. "How on earth did you hear?"

"Everybody knows," said Sam. "It's all over town."

"Really?"

"It was on the radio," said Sam. "WLGN was broadcasting live from the fairgrounds, keeping everybody up to date on prize-winning hogs and pickles and pies."

"And me," said Suzanne, secretly pleased.

"Gotta run and change," said Sam. He held up a plastic bag that contained his blue velvet Victorian cutaway suit, borrowed from another theater company in nearby Cornucopia.

"Go get gorgeous," she told him. Even though she knew he already was.

THE first guests began to trickle in around six-forty. By six-forty-five it turned into a torrent. Toni, wearing a sleek white blouse and long black skirt, clipboard in hand, checked off each guest's name and then led them to their seat.

Suzanne, Petra, Kit, and Ricky worked frantically in the kitchen. Because they'd be handling most of the serving duties, Suzanne and Kit were dressed in white blouses and slim black pants, while Petra and Ricky were dressed casually. Junior languished on the back porch, whittling a hunk of wood. The actors had tired of his incessant jabbering and kicked him out of the office.

Petra stirred a bowl of chutney that she was pairing with her first course, while Suzanne laid out small white plates. Kit was in a state of high excitement as she peeked out the pass-through.

"Did you guys know Sheriff Doogie was here?" Kit asked, her excitement suddenly shifting to nervousness.

"Doogie bought a ticket?" said Suzanne. Doogie had never bought a ticket to anything in his life. He just showed up and insinuated himself in whatever was happening, whether it was a church supper, fish fry at the VFW, or town picnic.

"I called and invited him," said Petra. "Right after I

looked at the list of ticket holders. I figured we might need a little extra security."

"What are you talking about?" said Suzanne. It was a fancy dinner theater event, for gosh sakes. They were using napkin rings and serving wine.

"Take a gander at the crowd out there," said Petra. "Tell me who you see."

Suzanne peeped through the pass-through and studied the crowd. "Bruce Winthrop's here, which is nice. It's good that he's getting out and mingling, not fretting about the fire."

"I'm not talking about him," said Petra. "Keep looking."

Suzanne continued to scan the room. Half the guests were already seated while the other half were still mingling and exchanging pleasantries. "Oh jeez, Jack Venable's here." Her eyes followed him for a few seconds. "But nobody seems to be talking to him."

"Uh-huh," said Petra. "Keep looking."

When Suzanne caught a glimpse of a woman with long blond hair, she suddenly puckered her brows. "Is that Annie Wolfson?"

"With her husband," Petra said. There was a distinct *tone* to her voice.

"They're back together?"

"Personally," said Petra, "I think they're just trying to put on a good show."

"Do you think Marty Wolfson is the one who set the fire?" asked Kit. She glanced hastily at Ricky and then at Petra.

"Who knows?" said Petra. She opened her oven and pulled out a baking sheet filled with miniature meat pies. They were golden brown and looked like small apple turnovers.

"I guess we'll just have to keep an eye on Wolfson," said Suzanne.

Petra pulled out a second sheet. "Keep looking, sweetie."

"What?" said Suzanne just as Darrel Fuhrman ducked through the front door.

"Is he out there?" said Petra.

"You mean Darrel Fuhrman?" said Suzanne.

Petra nodded briskly as she stepped to the stove and gave a stir to her bubble and squeak.

"He just came in," said Suzanne.

"You see why I called Doogie?" said Petra. "This isn't just dinner theater with *Blithe Spirit*, it's a real-life game of Clue. Or that movie version."

"Hah," said Toni as she slalomed through the swinging door and into the kitchen. "With Colonel Mustard in the library?"

"And Professor Plum poised with a lethal candlestick," grunted Petra.

Or a can of kerosene, thought Suzanne. She pushed her way into the café and slipped behind the counter. Sheriff Doogie was sitting on his favorite stool, his back against the marble counter as he gazed over the crowd with cool law enforcement eyes.

"Doogie," Suzanne said in a low whisper.

His head swiveled around. Then the rest of his khaki bulk followed.

"Thanks for coming."

Doogie gave an imperceptible nod. "Petra thought there might be trouble."

"She's a worrywart," said Suzanne. "Nothing's going to happen. There are way too many people here tonight."

"Suit yourself," said Doogie as he swiveled back around.

Toni dimmed the overhead lights and a murmur of anticipation swept through the audience. Now the room was illuminated mostly by candlelight, which lent a flattering glow to all their guests' faces and made the room look elegant and theatrical.

As Connie Halpern stepped in front of the curtain, introducing herself and giving a heartfelt welcome, Toni, Suzanne, and Kit began pouring wine and serving their first course, the miniature meat pies.

And then, as wine was sipped and forks began to clank, the velvet curtain was swept aside, and a hush fell over the audience. Junior hit a button on the CD player, music filled the room, and their drawing-room comedy kicked off with a flourish.

Even though Carmen Copeland was a pill to deal with personally, Suzanne had to admit that she made a wonderfully credible Madame Arcati, a role that Angela Lansbury had made famous on Broadway. Her voice rose and fell melodically as she summoned the spirits to make their appearance. Of course, Sam was delightful as the irascible Dr. Bradman, and the actors who played the parts of Elvira, Ruth, and Charles were terrific as well.

"This feels like real dinner theater," Toni whispered to Suzanne as they delivered their second course of bubble and squeak.

"Doesn't it?" said Suzanne. She was thrilled they'd drawn a full house tonight and tickled that their guests were entranced by the play. She decided, then and there, to do this again. Perhaps the Kindred Community Players could even stage *A Christmas Carol* for the holidays.

Back in the kitchen, Petra was busy slicing roast beef while Ricky was tasked with checking the scorched eggs.

"Are they cooked?" asked Petra.

Ricky shook his head, looking befuddled. "How do I tell?"

"Grab a knife and slice one open," Petra instructed.

"Here," said Kit. She handed Ricky a large butcher knife

and watched as he balanced the knife in his right hand and then, in one swift motion, whacked a baked egg in half.

"Looks good," said Ricky. "Cooked all the way through anyway, just like a hard-boiled egg."

"One more thing gone right," Petra murmured.

Then Suzanne and Toni were there to grab the third course and deliver it to their dinner guests.

As Suzanne slipped quietly around the tables, she marveled at the play. It really had a professional quality to it. Lights dimmed and winked out exactly on cue, the Victorian costumes were elegant, and the actors played their roles to the hilt.

Definitely have to do this again, she decided.

At intermission, just before the final act and the dishing up of the pudding trifle, Suzanne took a short breather. She slipped out the back door with the cardboard box containing her baby owl.

Junior, Ricky, and Bruce Winthrop were all sitting on the back steps under a yellow bug light that cast an eerie glow and made them all look like aliens. The sun had long since dropped below the horizon and there was just a faint remnant of pink backlighting the woods.

"Working hard, gents?" Suzanne said.

Winthrop was smoking a cigarette while Junior was kvetching about hops and bitters and fermentation problems. Only Ricky stood up politely and moved from his spot, the better to let Suzanne pass.

"You need help with that?" asked Ricky.

At that exact moment, Toni stuck her head out the back door and shrilled, "Junior! Ricky! Get your lazy butts in here. There's work to be done!"

"Ain't she a slave driver?" Junior said to Ricky. "Come on, kid, we better haul anchor."

Bruce Winthrop saw Suzanne walk toward the ladder

and said, "Help you with that?" He took a final puff of his cigarette, flicked it away, and stomped it out carefully.

"Sure," said Suzanne. "I want to try to put this baby owl back up in the tree with his momma."

Winthrop peered into the box and smiled. "Cute little thing. You think she'll take him back?"

"That's what I'm about to find out," said Suzanne. She tucked the box under her left arm, grasped the rail of the ladder with her right hand, and started to climb.

"Careful," Winthrop cautioned.

Suzanne was twelve rungs up when she turned and made a face. "Ugh, this ladder's wiggly. Can you steady it?"

"Sure."

Suzanne climbed up another ten rungs. For some reason, she hadn't realized how high up the hollow in the tree was, or that she'd be climbing a rickety extension ladder. Now, instead of high hopes at reuniting mother and baby, she was suddenly nervous. From where she was perched, hanging on with just one hand, it seemed like a long way down. It *was* a long way down.

"Please hold the ladder steady," she begged Winthrop. "If I fall now I'm afraid I'll drop like a sack of flour."

"We wouldn't want that, would we?" said Winthrop.

Something about the tone of his voice made Suzanne hesitate. She looked down and saw that he had taken a step back from the ladder. His hands were shoved deep in his pockets and he was jingling change. His lips were pursed as he blew a tuneless whistle.

"Bruce?" Suzanne said. The night air suddenly seemed chillier and the atmosphere felt electrically charged. Which made her perch feel all the more precarious and unstable.

"Yup?" Winthrop said as he looked up at her. His face was a pale oval beneath her and there was a strange light in his eyes.

"Are you okay?" she asked.

"You bet, Suzanne," said Bruce as he stared up at her, his jaw tightening.

As Suzanne balanced against the ladder, clutching her cardboard box, she felt a vague sense of unease. Was something going on? Wait a minute . . . Bruce wouldn't *do* anything, would he?

No, of course not. I'm just having a paranoid moment brought on by a busy day and my slightly ditzy fear of heights.

"Bruce," said Suzanne, trying to sound cool and calm, attempting to work past her fears, "I'd appreciate it if you'd grab hold of this ladder and keep it steady. I'm all the way up here trying to balance . . ."

Winthrop pulled his hands from his pockets and a spatter of change tumbled out. The coins hit the dirt with soft *plops.* Only, as Suzanne gazed down, she saw it wasn't change at all that had come loose.

They were casino chips.

Winthrop saw her looking and gave a low chuckle. "Oops," he said. But now there was an undercurrent of menace in his voice.

Comprehension suddenly dawned for Suzanne. And she knew she was staring at the same kind of chip she'd found in the wreckage of the fire.

Winthrop's a gambler? Suzanne thought. And then, as that one thought suddenly crystalized in her mind, she also experienced a wave of suspicion and then fear. "You're a gambler?" she croaked out.

Winthrop let loose a noise somewhere between a bark and a chuckle.

"Yeah," he said. "Sometimes a little too much for my own good."

Oh dear Lord, Suzanne thought, her thoughts tumbling one on top of the other. *And sometimes gamblers get into deep trouble, deep debt.* And on the heels of that terrifying realization—*And they cook the books. And then they're forced to cover it up.*

Suzanne looked down at Winthrop again and saw the cold, hard truth shining in his dark eyes. And she knew, deep down in the limbic portion of her brain, that Bruce Winthrop had set the fire that had killed Hannah. Because Hannah had known what he was up to. Hannah had discovered Winthrop siphoning off money, which meant she'd been bound and determined to reveal his thieving ways to the county attorney.

Only Winthrop had killed Hannah first. He'd set the fire, burned down the building, and murdered his only witness!

Winthrop smiled up at Suzanne with the cold, hard smile of a reptile. He knew that she knew exactly what he'd done.

"Have you ever done any hunting, Suzanne?" Winthrop asked.

"No." Suzanne's throat was so constricted with fear she could barely manage a sound.

"Well, I happen to have a particular taste for hasenpfeffer," Winthrop said.

Rabbit, Suzanne thought wildly. *What's with the non sequitur? Why is he suddenly talking about rabbits?*

"The best way to catch yourself a nice, plump rabbit is with a snare," said Winthrop. He placed his size-twelve shoe on the bottom rung, causing the ladder to creak noisily. "You get yourself a length of galvanized wire." He reached into his jacket pocket and pulled out a coil of thin wire. It glistened dully and dangerously in the dim light. "Something that's pliable, but still strong."

"Bruce . . . ?" Suzanne was shaking so badly she could barely hang on to her cardboard box.

Winthrop sighed deeply, almost a sigh of resignation at the effort he was going to have to put forth. And then he came up the ladder after her, climbing relentlessly, murder in his eye.

"Doogie! Sam!" Suzanne croaked out. But she couldn't be heard over the thunderous laughter and applause that suddenly rang from inside the café.

Five rungs below her, the ladder thrashing and shaking like crazy, Winthrop stretched out an arm and made a grab for her ankle.

Suzanne struck out wildly with her foot, kicking at his hand. She knew she didn't dare let herself be caught and dragged down. She knew that if he got his hands on her, he'd strangle her with insane detachment, and then drop her body to the ground like a discarded doll.

"Help!" Suzanne shrieked, finally finding her voice and managing to hang on to the box while she scrambled up two more rungs.

"You think you're so smart," Winthrop seethed through gritted teeth. "You think . . ."

He leaned dangerously backward and shook the ladder with all his might. Then he was bellowing like a madman, his face a blotchy red, his mouth making rabid, almost unintelligible sounds.

There was a roaring in Suzanne's head and her legs shook like Jell-O. As she shifted precariously on the ladder, she tilted the box and almost dropped the little owl. Terrified as he slid to and fro, the owlet let loose a pitiful cry.

As if in answer, a loud squawk sounded right above them, reverberating through the treetops, its piercing cry riding on the night air.

Then, seemingly out of nowhere, the mother owl swooped down. Her wingspread had to be at least four feet across, the tips of her feathers curling aerodynamically as she dropped faster and faster. Talons extended, her aim dead-on, she went straight for Winthrop's eyes without hesitation!

Winthrop threw up an arm in a belated attempt to protect himself, and let loose a howl like a crazed banshee. But the gigantic owl never let up. Her wings sounded a terrifying drumbeat as she clawed furiously at his face.

CHAPTER 26

ALL hell broke loose as Junior, Ricky Wilcox, and Sheriff Doogie came tumbling out the back door.

Doogie took one look at the struggle between Winthrop and the owl and drew his pistol.

"No! Don't shoot her!" Suzanne cried out as the mother owl gave one powerful flap of her wings and disappeared into the treetops.

Doogie lowered his gun.

"Just get him off me!" Suzanne screamed. "Winthrop tried to kill me, he tried to strangle me with that hunk of wire in his hand."

"What are you sayin'?" screamed Doogie.

"He killed Hannah, too," Suzanne yelled down from her shaky perch. "Set fire to the County Services Building and killed her so she couldn't rat him out over gambling debts. I bet if you can reconstruct county records, you'll find he's been embezzling like crazy."

"She's lying!" Winthrop screamed. He put a hand up to

wipe his face, saw that he was bleeding, and cried, "My eyes! That owl clawed out my eyes!"

Doogie started for the ladder, but Ricky Wilcox beat him to it. "I'll get that bugger down," said Ricky. He climbed up, grabbed hold of Winthrop's belt, and yanked him hard. "Get down here, you varmint!" he ordered. He was no longer Ricky the suspect, now he was Ricky the avenging, self-appointed deputy.

"Holy guacamole!" cried Toni as she flung open the back door and took in the scene. She saw Ricky yanking Winthrop down, Doogie still in combat stance, Junior's blank stare, and Suzanne hanging on for dear life. "I'm gonna get Sam," she cried out. "Hang on, honey!"

SUZANNE did hang on. After Winthrop was dragged down, after Doogie put handcuffs on him, she scrabbled down carefully, still clutching the box with her owl. When her feet finally touched solid ground, she let out a huge sigh of relief.

At which point the door burst open again and Sam, Toni, and Petra came rushing out.

Sam wasted no time. He brushed past everyone and swept Suzanne into his arms. "Are you okay?" he asked as she hiccupped and nodded against his chest. "Are you okay?"

"Holy crumb cake," said Petra. "Looks like we got ourselves a melodrama going on out here, too."

"You have no idea," said Ricky. He was aligned tightly with Doogie now. And Doogie, experienced law officer that he was, was managing to wring a halting confession out of Bruce Winthrop. Yes, Winthrop had embezzled money; yes, he'd set the fire, but only as a sort of smoke screen to try to delay any sort of investigation until he could pay all the money back.

"Lie!" shouted Suzanne. She'd thrown in her two cents' worth during the questioning and it was quite clear whose story had won out.

"What a jerk," said Toni.

Suzanne poked an index finger into the middle of Winthrop's chest. "Were you the clown?" she asked.

"I'd say he's more than a clown," said Doogie. "More like a murdering skunk who . . ."

"No," said Suzanne. "I'm asking if he was the one who chased me in his clown costume last night."

"You were chased?" said Sam. He shot a murderous glance at Winthrop.

"I can explain," said Winthrop. "A simple joke . . ."

"I might just lock this boy up and throw away the key," said Doogie.

"Were you responsible for the fire at the vet's clinic, too?" Suzanne prodded. "Did you plant those blasting caps in Ricky's car? Did you shoot at me as I rode my horse through the woods?" But Winthrop had suddenly clammed up.

"It was him," said Sam. "Just look at his face."

"Guilty as sin," said Petra.

Doogie, looking angry but satisfied that the case had mostly been solved, grabbed Winthrop and dragged him across the parking lot. He opened the back door of his cruiser and did everything but boot Winthrop inside.

"I need an ambulance!" Winthrop implored. "I was attacked by a vicious animal. Look at me, I'm all scratched and bleeding."

"Bull dingers," scoffed Doogie. "You ain't hurt bad at all. You're gonna ride to jail like any other common criminal. And don't you dare get a drop of blood on my fine plastic upholstery. There's been enough blood shed in this town already."

More and more people had heard the commotion and were spilling outside into the back parking lot. Some of the seriously curious had wandered through Petra's kitchen, others had gone out the front door of the Cackleberry Club and found their way around the side.

Doogie took over again. "That's it, show's over," he said, clapping his hands loudly. "Everybody back inside." He glanced at Ricky. "Son, can you kind of herd 'em around toward the front?"

"Yes, sir!" said Ricky.

"Oh my gosh," said Toni, grabbing Kit and hugging her tight. "Ricky's off the hook for sure."

"So are a lot of other people," said Petra. "Looks like Jack Venable might have been unfaithful to Hannah, but at least he wasn't her killer."

"Neither is Marty Wolfson or Darrel Fuhrman," said Toni. "And those are the two guys we thought might cause trouble tonight."

"Who says they won't cause trouble in the future?" said Suzanne. She remained in the safe embrace of Sam.

"You never know," said Toni. She grabbed Kit's hand, and motioned for Petra to follow. "Come on," she said, glancing at Suzanne and Sam, "let's give these two lovebirds a little space."

Alone in the back lot now, Sam furrowed his brow and gazed at Suzanne. "Are you really okay?"

She nodded. "I think so." She gestured toward the ladder. "All I wanted to do . . ." She sniffled and tried to manage a smile.

"The baby owl," said Sam. "I know."

"Just trying to reunite it," she said. She felt a profound sadness. For the owl, for Hannah, for everyone who'd been dragged into this mess.

Sam picked up the cardboard box from where Suzanne had set it down. He hooked one arm around it and started up the ladder.

"You're going to . . . ?" Suzanne said. Then, "Please be careful."

"No problem, I'm an old hand at this," said Sam. "I once built a tree house as a kid." He climbed surely and swiftly, up, up, up, almost to the very top of the ladder. "There's a hollow in the tree up here," he called out, his voice drifting down to Suzanne.

"That's it," she said. "That's their nest. Can you put it . . . can you put the baby owl in there?" She was on pins and needles, practically dancing in place, her fingers crossed.

"It's done," said Sam.

"Thank goodness," she breathed. What a finale to a crazy, weird evening. A crazy, weird week!

Sam was barely ten rungs down the ladder when there was a wild rush of wings as the mother owl flew down. She eased her way into the hollow tree and settled next to the baby owlet.

"What's happening?" Suzanne called up.

"She's touching it," said Sam. "But gently. Making sure it's okay."

Suzanne wasn't sure, but she thought she could detect a slight catch in his voice.

"Be careful," Suzanne warned as Sam continued to climb down. When he was back on terra firma, she said, "I can't wait to tell you . . ."

But Sam held up a hand to interrupt her. "Hang on a minute."

"What?" Suzanne asked, suddenly feeling nervous and jittery. Was there a problem? Was Sam angry with her for coming out here all by herself and getting suckered in by Bruce Winthrop?

Sam dug in his pocket. "I've got this . . ."

"What?" she said again, her voice a little sharper this time. But she was really thinking, *Please don't be mad. Please don't say you want to break up with me, or something really awful like that.*

"I've actually got something for you," said Sam. "I'm thinking this might be the right time to . . ." He pulled a small black velvet box from his pocket and cradled it in the palm of his outstretched hand.

Suzanne gasped.

Then, as if she had suddenly slipped into a wonderful dream, the ring box seemed to magically open. And there, nestled on a pillow of sleek white silk, was the most gorgeous Asscher-cut diamond ring she had ever laid eyes on. It sparkled and glimmered with precise shards of light, like the aurora borealis on a frozen winter night.

Suzanne gazed in awe at the ring, and then looked up at Sam, her eyes brimming with tears.

"Oh," she said, her voice a slight squeak.

She couldn't quite believe it. Was this moment really happening? Had a handsome man in a cutaway velvet coat, looking very Victorian and serious, gotten down on bended knee and offered her this gorgeous engagement ring? And, quite probably, a lifetime filled with happiness?

It was almost too much for Suzanne to bear. She wanted to sing, dance, cry hysterically, and shout for joy. But most of all, she wanted to sink to *her* knees and offer up a prayer to Heaven. Because right in the middle of a perfectly lovely, yet ordinary existence, life had handed her a fairy tale!

"I'm encouraged by that big smile on your face," said Sam. He rose to his feet and touched a hand to her cheek, gently brushing away her tears of joy. "But I would love to hear your answer."

"*Woo-hoo*," the mother owl hooted softly from up above, where leaves rustled and the little owl snuggled contentedly.

"Yes, Sam!" Suzanne finally cried, throwing her arms around him and hugging him as tight as she possibly could. "Absolutely I will marry you!" She hesitated. "Except . . ."

"Except what?" he asked, looking nervous.

"You're not going to expect beef bourguignon and chicken marsala for dinner every night, are you?"

"Sweetheart," Sam said, his lips poised above hers. "The only thing I really expect is to be ravenously happy with you."

And as Suzanne kissed him back, she whispered a silent prayer. *Thank you, dear Lord, for giving me a second chance at love. Because this time I know it will last for a very long time!*

Favorite Recipes from the
Cackleberry Club

Sour Cream Coffee Cake

½ cup butter, softened
1 cup sugar
2 eggs
1 cup sour cream
1 tsp. vanilla extract
2 cups all-purpose flour
1 tsp. baking powder
½ tsp. baking soda
¼ tsp. salt

TOPPING:

¼ cup sugar
⅓ cup brown sugar
1 tsp. ground cinnamon
½ cup chopped pecans

Preheat oven to 325 degrees. Cream together butter and sugar. Beat in eggs, sour cream, and vanilla. Combine flour, baking powder, baking soda, and salt. Add to creamed mixture and beat until combined. Pour half the mixture into a greased 9" × 13" baking pan. In a small bowl, combine all topping ingredients. Sprinkle topping on top of batter. Add remaining batter and bake for 40 minutes. Cool on wire rack. Makes 12 servings.

Eggs in a Frame

Whole red pepper, sliced into "rings"
Cooking oil
Eggs
Parmesan cheese, grated

Slice a whole red pepper horizontally into "rings" and place 3 or 4 in your frying pan. Sizzle in hot oil for a few minutes, then flip rings over. Now crack an egg into each ring and sprinkle on a pinch of grated Parmesan cheese. Fry as you would any sunny-side egg.

Cheese Popovers

4 eggs
1 cup all-purpose flour
½ tsp. salt
1 cup milk
1 tbsp. melted butter
1 cup cheddar cheese, grated

Preheat oven to 400 degrees. Break eggs into small bowl and beat with a fork. Place eggs in food processor and add in flour, salt, milk, and butter. Process for about 20 seconds.

Stir in cheese. Pour into well-greased popover pan. Bake for approximately 45 minutes—but don't open your oven until they're done or they might collapse! Makes 4 to 6 popovers.

Chicken Paprikash

1 medium onion, sliced
2 tbsp. paprika
4 tbsp. butter
1 whole chicken, cut into pieces
1½ cups chicken broth
4 tbsp. sour cream
1 tomato, chopped

In a fry pan, brown sliced onion and paprika in butter, then remove onions. Add chicken to pan and brown, adding a little more butter if needed. Add chicken broth and browned onions. Cover and simmer for 1 hour. After chicken is cooked, add in sour cream and sprinkle on chopped tomato. Serve with noodles, rice, or spaetzles. Serves 4.

Strawberry and Ritz Cracker Pie

3 egg whites
1 cup sugar
20 Ritz crackers, crushed
½ cup walnuts, crushed
1 tsp. baking powder
1 (10-oz.) pkg. frozen strawberries
½ pint heavy cream, whipped

Preheat oven to 350 degrees. Beat egg whites, gradually adding sugar until stiff. Fold in crushed Ritz crackers, walnuts, and baking powder. Gently press mixture into greased 9" pie plate. Bake for 20 minutes. While pie shell is baking, drain frozen strawberries and fold into whipped cream. Pour into pie shell when it's slightly cooled and chill in refrigerator for 2 hours.

Baked Omelet Roll

6 eggs
1 cup milk
½ cup all-purpose flour
½ tsp. salt
¼ tsp. ground black pepper
1 cup shredded cheddar cheese

Preheat oven to 450 degrees. In blender, combine eggs, milk, flour, salt, and pepper until smooth. Pour egg mixture into a lightly greased 9" × 13" baking pan. Bake for approximately 20 minutes until set. Remove omelet from oven and sprinkle on cheese. Carefully loosen all edges of omelet from pan, then gently roll up the omelet. Cut into 6 equal-sized pieces and garnish with sour cream, salsa, or fresh fruit. Serves 6.

Sunflower Cheese Spread

4 oz. cream cheese, room temperature
4 oz. goat cheese (or other soft cheese)
1 tbsp. cream

½ tsp. Worcestershire sauce
¼ tsp. paprika
⅔ cup roasted, salted sunflower kernels

Combine cheeses, cream, Worcestershire sauce, and paprika. Gently blend in sunflower kernels. If consistency is too thick, mix in a little more cream. Spread on bread for tea sandwiches, or serve as a dip with crackers or bread sticks.

Sweet and Spicy Glazed Sausages

1 (12-oz.) pkg. breakfast sausage links
¼ cup orange marmalade (or apricot preserves)
2 tbsp. sweet and spicy mustard

Sauté sausages in pan until lightly browned and fully cooked. Remove sausages from pan and drain. Wipe pan to remove cooking fat. Add marmalade and mustard to pan and blend over medium heat. Return sausages to pan and stir gently to glaze.

Petra's Baking Powder Biscuits

2¼ cups self-rising flour
¾ cup butter
1 cup milk
1 tsp. baking powder

Preheat oven to 425 degrees. Mix all ingredients together until dough comes together. Place on floured surface and gently pat out into a circle. Now fold in half and cut out your biscuits using a biscuit cutter. Bake on greased pan for 20 to 25 minutes. Yields 8 to 12.

Chilled Blueberry Soup

1 cup sour cream
2 (10-oz.) pkg. frozen blueberries, slightly thawed
4 tbsp. granulated sugar
2 tbsp. brown sugar (optional)

Put sour cream, blueberries, and sugar in food processor and pulse for 30 seconds or so. Then check for consistency and taste. If you'd like soup thinner, add ¼ cup of cream. If you'd like it sweeter, add 2 tbsp. brown sugar. Pulse again and serve chilled. Makes 4 servings.

Old-fashioned Soda Bread

3 cups flour, sifted
²/₃ cup sugar
1 tbsp. baking powder
1 tsp. baking soda
1 tsp. salt
1½ cups currants or dark raisins
2 eggs, beaten
2 cups buttermilk
2 tbsp. melted butter

Preheat oven to 350 degrees. In large bowl, mix together flour, sugar, baking powder, baking soda, and salt. Stir in currants or raisins. In separate bowl, combine eggs, buttermilk, and melted butter. Add liquid mixture to dry mixture and mix just until moistened. Place batter in 5¼" × 9½" loaf pan and bake for approximately 60 minutes. Remove bread from pan immediately and let cool before slicing.

Scorched Eggs

1 lb. sweet Italian-style ground sausage
Salt and pepper
8 hard-boiled eggs
½ cup bread crumbs
1 egg, beaten

Preheat oven to 375 degrees. Season sausage with salt and pepper and divide into 8 portions. Pat out each portion of sausage to about a ⅛"-thick patty. Wrap sausage patty around each hard-boiled egg, pressing edges together to seal. Roll sausage-covered eggs in bread crumbs and then dip in beaten egg. Place on greased baking sheet and bake for 20 minutes or until lightly browned. Makes 8 servings.

Resources

BOOKS AND MAGAZINES

The Good Egg—Author Marie Simmons offers two hundred fresh approaches to preparing eggs—everything from breakfast to dessert.

The Fresh Egg Cookbook—Jennifer Trainer Thompson explores recipes for using eggs sourced from farmers' markets, local farms, and your own backyard.

Home-Made Vintage—Christina Strutt provides a guide to giving your home a vintage air and a country cottage appeal.

Modern Country—Nancy Ingram and Jennifer Jordan show how to add a clean, modernist edge to classic country décor.

Country Home—Magazine with country-inspired home design, collecting, craft projects, and recipes. (countryhome.com)

Country Living—Magazine devoted to home and decorating, food and entertaining, antiques and collectibles. (countryliving.com)

Country Sampler—Magazine with country decorating and lifestyle articles. (countrysampler.com)

Living the Country Life—Homes, gardening, and country life. (livingthecountrylife.com)

Flea Market Style—Magazine dedicated to flea market shopping and repurposing unique finds. (fleamarketstylemag.blogspot.com)

MaryJanesFarm—Charming magazine about crafts, décor, and organic living. (maryjanesfarm.org)

WEBSITES AND INTERESTING BLOGS

Cottagehomedecorating.com—How to turn secondhand and rescued furniture and objects into charming, comfortable cottage style.

Mypetchicken.com—The how-tos of raising chickens in your own backyard.

Joyofbaking.com/eggs.html—All about cooking and baking with eggs.

Incredibleegg.org—American Egg Board's site with egg facts, fun, and lots of recipes.

Fresh-eggs-daily.com—Blog about eggs, chickens, and tasty recipes.

Beadandbreakfast.com—Your getaway guide to more than 11,000 country inns and bed-and-breakfasts.

Cookingwithideas.typepad.com—Recipes and book reviews for the bibliochef.

Jennybakes.com—Fabulous recipes from a real make-it-from-scratch baker.

Baking.about.com—Carroll Pellegrinelli writes a wonderful baking blog complete with recipes and photo instructions.

Garden-of-books.com—Terrific book reviews by an entertainment journalist.

Lattesandlife.com—Witty musings on life.

Thepioneerwoman.com—Real ranch cooking. What more could you ask for!

Lovintheoven.com—Baked goods, easy meals, and lots of great step-by-step photos.

RTbookreviews.com—Wonderful romance and mystery book review site.

Turn the page for a preview of
Laura Childs's next Tea Shop Mystery . . .

Ming Tea Murder

Coming soon in hardcover
from Berkley Prime Crime!

DRUMS banging, sweet notes of a Chinese violin trembling in the air, the enormous red and gold dragon shook its great head and danced its way through the rotunda of the Gibbes Museum in Charleston, South Carolina. It was the opening night celebration for the reconstruction of a genuine eighteenth-century Chinese teahouse, and the crème de la crème of society had turned out in full force for this most auspicious occasion.

And even though black-tie events weren't exactly topmost in Theodosia Browning's comfort zone, there had been no easy way to refuse this particular invitation, especially when your handsome, hunky boyfriend was the museum's PR director. So here she was, applauding the music, mesmerized by the spectacle of the enormous dragon's gaping jaws snapping and slapping above the heads of the excited crowd.

Yes, the event was most impressive, Theodosia decided. Glowing red Chinese lanterns, stands of bamboo, dozens of elegant orchids, and miniature Penjing trees had transformed the cold, marble rotunda into an elegant Asian garden. And then there was the food. Serving tables were laden with tempting bites such as shrimp dumplings, honey-glazed pork buns, chicken satays, and miniature crispy duck rolls. Delicious!

Of course, the real treasure was the teahouse itself, purchased and deconstructed in Shanghai, then rebuilt board-by-board inside the museum. The blue-tiled, exotically peaked roof, gleaming cypress walls, and intricately carved sandalwood screens seemed tailor-made for an emperor and his courtesans.

"I'm anxious to take a look inside," Theodosia told Max, who was gazing about proudly if not a little distractedly.

"We pulled it off," said Max. "I can't believe we actually pulled it off." He sounded surprised that his PR efforts had yielded such a turnout.

"Of course you did," Theodosia told him. "Because nobody would pass up an opportunity to enjoy a fancy celebration like this." *Except . . . maybe me?*

Theodosia had a smile that could light up a tearoom—and often did, since she was the proprietor of the Indigo Tea Shop on nearby Church Street. But tonight she'd been smiling so exuberantly that her face felt like it was about ready to crack. She'd flitted about on Max's arm, chatting and rubbing shoulders with Charleston's old guard, most of them big-buck donors who were thrilled that their money had helped make it possible to import this masterpiece of a teahouse.

But Theodosia was also counting the seconds to midnight.

Because when the clock struck the proverbial witching hour, she planned to cut and run like Cinderella. She'd kick off her pinchy black satin heels, climb into her pumpkin coach, which, in this case, was her venerable six-year-old Jeep, and head home to her cozy little cottage where her dog, Earl Grey, awaited her.

Shaking her head, forcing another smile, because Max was saying something to her again, she leaned toward him and said, "Excuse me?"

"I need to schmooze a couple more board members," said Max. "You'll be okay?"

"I'll be perfect," said Theodosia.

"Go check out the photo booth," Max urged. "While I huddle with Edgar Webster, one of our illustrious donors." He grinned. "Maybe take a selfie." As a fun perk for the guests, Max had convinced the museum director to let him bring in a photo booth. And just as he'd predicted, there'd been a constant parade of guests in and out of the booth all night long. Everyone was seemingly thrilled with the notion of immortalizing themselves in photos, even if they were the small black-and-white variety.

"I'll do that," Theodosia told him. "That'll be fun." As she turned to push her way through the crowd, she caught sight of herself in a fragment of mirror. And as always, the image gave her pause.

Is that really me with that mass of auburn hair framing my face and blue eyes looking so expectant? Hmm, I don't look half bad for being in my mid-thirties.

She'd swooped a hint of blusher on the apples of her cheeks, smudged on the bare minimum of mascara. But with her confident bearing, winning smile, and fair Southern belle skin, she looked almost like a noblewoman who might have been portrayed in some delectable English painting. Perhaps something James Constable might have done.

"You're looking very lovely tonight," said a voice behind her.

Theodosia whirled about to find Drayton, her dear friend and tea master, smiling at her.

"If not a bit mischievous," continued Drayton.

Theodosia smiled and gave an offhand wave. "Ah, I think I might be a tad underdressed." She'd worn a simple black cocktail dress, an armful of colorful bead bracelets, and heels, while most of the other women were glitzed and glammed in the latest runway creations from Dior and Oscar de la Renta.

"Nonsense," said Drayton. "An LBD is always perfectly appropriate." Drayton was sixtyish, tall, and debonair. Tonight his gray hair was slicked back straight and he wore a slim-cut tuxedo with his trademark bow tie. He was the buttoned-up old guard to Theodosia's more playful boho cool.

"Did you get a gander at all the jewels these women are wearing?" Theodosia asked him. "I mean, a cat burglar would have a field day here."

Drayton's bushy brows rose in twin arcs. "Please don't interject a criminal element into the occasion. Even if it is only imaginary."

"Okay, then I'll just compliment you on all your lovely Penjing, because they certainly help add to the Asian atmosphere." Penjing were basically Chinese bonsai, miniature trees that had been cut, trimmed, and wired so they could exist in small, moss-encrusted ceramic pots. Drayton, a master at creating windblown-styled trees and miniature forests, had lent the museum a dozen of his trees. Most had spectacularly twisted trunks and leaves that were smaller than a lady's pinky nail.

"They do look nice, don't they? Particularly my Chinese elm." Drayton prided himself on his composure and modesty, but he also appreciated a compliment now and then.

"You've been inside the teahouse?" said Theodosia. They both had to take a step back since the crowd was pressing so hard around them.

"It's a marvel," exclaimed Drayton. "I took the liberty of exploring while all that Chinese dragon business was going on." He paused and smiled. "You should run over and take a quick peek, too. You'll love it."

"I'm going to," said Theodosia. "But first I promised Max I'd check out his photo booth." She looked around, saw that Max was backed up against a wall, talking to a rather red-faced man, a board member by the name of Edgar Webster. Neither of them looked happy.

"*Photo* booth?" spat out Drayton. Clearly he wasn't a fan. "What is this fixation everyone has today with memorializing themselves? And then posting every single silly photograph on . . ." Drayton made a face. "On the *Internet*?"

"Come on," Theodosia cajoled. "It's not as bad as all that."

"I'm just not sure a photo booth is apropos for an event such as this."

"Still, it's fun. And everyone seems to love it."

"You see," said Drayton, "that's why I'm not everyone." Drayton was a self-proclaimed Luddite who mistrusted smartphones, DVDs, and CDs. In fact, he was an old-fashioned, vinyl record kind of guy.

"But you're perfect just the way you are," Theodosia assured him. She glanced around again, but didn't see Max.

"Oh my," said Drayton. As he gazed out into the crowd his placid expression suddenly changed to one of horror.

"What?" Then Theodosia caught sight of the small, blond woman speed-balling toward them on clacking kitten heels.

"I'm going to let *you* handle this encounter," said Drayton as he quickly slipped away.

"You look like you're having a *marvelous* time," cooed Charlotte Webster. She slalomed to a stop in front of Theodosia and grinned like a Cheshire cat, practically upending her glass of champagne in the process. Charlotte was the bubbly socialite who presided over the Broad Street Garden Club, was a sometime customer at Theodosia's Indigo Tea Shop, and was married to Edgar Webster.

"It's a thrilling night," Theodosia told Charlotte, mustering yet another smile. Since Charlotte's husband, a prominent businessman and philanthropist, had put up the largest chunk of money to import the teahouse, she pretty much had to make nice with his wife.

"I was just chatting with Percy Capers," said Charlotte. She fluttered a pudgy hand and adjusted her necklace, a string of sparkling diamonds with a large yellow diamond as the center stone. "You know, the museum's curator of Asian art?"

Theodosia nodded. She'd met Capers a couple of times.

"Anyway, Mr. Capers was regaling me with horror stories about importing this lovely teahouse. Shipping it across the Pacific, shepherding it through customs, misplacing some of the actual parts. Why, do you know there are no *nails* whatsoever in the construction? That the entire thing is held together with dozens of wooden pegs?"

"I've heard that."

"Isn't that the craziest thing ever?" said Charlotte. "Wooden pegs?"

"I guess that's how they built them two hundred years ago," said Theodosia.

"Two hundred years? That's how old that thing is?" said Charlotte. She took a quick glug of champagne. "Well, I certainly hope we got our money's worth then." She giggled loudly, patted Theodosia on the arm, and toddled off.

Charlotte was a real character, Theodosia thought to herself. And then, because she really didn't want to be unkind, decided that the Websters, as civic-minded underwriters of the teahouse, really had done a wonderful thing.

As Theodosia slipped past one of the food tables, she accepted a miniature egg roll from a black-uniformed waiter. Then, when another waiter held out a tray filled with champagne glasses, she took a glass. As she sipped and surveyed the crowd, she was struck again by how fancy and formal everyone looked. Of course, many of the guests, board members as well as donors, were friends and neighbors who lived in the nearby historic district. There was one of the Ravenels conspiring with a Clayton and a Tisdale. And Mr. Pinckney was talking to a rather large man with a pronounced Texas bray.

The pounding of drums suddenly started up again, loud and hard, and Theodosia turned to see what was going on now. Oops, it was dragon time again. The Chinese dragon was humping its way through the crowd once more, tossing its head from side to side, its dragon beard fluttering with every move.

Theodosia had witnessed a dragon parade in San Francisco's Chinatown once, when she'd been roaming up and down Grant Street, popping into tea shops, looking for unusual varieties and blends. But seeing this guy up close and personal was a lot more fun. And from the enthusiasm generated by the crowd, they obviously thought so, too.

Edging her way through a clutch of suitably enthralled guests, Theodosia headed for the photo booth. Maybe she could slip in and take a quick photo right now. She wasn't all that hot to pose, but it would make Max happy. Give him a small souvenir of tonight's museum triumph.

Dodging around an enormous celadon pot filled with leafy bamboo plants, Theodosia darted past a red Chinese lantern supported by a heavy wooden post. Over here, in an alcove off the rotunda where the photo booth was located, it was a little darker, a little quieter.

Perfect.

Theodosia rounded a stone lion-dog statue, heading for the photo booth. The drums were pounding furiously now, the erhu, or Chinese violin, pouring out urgent notes. Finishing the last sip of champagne, she set her glass down on a small rosewood table and turned toward the photo booth.

Was it still occupied? she wondered. Or could she dart in for a quick photo?

"Hello?" Theodosia called out, giving a couple of sharp knocks on the shiny, bright yellow exterior. She didn't want to go crashing in and photo bomb someone. That would be just plain rude.

"Is someone in there?" she called again.

When there was no reply, Theodosia took a step forward. And just before her hand parted the flimsy black curtain, the toe of her strappy black stiletto slid into a patch of something sticky.

Oh no, she groaned. All she needed was to ruin her best pair of shoes because some exuberant guest had spilled a glop of sweet-and-sour sauce.

Theodosia glanced down, expecting to see sauce, fragments of an exploded pork bun, or a puddle of champagne. After all, this art opening had turned into a fairly raucous party.

Only what she saw instead was a small, dark puddle.

A spilled drink?

No, Theodosia decided. Champagne or tea would be much more translucent.

As she pulled her foot back and stared at the floor again, taking a longer, harder look, her heart began to flutter. Then it began to dance a little jitterbug. Because whatever was on the floor was decidedly dark and sticky.

No, it couldn't be. Could it?

Slowly, tentatively, her heart in her throat, Theodosia reached forward and parted the curtains. And saw . . . nothing.

It was pitch-black inside the photo booth. Lights out.

Somehow that didn't feel right to her. What was going on? She pushed the curtains a little farther apart.

And that's when she saw him. A large man, sprawled on a narrow wooden bench, bent all the way forward so his forehead pressed tightly against the front panel of the booth. His eyes were closed and he looked like he was passed out cold.

"Excuse me," said Theodosia. "Sir?" Her mouth felt dry, her breathing was fast and thready. "Are you okay, sir?" She paused. "Do you need help?"

No answer.

Theodosia glanced backward, looking for a museum

guard, one of the museum staff, anyone who might be able to lend a hand.

But everyone had their backs to her. They were still cheering and clapping like mad as the musicians played wildly and the Chinese dragon continued his energetic prance.

Tentatively now, Theodosia touched a finger to the side of the man's throat. To where she figured a pulse point might be.

She felt . . . nothing. In fact, he felt cool. Practically lifeless.

A loud pounding sounded inside Theodosia's head and she could feel the tiny hairs on the back of her neck prickle and rise.

No . . . please no.

And, as her eyes gradually adjusted to the darkness inside the photo booth, as her mind slowly wrapped itself around what might have just happened, that's when she saw the first telltale evidence of foul play. Just above where her fingertip had come into contact with the man's throat, a trail of dark sticky liquid dribbled from his ear!

Blood? Has to be.

Theodosia snatched her hand away and backed out of the photo booth as fast as humanly possible. Then she screamed as loud as she could, her voice rising in volume as it mingled with the shrill notes of the erhu.

Watch for the next Cackleberry Club Mystery

Egg Drop Dead

When Suzanne goes to Mike Mullen's dairy farm to pick up wheels of cheese, nobody's around. She steps into his barn only to be greeted by the urgent, upturned faces of cows that haven't been milked. As the cows wail, Suzanne tiptoes down the aisle and discovers Mike's dead body—and the body of his wife. What kind of maniac would murder this mild-mannered farm couple? And who is coming after Suzanne now that she's hot on the trail of a double murder?

And be sure to catch the next Scrapbooking Mystery, also from Laura Childs and Berkley Prime Crime

Parchment and Old Lace

A scrap of parchment, a snippet of old lace. What look like pieces for a scrapbook collage are really clues to a murder.

Find out more about the author and her mysteries at laurachilds.com or become a friend on Facebook.